**Alexandre Dumas** (24 July 1802 – 5 December 1870), also known as Alexandre Dumas père (French for 'father'), was a French writer. His works have been translated into many languages, and he is one of the most widely read French authors. Many of his historical novels of high adventure were originally published as serials, including The Count of Monte Cristo, The Three Musketeers, Twenty Years After, and The Vicomte of Bragelonne: Ten Years Later. His novels have been adapted since the early twentieth century for nearly 200 films. Dumas' last novel, The Knight of Sainte-Hermine, unfinished at his death, was completed by scholar Claude Schopp and published in 2005. It was published in English in 2008 as The Last Cavalier. Prolific in several genres, Dumas began his career by writing plays, which were successfully produced from the first. He also wrote numerous magazine articles and travel books; his published works totalled 100,000 pages. In the 1840s, Dumas founded the Théâtre Historique in Paris. (Source: Wikipedia)

**Literary works:**
The Three Musketeers
Twenty Years After
The Vicomte of Bragelonne
Ten Years Later
Louise de la Valliere
The Man in the Iron Mask
The Count of Monte Cristo
The Women's War
The Pale Lady
The Black Tulip
Olympe de Cleves
Isaac Laquedem
Catherine Blum
Georges
Amaury

# The Prussian Terror

ALEXANDRE DUMAS

PRINCE CLASSICS

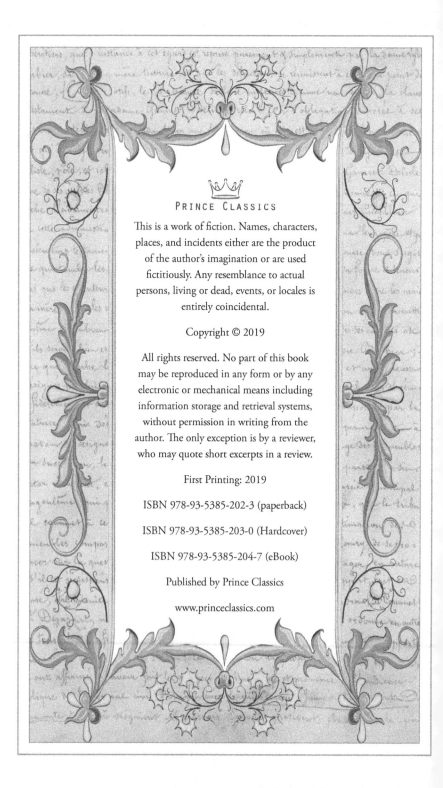

PRINCE CLASSICS

First Printing: 2019

ISBN 978-93-5385-202-3 (paperback)

ISBN 978-93-5385-203-0 (Hardcover)

ISBN 978-93-5385-204-7 (eBook)

Published by Prince Classics

www.princeclassics.com

# Contents

INTRODUCTION 11

CHAPTER I. BERLIN 17

CHAPTER II. THE HOUSE OF HOHENZOLLERN 22

CHAPTER III. COUNT VON BISMARCK 30

CHAPTER IV. IN WHICH BISMARCK EMERGES FROM AN IMPOSSIBLE

POSITION 35

CHAPTER V. A SPORTSMAN AND A SPANIEL 46

CHAPTER VI. BENEDICT TURPIN 53

CHAPTER VII. KAULBACH'S STUDIO 62

CHAPTER VIII. THE CHALLENGE 68

CHAPTER IX. THE TWO DUELS 73

CHAPTER X. "WHAT WAS WRITTEN IN A KING'S HAND" 82

CHAPTER XI. BARON FREDERIC VON BÜLOW 92

CHAPTER XII. HELEN 100

CHAPTER XIII. COUNT KARL VON FREYBERG 108

CHAPTER XIV. THE GRANDMOTHER 117

CHAPTER XV. FRANKFORT-ON-MAIN 123

CHAPTER XVI. THE DEPARTURE 129

CHAPTER XVII. AUSTRIANS AND PRUSSIANS 136

CHAPTER XVIII. THE DECLARATION OF WAR 142

CHAPTER XIX. THE BATTLE OF LANGENSALZA 149

CHAPTER XX. IN WHICH BENEDICT'S PREDICTION CONTINUES TO BE FULFILLED    156

CHAPTER XXI. WHAT PASSED AT FRANKFORT BETWEEN THE BATTLES OF LANGENSALZA AND SADOWA    160

CHAPTER XXII. THE FREE MEAL    167

CHAPTER XXIII. THE BATTLE OF ASCHAFFENBURG    172

CHAPTER XXIV. THE EXECUTOR    179

CHAPTER XXV. FRISK    187

CHAPTER XXVI. THE WOUNDED MAN    194

CHAPTER XXVII. THE PRUSSIANS AT FRANKFORT    201

CHAPTER XXVIII. GENERAL MANTEUFFEL'S THREATS    210

CHAPTER XXIX. GENERAL STURM    215

CHAPTER XXX. THE BREAKING OF THE STORM    222

CHAPTER XXXI. THE BURGOMASTER    229

CHAPTER XXXII. QUEEN AUGUSTA    233

CHAPTER XXXIII. THE TWO PROCESSIONS    240

CHAPTER XXXIV. THE TRANSFUSION OF BLOOD.    247

CHAPTER XXXV. THE MARRIAGE IN EXTREMIS    253

CHAPTER XXXVI. "WAIT AND SEE"    263

CONCLUSION    269

EPILOGUE    273

About Author    283

# The Prussian Terror

# INTRODUCTION

"The enemy passed beneath our window and then out of view. A moment afterwards we heard the sound as it were of a hurricane; the house trembled to the gallop of horses. At the end of the street the enemy had been charged by our cavalry; and, not knowing our small numbers, they were returning at full speed hotly pursued by our men. Pell-mell they all passed by—a whirlwind of smoke and noise. Our soldiers fired and slashed away, the enemy on their side fired as they fled. Two or three bullets struck the house, one of them shattering a bar of the window-shutter through which I was looking on. The spectacle was at once magnificent and terrible. Pursued too closely the enemy had decided to face about, and there, twenty paces from us, was going on a combat life for life. I saw five or six of the enemy fall, and two or three of our men. Then, defeated after a ten minutes' struggle, the enemy trusted themselves again to the swiftness of their horses, and cleared off at full gallop. The pursuit recommenced, the whirlwind resumed its course, leaving, before it disappeared, three or four men strewn on the pavement. Suddenly we heard the drum beating to the charge. It was our hundred infantry soldiers who were coming up in their turn. They marched with fixed bayonets and disappeared at the bend of the road. Five minutes later we heard a sharp platoon firing. Then we saw our hussars reappearing, driven by five or six hundred cavalry; they reappeared the pursued, as they had started the pursuers. Amid this second tempest of men it was impossible to see or distinguish anything; only, when it was past, three or four dead bodies more lay stretched on the ground."

The boy who saw these scenes, to record them in his Memoirs many years later, was living with his mother at Villers-Cotterets, on the Soissons road in the Aisne, where fierce fighting between our little army and our allies the French on the one hand, and the Germans on the other, is taking place as these lines are being written. The time was 1814. Napoleon had retreated from Moscow and had lost the battle of Leipzig, and the Russians, Prussians, and Austrians in alliance were gradually closing in on France. All confidence in Napoleon's star had disappeared. Every hour was bringing the roar of cannon nearer to Paris: in a few days the Allies were to enter it and Napoleon to sign the decree of abdication and leave for Elba.

The name of the boy was Alexandre Dumas. His mother had filled her cellar with furniture, bedding, and household goods, and had then had a new plank floor made for the room above, so that treasure seekers might look in vain, and had buried her little store of money in a box in the middle of the garden. She was as much in terror of Napoleon as she was of the Prussian and Russian troops. If her own countrymen, the French, were beaten, she and her son might be killed, but if Napoleon was victorious he would want her son as a soldier. Now Alexandre was twelve and conscription began at sixteen.

The boy's father, General Alexandre Dumas, was dead, and as on account of his republican principles the First Consul had disgraced, exiled, and ruined him, so by the Emperor the widow and her son were disowned, forgotten and left to starve. In spite of this Madame Dumas's neighbours called her a Bonapartist, her husband having fought under Bonaparte, and the term Bonapartist was one which was presently to amount to an accusation as Louis XVIII neared the throne.

The enemy seen by the boy fighting in the street were Prussians—Prussians long expected by his mother, who had made three successive enormous dishes of haricot mutton for their pacification. Although young Alexandre had partaken of the mutton and thought very little of the threatened danger before it occurred, he never forgot the sudden Prussian inroad and the dead men left outside this door. And he often said that the Valley of the Aisne might see the Prussians again.

In 1848, when a candidate for the Chamber of Deputies, Dumas lost many votes by making a speech in the course of which, when passing the state of Europe in review, he said. "Geographically, Prussia has the shape of a serpent, and like a serpent it seems always to sleep and prepare to swallow everything around it—Denmark, Holland, and Belgium; and when it has engulfed them all you will see that Austria will pass in its turn and perhaps, alas! France also."

In June 1866 Prussia's rapid campaign against Austria startled Europe.

Every thoughtful man was calculating the consequences of the preponderance of Prussia in Germany, and Dumas was one of those Frenchmen who were seized with sad presentiments of the future for their own country. Particularly does he appear to have been struck with the barbarous conduct of the Prussians in the free city of Frankfort[1] which the newspapers were daily reporting. Unable to remain at home while such events were occurring, he travelled to Frankfort and observed them for himself. Then he went to Gotha, Hanover, and Berlin; he visited the battlefields of Langensalza and Sadowa and returned to Paris with his notebooks crammed with precious details, his pockets bulging with unpublished documents.

Then M. Hollander, the owner of the political journal "The Situation," came running to the author of "The Three Musketeers," "Queen Margot," and of so many other famous historical romances to ask for one to be called "The Prussian Terror." Dumas, who like M. Hollander was anxious to do all he could to arouse France, fast crumbling under the Second Empire, to a sense of her danger from Prussia, gladly complied. Such is the genesis of this book in which on every page the author seems to say—"Awake! the danger is at hand."

To render it more easily intelligible to readers of the present day who appear to us to know very little of the Austro-Prussian War of 1866, let us glance at the important events which the newspaper proprietor and the historical romancer had in mind.

The death of the King of Denmark occurred in 1863[2] and North Germany buzzed like a swarm of angry bees over the Duchies of Schleswig, Holstein, and Luxemburg. By the treaty of London (1852), which fixed the succession to the Danish Crown, Austria and Prussia, although signatories to it, denied the right of the new king to those duchies and claimed them as part of Germany. In February 1864 Austrian and Prussian troops crossed the Danish border. The Danes fought well, but were forced to submit and eventually the duchies were made over to their enemies.

Then Prussia, which had long looked with jealousy on the power of Austria and considered a war with her inevitable sooner or later, opposed her desire to form the duchies into a separate state under the Duke of Augustenburg. Austria referred the matter to the Frankfort Diet, which decided in favour of the duke, but Bismarck, as Prussia's Prime Minister, to secure the complete control of North Germany, required that, not only the duchies but the whole of Hanover, Hesse Cassel, Hesse Nassau, and the city of Frankfort should be absorbed in Prussia. Both Prussia and Austria prepared for war, Prussia entering into an alliance with Victor Emanuel. On June 7th Prussian troops entered Holstein.

On June 14th, in regard to the decisive question whether the federal army should be mobilized, Hanover voted in the Diet with Austria, and by so doing irrevocably declared on which side she would range herself in the approaching struggle. Prussia at once issued an ultimatum to Hanover, requesting her to maintain neutrality and to accept her scheme for the reformation of the Confederation. Hanover immediately rejected these demands and Prussian troops at once crossed the frontier. The resulting battles are known as those of Langensalza and Aschaffenburg. The Austrians were disastrously defeated in the terrific battle of Sadowa or Königsrätz, and Bismarck was thus nearer to the formation of German Unity under Prussia.

After Sadowa, the first act of the Prussians was to enter the "free" city of Frankfort, which did not attempt any defence, relying as it did on its treaties, and terrorise its inhabitants. It was these "acts of terror," then, of which M. Hollander and Dumas were particularly thinking, hoping that the recital of them in a popular romance would do something to awaken France.

It has been repeatedly stated that before the Franco-German War of 1870 the German soldiers were guiltless of acts of atrocity. This story proves the contrary, and it is not a little curious that no work in the English language, save books of reference, covering the ground traversed by "The Prussian Terror," appears to be now accessible. For this reason alone Dumas's book, which, though in story form, is an authoritative contribution to history, deserves attention at the present time. Apart from this, it is so spirited and interesting that it is quite surprising that at so late a date—forty-seven years after its original issue—I should be the first to offer a version[3] to the British public.

14

Dumas was still living in Paris when, in the summer of 1869, war was declared with Germany. His health was now bad, and his son, the author of "La Dame aux Camélias," did not wish him to remain during the siege. In the autumn he took his father with him to Puys near Dieppe, where he had a villa. There Dumas died on December 5th, 1870.

He did not know it—news being kept from him—but during his last days his worst prognostications had been verified. A detachment of the Prussian army was actually taking possession of Dieppe as he breathed his last. While the soldiers marched along the streets, their bands playing German airs and the inhabitants hid in their houses behind shuttered windows, the news flew round the town that the country had lost Alexandre Dumas, the most typically French writer who has ever existed. The coffin was borne to the grave at Neuville, where the German soldiers were in occupation, before a Prussian patrol. In 1872 the body was exhumed, and buried in the family tomb at Villers-Cotterets. Hard by, where as a boy of twelve Dumas heard the Prussian cannon, three nations are now fighting.

R.S. GARNETT.

[1] Dumas knew Frankfort well, having lived there for some time in 1838 with Gérard de Nerval, the author of "Les Filles de Feu."

[2] These facts are taken from the "Encyclopædia Britannica."

[3] It should be stated that M. Hollander, who wished the brilliant name of Dumas to shine on as many issues of his newspaper as possible, stipulated for not less than sixty feuilletons. Dumas complied, but was forced to include some hunting stories which he puts into the mouth of his hero, Benedict Turpin. These stories will not be found in the present volume.

# CHAPTER I. BERLIN

The architect of Berlin appears to have carefully designed his plan according to line and rule in order to produce a capital of dullness as far removed from the picturesque as his ingenuity could accomplish. Seen from the cathedral, which is the loftiest point attainable, the place suggests an enormous chess-board on which the Royal Palace, the Museum, Cathedral, and other important buildings fairly represent kings, queens, and castles. And, much as Paris is intersected by the Seine, so is Berlin divided by the Spree, except that instead of surrounding one island, as does the former river, two artificial canals branch out right and left like the handles of a vase, and form two islands of unequal size in the centre of the town. Berlin being the capital of Privilege, one of these islands is distinguished by possessing the Royal Palace, the Cathedral, the Museum, the Bourse, most other public buildings, and a score of houses which in Turin, the Berlin of Italy, would certainly be called palaces; the other contains nothing remarkable, corresponding to the Parisian Rue Saint-Jacques and the quarter Saint-André-des-Arts.

The aristocratic, the smart Berlin lies to the right and left of the Friedrich Strasse, which extends from the Place de La Belle Alliance by which one enters Berlin to that of Oranienburg by which one leaves it, and which is crossed nearly in the middle by the Unter den Linden. This famous promenade traverses the fashionable quarter and extends from the Royal Palace to the Place d'Armes. It owes its name to two rows of magnificent lime trees which form a charming promenade on each side of the broad carriage-way. Both sides abound in cafés and restaurants, whose crowds of customers, overflowing in summer on to the public road, cause a considerable amount of lively motion. This, however, never rises into noisy horse-play or clamour, for the Prussian prefers to amuse himself sub rosa, and keeps his gaiety within doors.

But on June 7th, 1866, as beautiful a day as Prussia can produce, Unter den Linden, at about six in the evening, presented a scene of most unusual commotion. The excitement was caused in the first place by the increasingly hostile attitude assumed by Prussia towards Austria, in refusing to allow the States of Holstein to proceed to the election of the Duke of Augustenburg, also by the general arming on all sides, by reports concerning the immediate calling up of the Landwehr and the dissolution of the Chamber, and finally by rumours of telegrams from France containing threats against Prussia, said to have been made by Louis Napoleon himself.

It is necessary to travel in Prussia before one can in the least comprehend the sort of hatred therein cherished against the French. It is a species of monomania which distorts even the very clearest vision. No minister can be popular, no orator will gain a hearing unless the one lets it be supposed his policy is for war, and the other can produce some brilliant epigram or clever sous-entendu levelled against France. Nor will the title of poet be allowed, unless the claimant can qualify by being the author of some popular rhyme, entitled "The Rhine," "Leipzig," or "Waterloo."

Whence comes this hatred for France—a deep, inveterate, indestructible hatred which seems to pervade the very earth and air? It is impossible to say. Can it date from the time when a legion from Gaul, the advanced guard of the Roman army, first entered Germany? Abandoning this idea we come down to the battle of Rosbach as a possible cause, in which case the German national character must be an uncommonly bad one, seeing they beat us there. Still later, it might possibly be explained by the military inferiority shown by the pupils of Frederic the Great ever since the Duke of Brunswick's famous manifesto threatening that not one stone of Paris should be left on another! One battle, that of Valmy, expelled the Prussians from France in 1792; and another, that of Jena, opened the gates of Berlin to us in 1806. Still, to these dates, our enemies—no, our rivals—can oppose the names of Leipzig and of Waterloo. Of Leipzig, however, they cannot claim more than a quarter, seeing their army was combined with those of Russia, Austria, and Sweden, to say nothing of that of Saxony, which also deserves to be remembered. Nor is more than one-half of Waterloo to their credit, for Napoleon, who till then had the advantage, was already exhausted by a six hours' struggle with the English when they arrived.

Consequently, remembering this heritage of hate, which, indeed, they have always shown quite openly—one could not be surprised at the popular emotion caused by a rumour, non-official but widely spread, that France would throw down the gauntlet and join in the impending conflict. Many, however, doubted the news, as not a word of it had appeared in the "Staat's Anzeiger" that morning. Berlin, like Paris, has its faithful adherents to the Government and the "Moniteur," who believe that the latter cannot lie, and that a paternal Government would never, never keep back news interesting to its affectionate subjects. These were joined by the readers of the "Tages Telegraphe" ("Daily Telegraphic News"), certain that their special organ would have known whatever was to be known, and also by those of the ministerial and aristocratic "Kreuz Zeitung," who equally declined to believe anything not contained in its usually well-informed columns. And besides these one heard the names of a dozen other daily or weekly issues bandied from side to side in the excited crowd, until suddenly a harsh cry of "French news! French news! Telegraphic News" "One kreutzer," succeeded in dominating the din.

The effect produced on the crowd may be imagined. Despite the proverbial Prussian economy, every hand sought its pocket and drawing forth a kreutzer, proceeded to exchange it for the square bit of paper containing the long-desired news. And indeed the importance of the contents made amends for the delay in obtaining it. The dispatch ran as follows:

"June 6th, 1866. His Majesty the Emperor Napoleon III, having gone to Auxerre, in order to be present at the provincial assembly, was met at the gates of the town by the mayor, who presented an address, offering the respectful homage of himself and the inhabitants. His Majesty replied in the following terms, which do not require to be explained to our countrymen. Their meaning must be sufficiently clear to all.

"I see with much pleasure that Auxerre still remembers the First Empire. Let me assure you that I, on my side, have inherited the feelings of affection entertained by the Chief of our family for the patriotic and energetic communities which supported him alike through good and evil. And I myself owe a debt of gratitude to the department of the Yonne as being one of the first to declare for me in 1848. It knew, as indeed the greater part of the nation knew, that its interests and mine were identical and that we both equally detested those treaties of 1815, which are used to-day as a means of controlling our external policy."

Here the dispatch broke off, the sender evidently not considering the remainder of the emperor's discourse worth transcribing. Certainly his meaning was sufficiently clear without it. Nevertheless some minutes elapsed before the sense of the communication was understood by the readers, and evoked the display of hatred which naturally followed.

When at last they began to comprehend and to see the hand of the nephew of Napoleon the Great overshadowing their beloved Rhine, there arose from one end of Unter den Linden to the other such a tempest of threats, howls, and hurrahs, that, to borrow Schiller's lively expression, one would have thought the encircling hoops of the heavenly concave must all be burst asunder. Threatening toasts were called, curses shouted, and fists shaken against offending France. A Göttingen student springing on a table began to recite with due emphasis Rückert's ferocious poem entitled "The Return," in which a Prussian soldier, having returned home in consequence of peace being declared, bitterly regrets the various outrages he is in consequence debarred from committing. Needless to say, this recital was enthusiastically applauded. Shouts of "Bravo!" and "Hurrah!" mixed with cries of "Long live King William!" "Hurrah for Prussia!" "Down with France!" formed an accompaniment which would doubtless have been continued to the next piece, the reciter proposing to give a lyric by Theodor Körner. The announcement was received with loud applause.

It was, however, by no means the only safety valve at which the passion of the surging crowd, now at white heat, sought and found a vent. A little lower down, at the corner of the Friedrich Strasse, a well-known singer happened to be returning from rehearsal, and as he chanced on one occasion to have made a hit by singing "The German Rhine" some one who remembered this raised a cry of "The German Rhine! the German Rhine! Heinrich! sing 'The German Rhine!'" The crowd instantly recognized and surrounded the artist, who, owning a fine voice, and being familiar with the piece demanded, did not wait to be asked twice, but gratified his audience by singing his very best, thereby far surpassing the Return in the tremendous reception he obtained.

But all at once a loud and furious hiss which might have issued from the throttle of a steam engine was heard above all the wild applause, and produced the effect of a blow in the face bestowed on the singer. A bomb suddenly exploding in the crowd could hardly have been more effective; the hiss was answered by a dull roar something like that which precedes a hurricane and every eye was turned towards the quarter whence it proceeded.

Standing by a solitary table was a handsome young man, apparently about five-and-twenty, fair-haired, fair-skinned, rather slightly built, and in face, moustache and costume somewhat resembling the portrait of Vandyke. He had just opened a bottle of champagne and held a foaming glass aloft. Undisturbed by angry looks and threatening gestures he drew himself up, placed one foot on his chair, and raising his glass above his head cried loudly, "Vive la France!" then swallowed the contents at one draught.

## CHAPTER II. THE HOUSE OF HOHENZOLLERN

The immense crowd surrounding the young Frenchman remained for a moment dumb with stupefaction. Many, not understanding French, failed to comprehend his meaning, and others who did understand, appreciating his courage in thug braving a furious crowd, surveyed him with more astonishment than anger. Others again, who realized that a dire insult had been offered them, would nevertheless with typical German deliberation have allowed him time to escape had he wished. But the young man's demeanour showed that, whatever the consequences of his bravado, he intended to face them. Presently a threatening murmur of "Franzose, Franzose," arose from the crowd.

"Yes," said he, in as good German as might be heard anywhere between Thionville and Memel. "Yes, I am French. My name is Benedict Turpin. I have studied at Heidelberg and might pass for a German since I can speak your language as well as most of those here, and better than some. Also I can use a rapier, pistol, sword, sabre, single-stick, boxing gloves, or any other weapon you like to choose. Any one wishing for satisfaction may find me at the Black Eagle."

The young man had hardly finished his audacious defiance when four men of the lower class advanced upon him. The crowd kept silence, and the contemptuous words, "What! four to one? Leipzig again! Come on! I am ready!" were distinctly heard. Then, not waiting to be attacked, the young Frenchman sprang at the nearest and broke the bottle of champagne over his head, blinding him with foam. The second he tripped up, throwing him a good ten paces off, and disposed of the third with a vigorous blow in the ribs which hurled him against a chair. Then, seizing the fourth by the collar and grasping his waist he actually held him aloft in the air for a moment, then flinging him on the ground he placed a foot on his chest.

"Is not Leipzig avenged?" said he.

Then at last the tempest burst. A rush was made for the Frenchman, but he, still keeping a foot on his fallen enemy, seized a chair and whirled it round him so vigorously that for a moment the crowd was held at bay and only ventured on threats. But the circle drew closer, some one grasped the chair and succeeded in stopping it. A few moments more and the audacious Frenchman would probably have been torn to pieces had not two or three Prussian officers intervened. They forced their way through the crowd and formed a guard around the young man, one of them addressed the crowd thus:

"Come, come, my friends, don't murder a brave young man because he does not forget he is a Frenchman and has cried 'Vive la France!' He will now cry 'Vive Guillaume IV!' and we will let him off." Then, whispering to Benedict, "Cry 'Vive Guillaume IV!' or I can't answer for your life."

"Yes!" bawled the crowd, "let him cry 'Vive Guillaume IV!—Vive la Prusse!' and we will let him go."

"Very well," said Benedict, "but I prefer to do so freely, and without compulsion. Leave me alone and let me speak from a table."

"Stand aside and let him pass," said the officers, releasing Benedict and leaving him free. "He wishes to address you."

"Let him speak! let him speak!" cried the crowd.

"Gentlemen!" said Benedict, mounting the table nearest to the open windows of the café, "oblige me by listening. I cannot cry 'Vive la Prusse,' because at this very moment my country may be at war with yours, in which case a Frenchman would disgrace himself if he cried anything except 'Vive la France.' Nor can I very well cry 'Vive le roi Guillaume,' because, not being my king, it does not matter to me whether he lives or dies. But I will recite some charming verses in answer to your 'German Rhine!'"

The audience heard him impatiently, not knowing what he meant to recite. They had another disappointment in discovering that the lines in question were not German but French. However, they listened with all the more attention. In enumerating his accomplishments Benedict had omitted those of amateur actor and elocutionist. The lines were those written by de

Musset in response to the "German Rhine," and they lost nothing in his impassioned delivery. Those among his hearers able to follow the reciter soon perceived that they had been tricked into listening to truths they had no desire to hear. Once this was understood, the storm, momentarily lulled, burst forth with redoubled violence.

Knowing that there would be no further chance of protection, Benedict was carefully considering the distance between his table and the nearest window, when suddenly the attention of the crowd was diverted by the report of several pistol-shots rapidly fired in the immediate vicinity. Turning towards the sound they perceived a well-dressed young civilian, struggling desperately with a much older man in colonel's uniform. The young man fired again, with the only result of further exasperating his adversary, who seized him with a grasp of iron, and, disdaining to call for help, shook him as a terrier shakes a rat. Then, throwing him down, he knelt upon the would-be murderer's chest, tore the now useless revolver from his hand, and placed the barrel against his forehead. "Yes, fire, fire!" gasped the young man. But the colonel, in whom the bystanders now recognized the powerful minister, Count von Bismarck, changed his mind. He pocketed the revolver, and beckoning to two officers, "Gentlemen," said he, "this young man is probably mad, or at any rate he is a clumsy fool. He attacked me without the slightest provocation and has fired five times without hitting me. You had better consign him to the nearest prison whilst I acquaint the king with what has happened. I think I need hardly mention my name—Count von Bismarck."

Then, wrapping his handkerchief round his hand which had been slightly scratched in the conflict, the count retraced his steps towards the royal palace hardly a hundred yards distant, while the two officers handed the assassin over to the police. One of them accompanied him to the prison, where he was at once incarcerated. The crowd having now time to remember Benedict Turpin found that he had vanished. However, this did not trouble them much, for the excitement of the more recent event had changed the course of their ideas. Let us profit by the interval and glance at the characters who are destined to appear in our recital. But, first let us examine the stage on which they will play their several parts.

24

Least German of all Germanic states, Prussia is inhabited by a mixture of races. Besides Germans proper, numbers of Slavonians are found there. There are also descendants of the Wends, Letts, Lithuanians, Poles, and other early tribes, and a mixture of Frankish refugees. The prosperity, though not perhaps the grandeur of the House of Hohenzollern, began with Duke Frederic, the greatest usurer of his day. It is as impossible to calculate the enormous sums wrung from the Jews as to narrate the means by which they were extorted. At first a vassal of the Emperor Wenceslaus, when that monarch's impending fall became evident Frederic deserted his camp for that of his rival Otho, and when Otho's crown began to totter, he passed over to Sigismund, brother of Wenceslaus.

In 1400 A.D., the same year in which Charles VI ennobled the goldsmith Raoul, as a reward for financial help, Sigismund, equally embarrassed, borrowed 100,000 florins from Frederic, giving him the Margravate of Brandenburg as security. Fifteen years later, Sigismund having had to provide for the extravagance of the Council of Constance, found himself in debt to Frederic for 400,000 florins. Utterly unable to pay, he sold, or granted in compensation, both the Marches of Brandenburg and the dignity of Elector. In 1701 the electorate rose into a kingdom and the Duke Frederic III became the King Frederic I of Prussia.

The Hohenzollerns display the faults and the characteristics of their race. Their exchequer is admirably managed, but the moral balance-sheet of their administration can rarely be compared with the financial one. They have advanced on the lines of Duke Frederic, with more or less hypocrisy, but with ever-increasing rapacity. Thus in 1525, Albert of Hohenzollern, Grand Master of the Teutonic knights, then lords of Prussia, forsook his faith and became a Lutheran, receiving in return the rank of Hereditary Duke of Prussia, under the over-lordship of Poland. And in 1613, the Elector John Sigismund, wishing to obtain the duchy of Cleves, followed Albert's example and became a Calvinist.

The policy of the Great Elector has been summed up by Leibnitz in a single phrase: "I side with him who pays best." To him is due the formation of the European permanent standing army, and it was his second wife, the famous Dorothea, who started shops and taverns in Berlin for the disposal of her beer and dairy produce. The military genius of the Great Frederic is beyond dispute, but it was he who, in order to curry favour with the Russian Court, offered to "supply" the Grand Dukes with German princesses "at the lowest reasonable rate!" One lady thus "supplied" a princess of Anhalt, is known as "Catherine the Great." We may remark incidentally that he also is chiefly responsible for the partition of Poland, a crime which has weighted the Prussian crown with the malediction of nations, and which he celebrated by this scandalously impious summons to his brother Henry, "Come, let us receive the Eucharist of the body of Poland!" To Frederic also, we owe the economical maxim, "He dines best who eats at another's table!"

Frederic died childless, a fact for which, oddly enough, historians have seen fit to blame him. His nephew and successor, William II, invaded France in 1792. His entry, preceded by the famous manifesto of the Duke of Brunswick, was ostentatious to a degree, but his departure, accompanied by Danton and Dumouriez, was accomplished without sound of trumpet or drum.

He was succeeded by the "Man of Jena," Frederic William III. Among the numerous stupid, and servile letters received by the Emperor Napoleon in the days of his prosperity, must be counted those of William III.

Frederic William IV—we are rapidly approaching our own times—came to the throne in June 1840. According to the Hohenzollern custom his first ministry was a liberal one and on his accession he remarked to Alexander von Humboldt:

"As a noble I am the first gentleman in the kingdom; as a king I am only the first citizen."

Charles X had said much the same on succeeding to the crown of France, or, rather, M. de Martignac had said it for him.

The first proof the king gave of his liberalism was an attempt to drill properly the intellectual forces of the kingdom, which duty he entrusted to the Minister Eichhorn. The name—it means "squirrel"—was quite prophetic.

26

At the end of ten years the project had not advanced a step, although the minister himself had done wonders of perpetual revolution. On the other hand reaction had progressed. The press was persecuted, promotion and rewards were obtained only by hypocrites and informers. High office could only be acquired by becoming a servile instrument of the pietistic party, which was headed by the king.

Frederic William and King Louis of Bavaria were the two most literary of contemporary sovereigns. But Louis encouraged Art under whatever form it appeared, whereas Frederic William wished it to be drilled into a sort of auxiliary to despotism. Feeling himself constrained, like our great satirist Boileau, to give an example of good manners to both court and city, he began a correspondence with Louis, in the course of which he sent the latter a quatrain commenting on the scandal caused by his intimacy with Lola Montes. The King of Bavaria replied in another which made the round of all the courts of Europe.

"Contempteur de l'amour, dont adore l'ivresse,

Frère, tu dis que, roi sans pudeur, sans vertu,

Je garde à tort Lola, ma fille enchanteresse.

Je te l'enverrai bien.—Oui; mais qu'en ferais-tu?"

And, by general consent of the wits, the laugh remained on the side of the versatile King Louis.

After six years of domiciliary visits, suppressions, and summary expulsions of offending journalists, the Prussian Diet at length assembled at Berlin. In his opening speech the king addressed the deputies thus:

"Recollect, gentlemen, that you are here to represent the interests of the people, but not their sentiments."

A little later in the year, Frederic William inaugurated his Divine Right by observing as he tore up the Constitution:

"I shall not allow a scrap of paper to stand between my people and their

God!" meaning, though he did not dare to say it, "between my people and me."

Then the revolution of 1848 burst forth, and did not spare Berlin, which was soon in full revolt. The king lost his head completely. In leaving the town he had to drive past the dead bodies of rioters killed in the struggle. There was a shout of "Hats off!" and the king was obliged to remain uncovered while the people sang the famous hymn composed by the Great Electress.

"Jesus, my Redeemer lives."

Every one knows how Absolutism succeeded in dominating the National Assembly, and how presently reaction brought the following leaders into power:

Manteuffel, whose policy led to the unfortunate Austrian triumph at Olmutz.

Westphalen, who revived provincial councils, and brought the king to the famous Warsaw interview.

Statel, a converted Jew and Protestant Jesuit, a Grand Inquisitor who had missed his vocation.

And, lastly, the two Gerlachs, intriguers of the first water, whose history belongs to that of the two spies, Ladunberg and Techen.

Although the Constitution, establishing two Chambers, was sworn to by William IV, February 6th, 1850, it was not until his successor, William Louis, was on the throne that both Upper and Lower Chambers began to legislate.

A league was now formed by the bureaucracy, the orthodox clergy, the provincial squirearchy, and some of the proletariat. This was the origin of the famous association inappropriately designated the Patriotic Association, which had for its aim the annihilation of the Constitution.

There now appeared as First President of the Association at Königsberg, the Count von Bismarck, who has played so great a part in Prussian history.

We cannot do less for him than we have done for the Hohenzollerns, that is to say, we must devote an entire chapter to him and to the Prussia of to-day. For is not the Count von Bismarck a much greater monarch than the King of Prussia himself?

## CHAPTER III. COUNT VON BISMARCK

Many have sought, and some profess to have found, the reasons for the remarkable royal favour enjoyed by Count Bismarck, but the chief, and to our thinking the only one, is the extraordinary genius which even his enemies dare not dispute, notwithstanding the fact that genius is usually anything but a passport to the favour of kings.

We will relate one or two little anecdotes concerning the Prime Minister, beginning with one which does not refer to him personally, but may serve as a sort of preface to another. Every one knows the absurd point to which military etiquette is carried in Prussia.

A Pomeranian general—Pomerania may be called the Prussian Bœotia—being in garrison at Darmstadt and being bored even to the fullest possibility of Darmstadt boredom, was standing at his window, wishing for a conflagration, a revolution, an earthquake—anything—when he beheld an officer in the distance—an officer minus his sword! An awful breach of discipline! "Ah!" thought the delighted general, "here is a lieutenant to make a scapegoat of. Ten minutes' lecture and a fortnight's arrest! What luck!"

The unsuspecting officer drew nearer, and when within hail: "Lieutenant Rupert," shouted the general. The officer looked up, saw the general, and immediately remembering his missing sword, understood his terrible position. The general had seen him; he could not go back, and he felt he must brave the storm. The general beamed and rubbed his hands cheerfully at the prospect of some amusement at last. The lieutenant plucked up courage, entered the house, and arriving at the ante-room, beheld a regulation sword hanging on the wall. "What a mercy!" he murmured, unhooking the sword and quickly buckling it on. Then looking as innocent as possible, he entered the room, and standing at attention by the door,

"The general did me the honour to call," he said.

"Yes," said the general with severity, "I have to enquire—" he stopped suddenly, observing that the culprit's sword was at his side. His expression changed, and he said smiling:

"Yes, I wanted to ask, I wanted to ask—What on earth was it? Ah, yes. I wanted to ask after your family, Lieutenant Rupert. I particularly wished to enquire after your father."

"If my father could hear of your kind feeling towards him, general, he would be greatly gratified. Unhappily, he died twenty years ago."

The general looked considerably taken aback.

The young officer continued: "Have you any further commands, sir?"

"Why, no," said the general. "Only this. Never be seen without your sword. Had you been without it to-day, I should have given you a fortnight's arrest."

"I will take the greatest care, sir! You see?" answered the lieutenant, boldly indicating the sword which hung at his side.

"Yes, yes, I see. It is all right. You can go now."

The young man lost no time in profiting by the permission; he saluted, left the room, and carefully hung up the sword as he went through the ante-room. As he left the house the general, being again at the window, again saw that he had no sword. He summoned his wife:

"Look here," he said, "do you see that officer?"

"Certainly I do," she replied.

"Has he a sword or not?"

"He has not."

"Well then, you are mistaken; he looks as if he hadn't one, but he has."

The lady made no remark, being accustomed to accept whatever her husband said. The young officer escaped with the fright, and took good care not to forget his sword a second time.

Well, a similar misfortune—more, a real humiliation of this kind very nearly happened to the King of Prussia, when he was only the Prince Royal. Von Bismarck was then merely an attaché at the Frankfort Legation without any handle to his name. When the prince stopped at Frankfort on his way to a review at Mayence von Bismarck had the honour of being told off to accompany him.

It was a hot day in August and the railway carriages were stifling. Etiquette notwithstanding, everyone from the prince downward, unbuttoned his coat. On arriving at Mayence, where the troops were drawn up at the station to receive him, the prince refastened his coat but left one button undone. He was just leaving the carriage, when, luckily, von Bismarck noticed the oversight.

"Good heavens, prince!" he exclaimed, "what are you about?"

And, for once forgetting etiquette, which forbids the royal person to be contaminated by profane fingers, he sprang forward and fastened the offending button. Hence, according to some, came the royal favour, for the king, greatly embarrassed by the events of '58, reflected that the man who had saved his credit at Mayence might also save his crown at Berlin.

The count now became the leader of the "Junker" faction, voiced by the "Kreuz Zeitung." He was, in fact, the fittest man for the position, possessing oratorical eloquence, great mental and physical activity, and a complete conviction that any sort of means is justified by the end. And, the end accomplished, he flung from the height of his tribune this epigram in the face of an astonished Chamber: "Might is Right!" in three words summing up both his political creed and the direct consequences which followed.

The life-giving principles of humanity should be exemplified by three nations:

Commercial activity by England.

Moral expansion by Germany.

Intellectual brilliance by France.

If we ask why Germany does not occupy the great position assigned to her we find the answer in this: France has attained freedom of thought, but Germany is allowed only the freedom of a dreamer. The sole atmosphere in which she can breathe freely is that of the fortress or the prison. And if we wonder why the rest of Germany is ruled by the rod of Prussia the explanation may be found in this: German manners do not exist, but there is a national genius; a genius which desired no revolution, but peace and liberty, and, above all—intellectual independence. This desire was Prussia's greatest difficulty; she fought it, she weakened it, and she hopes to conquer it entirely. She boasts of her compulsory education; her children are indeed taught all they can be taught, but once out of school they are never permitted to think for themselves.

The Junker faction is composed chiefly of younger sons who have to seek either an official career or a military one. Failing this, they must depend on the head of the family for a decent maintenance. With very few exceptions there is no "old nobility" in Prussia, the aristocracy is not distinguished by either wealth or intellect. A few names here and there recall ancient Germanic history; others belong to Prussian military annals. But the rest of the nobility can claim no distinction, and have only owned their estates for a century or two.

Consequently, nearly all the liberal and progressive members of the Chamber depend, either by position or office, on the Government, and not one of them was strong enough to fight against a despotism which seizes a child at the moment of his birth, guides him through adolescence, and escorts him for the rest of his life. Therefore Count von Bismarck could insult both Chamber and deputies with impunity, knowing that their complaints would rouse no answering echo in the country, while at Court they were considered as being next door to the servants. On one occasion the President Grabow, being present at a state concert, was going to occupy a chair in one of the less crowded rooms, when a footman stopped him with "These chairs are meant for Excellencies, sir."

"Indeed, my friend," answered the President, "I am evidently out of place here."

From the advent of Hohenzollern supremacy may be dated the decay of moral independence, both in Prussia and the other Germanic states. Not only have the Hohenzollerns failed to exercise any civilizing influence by encouraging literature and purifying the language, but they have changed Minerva into Pallas, and the beneficent deity of knowledge and wisdom has become the Medusa-brandishing goddess of war.

# CHAPTER IV. IN WHICH BISMARCK EMERGES FROM AN IMPOSSIBLE POSITION

Now for three months past Bismarck had been in an impossible position, and no one could predict how he would emerge from it. Notwithstanding the important events which were being enacted from China to Mexico, it was upon him that the eyes of Europe were fixed.

Old ministers, experienced in all the wiles of diplomacy, followed him with their eyes, spyglass in hand, never doubting that the epoch-making minister had an accomplice on the throne in a policy of which they vainly sought for precedents in the world's history. If, however, there should prove to be no accomplice, they pronounced that he must be a fool without an equal.

Young diplomats, modestly aware that they did not quite rank with the Talleyrands, the Metternichs, or Nesselrodes, studied him more seriously, believing they desired the infancy of a new policy destined to carry their epoch to its zenith, whispering the question which Germany has asked for three hundred years: "Ist es der Mann?" (Can it be the Man?) To make this question comprehensible we must tell our readers that Germany awaits a liberator as the Jews awaited a Messiah. Whenever her chains gall her, she exclaims: "Wo bleibt der Mann?" (Where, then, is the Man?)

Now, some pretend that to-day in Germany a fourth party, which up to the present has been crouching in the gloom, is preparing to emerge—a horrible figure, if the poets of Germany are to be believed. Listen to Heine on the subject:

"There is thunder truly in Germany, yea, even in Germany: it comes slowly; it rolls up gradually from afar; but I doubt not it will come.

"And when you hear a crash, such a crash as the world has not heard in all history, you will know that the German thunder has done its work. At this uproar eagles will fall dead from the upper air; and lions in the pathless deserts of Africa will crouch terrified in their lairs. In Germany will be enacted a drama compared with which the French Revolution will seem but an innocent idyll."

Had Heinrich Heine been the only prophet I should not repeat his auguries, for Heine was a dreamer. But here is what Ludwig B—— says:

"In truth, Germany has accomplished nothing for three centuries, and has patiently endured all the suffering inflicted upon her. But, even so, her labours, sufferings, and joys have not subdued her virgin heart, nor her chaste spirit. She contains the reserve forces of liberty and will ensure its triumph.

"Her day will come; and to bring it about but little is necessary a flash of good-humour, a smile, a summer shower, a thaw, a fool the more, or a fool the less, a nothing; the bell of a mule is enough to bring down an avalanche. Then France, which is not easily astonished, France which accomplished in three days the work of three hundred years, and has ceased to wonder at her own work, will survey the German nation with astonishment which will not be merely surprise but admiration."

But whether it was the Man or was not the Man that the gallery watched as he weighed Europe in the scales, putting everything into one, nothing into the other, whether he belonged to the old or to the new diplomacy mattered little. The only question was—will von Bismarck demand a dissolution of the Chamber, or will the Chamber impeach the count?

The conquest of Schleswig-Holstein had carried him to the height of fortune, but the new complications arising à propos of the election of the Duke of Augustenburg, made everything seem doubtful even to the genius of von Bismarck. During a long interview with the king which took place the very day on which this story begins, he fancied that his influence was shaken, and he attributed the king's coldness to the persistent ill will of the queen.

It is true that until now the count had worked only for his own personal advancement, and, having kept entire silence as to his projects, was reserving an explanation for a favourable moment, when by the grandeur and clearness of his views he hoped to recover the goodwill of his sovereign, by an audacious coup d'état to build up a more solid and unassailable position than ever.

He had, then, just left the king, intending to unmask his new plan as soon as possible, counting on the telegraphic despatches to create an effect favourable to himself, which, by making war inevitable, would ensure his own safety.

He left the palace accordingly, immersed in these thoughts, and so preoccupied that not only did he scarcely observe the excitement in the crowded streets, but he did not notice a young man leaning against one of the columns of the theatre, who left his place as he passed, and followed him like his shadow in and out of the groups blocking the street. Twice or thrice, however, as if warned of this close pursuit by some magnetic current, the count turned his head, but seeing only a well-dressed young man apparently belonging to his own class in life, he paid no attention to him.

It was not until he had passed the Friedrich Strasse and was crossing the road that he really noticed that the young man seemed determined to follow him. He then decided as soon as he had reached the other side to stop and ask what his pursuer meant by shadowing him.

But the shadower did not give him an opportunity. The count had hardly proceeded three or four steps on his way when he heard a report, and felt the wind of a ball which just missed his coat collar. He stopped and turned sharply round, seeing in a flash the eddying smoke, the aimed revolver, the assassin with his finger on the trigger preparing to fire again.

But, as we have said, the count was naturally brave: it did not occur to him either to fly or to call for help. He threw himself upon his enemy, who, without an instant's delay, fired the second and third shots, which whistled harmlessly by. Whether the assassin's hand trembled under stress of emotion, or whether, as some say, Providence (which nevertheless permitted the assassinations of Henri IV and Gustavus Adolphus) forbade the accomplishment of such a crime, the two balls passed right and left of von Bismarck.

Then the murderer lost courage and turned to fly. But the count seized him by the collar with one hand and with the other clutched the barrel of the revolver. Once again a shot was fired; the count was slightly wounded, but kept his hold and grasped his adversary closely, throwing him on the ground, and finally handed him over to the Prussian officers.

Seizing the favourable occasion with the promptitude of genius, he again took his way to the palace, bent on making this event the turning point of the situation.

This time he passed through a double avenue of spectators, whereas previously in the public commotion no one had noticed him. It was now otherwise—the murderer's attempt, of which he had been the object and from which he had emerged with so much courage, attracted every one's attention, if not their sympathy, and whether loved or not loved, all made room and saluted him. Sympathy might be wanting, but the count could at all events read admiration upon every face.

Von Bismarck was at this time about fifty or fifty-two; tall, with a well-proportioned figure, slightly puffy, and almost bald except at the temples, with a thick moustache. One of his cheeks was furrowed by a scar, the legacy of a duel fought at the University of Göttingen.

The palace guard had already heard the news and turned out to receive the count, who, as colonel in the Army, was entitled to this mark of respect. He graciously responded, and went up the staircase leading to the king's audience chamber.

As prime minister, the count had the right of entry at any time. He was about to turn the door handle when the usher in waiting stopped him, saying:

"His Excellency will pardon me, but the king can see no one."

"Not even me?" asked the count.

"Not even your Excellency," replied the usher with a low bow.

The count stepped backward with a movement of the lips that might have passed for a smile, but was certainly not one. Then he began to study, but without seeing it, a large naval picture which decorated the ante-room, standing out by reason of its immense gilt frame from the official green paper which adorns all the royal apartments.

At the end of a quarter of an hour, the door opened, the count hearing the frou frou of a satin dress, turned and bowed low before a woman of forty to forty-five years of age, who had evidently possessed great beauty and was indeed still beautiful. Perhaps, if the "Almanach de Gotha" were consulted, it would be found that the lady was rather older than this, but as the proverb says: "A woman is as old as she looks," and I see no reason why queens should be excepted.

The lady was Queen Marie Louise Augusta Catherine, daughter of Charles Frederic, Grand Duke of Saxe-Weimar, and known throughout Europe as the Queen Augusta. She was of medium height—is best described by the essentially French word attrayant. She wore on her left arm the feminine Order of Queen Louise of Prussia. She passed the minister slowly and somewhat haughtily, saluting him indeed, but without her usual kindness. By the doors through which she passed the count understood she had been with the king, and was now returning to her own apartments.

The queen had left the door belonging to the king's apartment open behind her, and the usher now intimated that the minister might enter. He waited, however, until the door had closed upon the queen.

"Yes," he said, "it is true that I was not born a baron, but let us see what the future will do for me."

And then he passed forward. The various lackeys or chamberlains whom he met hastened to open the doors leading to the audience-room. Reaching it the chamberlain announced in a loud voice: "His Excellency Count von Bismarck."

The king started and turned round. He was standing before the chimney-piece, and heard the name of von Bismarck with some surprise, it being barely a quarter of an hour since the minister had left him. The count wondered if the king had already heard what had happened to him in the interval.

He bowed low before His Majesty.

"Sire," he said, "an event of great importance has recalled me to Your Majesty, but I see with regret that the moment is unfavourable—"

"Why?" enquired the king.

"Because I have just had the honour of meeting the queen in the ante-room, and not having the happiness of being in Her Majesty's good graces—"

"Well, count, I admit that she does not see eye to eye with you."

"She is wrong, sire, for my devotion belongs equally to my king and to my queen, and the one cannot become Emperor of Germany without the other becoming Empress."

"A dream, my dear count, in which Queen Augusta unfortunately believes, but which is not the dream of a reasonable being."

"Sire, the unity of Germany is as much decreed in the design of Providence as the unity of Italy."

"Excellent," said the king, laughing; "can there be a united Italy while the Italians possess neither Rome nor Venice?"

"Italy is in formation, sire. She began her march in '59 and will not stop on the way. If she looks like stopping, she is only taking breath. Indeed, have we not promised her Venice?"

"Yes, but it is not we who will give it her."

"Who then?"

"France? who has already given her Lombardy, and has let her take the duchies and Naples. France!" said the king. "France let her take all that with quite the best will in the world."

"Is Your Majesty aware of the contents of the telegraphic despatches which arrived when I was here and which were delivered as I left?"

"Yes, I know. The Emperor Napoleon's speech at Auxerre," answered the king with some embarrassment. "You refer to that, do you not?"

"Well, sire, the emperor's speech means war—war not only against Austria but against Germany. It means Venice for Italy and the Rhine provinces for France."

"You really think so?"

"I mean that if we give France time to arm, the question without becoming desperate becomes grave, but that if we fall promptly and vigorously upon Austria, we shall be on the Moldau with three hundred thousand men before France can reach the Rhine with fifty thousand."

"Count, you do not give the Austrians their proper value; the swagger of our young men has gone to your head."

"Sire, if I appear to adopt the opinions of the heir-apparent and of Prince Frederic Charles, I can only say that the prince having been born on June 29th, 1801, is scarcely a young man; but the fact is, that in these matters I rely on my own opinion only, and I say deliberately in a war against Prussia, Austria will certainly be beaten."

"Really?" said the king doubtfully. "Yet I have heard you speak in high terms of both their generals and their soldiers."

"Certainly."

"Well then, it does not seem to me so remarkably easy to conquer good soldiers commanded by good generals."

"They have good, soldiers, sire, they have good generals, but we shall beat them because our own organization and arrangement are superior to theirs. When I persuaded Your Majesty to undertake the war on Schleswig which Your Majesty did not desire to do—"

"If I had not desired to make war on Schleswig it would never have been made!"

"That is very true, sire, but Your Majesty hesitated; I had the courage to insist, and Your Majesty approved of my reasons."

"Yes, and what is the result of the war on Schleswig? War throughout Germany!"

"True, sire, in the first place I like a situation that calls for resolute action; and as I consider war in Germany inevitable, I congratulate you."

"Will you explain whence comes your confidence?"

"Your Majesty forgets that I made the campaign with the Prussian army. I did not do it for the mere pleasure of hearing cannon, of counting the dead, and of sleeping on the battlefield, where I assure you one sleeps very badly, or for the purpose of giving you what was nevertheless well worth having, two posts on the Baltic, of which Prussia stood in great need. No, I made the campaign with the object of trying the Austrians, and I repeat that they are behind us in everything—discipline, armaments, use of arms: they have bad rifles, bad artillery, and worse powder. In a war against us Austria will be beaten from the very commencement, for we have everything which she has not, and Austria once vanquished, the supremacy in Germany must inevitably fall from her hands into those of Prussia."

"And how is Prussia with a population of eighteen millions to maintain her superiority over sixty? Only look at her pitiful appearance on the map."

"That is exactly the point. I have looked at her for three years, and now is the time to mould her anew. Prussia is a great serpent whose head is at Thionville, while her tail is at Memel, and which has a lump in her stomach because she has swallowed half Saxony. She is a kingdom cut in two by another—Hanover—in such a fashion that you cannot get home without going abroad. You must understand, sire, Hanover is bound to become part of Prussia."

"But what will England say to this?"

"England is no longer in the age of Pitt and Cobourg. England is the very humble servant of the Manchester School, of Gladstone, Cobden, and their scholars; England will do no more for Hanover than she did for Denmark. Must we not take Saxony also?"

"France will never allow us to meddle with Saxony, if only in memory of the king who was faithful to her in 1813."

"Not if we took too big a mouthful; but if we only nibble she will shut both eyes, or at least one of them. And is not Hesse also very necessary?"

"The Confederation will not abandon all Hesse."

"But if it will let us take half, that is all we want. Now let us consider

Frankfort-on-the-Main."

"Frankfort-on-the-Main! The free town! The seat of the Diet!"

"The moment Prussia can reckon thirty millions of men instead of eighteen the Diet is dead. Prussia will then be the Diet. Only, instead of crying a decree she will say 'decree.'"

"We shall have the whole of the Confederation against us. It will side with Austria."

"So much the better!"

"And why?"

"Austria once beaten, the Confederation is beaten along with her."

"We shall have a million men against us."

"Let us count them."

"There are four hundred and fifty thousand in Austria—"

"Agreed."

"And four hundred and fifty thousand in Venetia."

"The emperor is too obstinate to recall troops from Venice before two or three battles if he is successful, before ten if he is beaten."

"Bavaria has one hundred and sixty thousand."

"I will answer for Bavaria—her king is too fond of music to love the sound of cannon."

"Hanover, twenty-five thousand men."

"Only a mouthful to swallow on our first march."

"Saxony, fifteen thousand."

"Another mouthful."

"And a hundred and fifty thousand belonging to the Confederation."

"The Confederation will have no time to arm them; only we must not lose a moment, sire; therefore I now say 'War, Victory, the supremacy of Prussia—myself—or-'"

"Or?"

"Or my resignation, which I lay very humbly at Your Majesty's feet."

"What is that on your hand, count?"

"Nothing, sire."

"It looks like blood."

"Perhaps it is."

"Is it true, then, that some one attempted your life by firing at you with a revolver?"

"Five times, sire."

"Five? Good gracious!"

"He thought it none too many for me."

"And you are unwounded?"

"Only a scratch on the little finger."

"And who was your assassin?"

"I do not know who he is."

"Did he refuse to give his name?"

"No, I forgot to ask him; besides, that is the Attorney-General's affair, not mine. I do not interfere with other people's concerns. Now, my own business is my King's business, and that is here."

"I am listening," said the king.

"To-morrow the chamber is dissolved; the following day we mobilize; in eight days hostilities are declared, or else—"

"Or else what?"

"Or else, as I have the honour to repeat to Your Majesty, my resignation."

Then, without waiting for the king's answer the Count von Bismarck bowed low, and according to etiquette retired backwards from the king's presence. The king said nothing to detain his minister, but before closing the door, that gentleman heard the bell rung loudly enough to rouse the whole palace.

# CHAPTER V. A SPORTSMAN AND A SPANIEL

On the day following the events just narrated, a young man about twenty-five years of age arrived in Brunswick by the eleven o'clock train from Berlin. Leaving his luggage, which was labelled "Hanover," in the station, he took a small knapsack on which were strapped a sketch-book and camp-stool, buckled on a cartridge belt, flung a baldric supporting a double-barrelled gun over his shoulder, and completed his toilet with a large grey felt hat. Altogether he appeared a sort of cross between sportsman and tourist. Accompanied by a beautiful jet-black spaniel he left the station and hailed an open carriage, whereupon the dog instantly justified his name of "Frisk" by springing joyously in, and installing himself on the front seat, while his master reclined on the back after the manner of one accustomed to do things comfortably. Courteously addressing the driver in excellent German:

"Coachman," said he, "kindly take me to the best hotel the town affords, or at any rate, to the one which provides the best lunch!"

The coachman nodded as if to say he required no further instructions, and the carriage rattled and bumped over the cobble stones to the Hôtel d'Angleterre. The dog, who had hardly been able to retain his position, instantly sprang out, and showing his relief by active gambols, besought his master to follow. The latter alighted, but left his knapsack and gun in the carriage. Turning to the driver:

"You may wait," he said, "and keep an eye on my things."

Hackney coachmen, all the world over, have a keen eye for good customers. This honest fellow was no exception.

"Excellency may be quite satisfied," he answered with a wink. "I will keep careful guard over them."

The traveller entered the inn, and passing straight through it arrived at a pleasant court shaded by lime-trees. Here he selected a small table with chairs for two, one of which was promptly occupied by Frisk; his master took possession of the other and the two proceeded to lunch. This occupied an hour, and no lady could have received more attention than the young man bestowed on Frisk. The dog ate whatever his master ate, only politely protesting when a hare, accompanied by currant jelly, appeared on the scene, that as a sporting dog he ought not to touch game, and personally had a serious objection to sweets. Meanwhile, the driver remaining on his box refreshed himself with bread, cheese, and a half bottle of wine. Consequently, when master and dog re-occupied the carriage the trio presented an appearance of general satisfaction.

"Where to, Excellency?" enquired the driver, wiping his mouth on his sleeve, with the air of a man ready to drive to the world's end if you wished.

"I don't quite know," was the answer, "it depends a little on you."

"How so?"

"Well, if I find you a good fellow, I might wish to keep you on for some time."

"Oh, a year if you like!"

"No, that is too long."

"Well, a month then."

"Neither a year nor a month, but a day or two."

"Oh, that's not enough. I really thought you meant to take me on lease."

"To begin with, what will you charge for going to Hanover?"

"It is six leagues, you know."

"Four and a half, you mean."

"But it is up and down hill the whole way."

"Nonsense! it is as flat as a billiard-table."

"One can't get round you," said the grinning driver.

"In one way you can."

"And which is that?"

"Simply by being honest."

"Ah, indeed! That is a new idea."

"It is one which has not before occurred to you, I think."

"Well, name your own price, then."

"Four florins."

"But you are not counting the drive from the station and the time for lunch."

"You are right, I will allow for that."

"And the pourboire."

"That is as I may choose."

"Agreed. I don't know why, but I trust you."

"Only, if I keep you more than a week it will then be three and a half florins per day, and no pourboire."

"I couldn't agree to that."

"Why not?"

"Because I see no reason for depriving you of the pleasure of doing the handsome thing when I have the misfortune of leaving you."

"The dickens! One would take you for a wit!"

"I've wit enough to look like a fool when I want to."

"Well done! Where do you come from?"

"From Sachsenhausen."

"And where may that be?"

"It is a suburb of Frankfort."

"Ah! yes, it is a Saxon colony from the days of Charlemagne."

"That is so. So you know that, do you?"

"I also know that you are a fine race, something like the Auvergnats of France. We will settle up when we part."

"That's suits me down to the ground."

"What's your name?

"Lenhart."

"Very well, Lenhart, let us get on then."

The carriage started, scattering the usual crowd of idle spectators. A few minutes brought it to the end of the street leading to the open country. The day was magnificent. The trees had just burst into leaf, and earth had assumed a mantle of green, the soft spring breeze seemed laden with the perfume of flowers. Overhead the birds were already seeking food for their little ones, and awakening Nature appeared to listen to their songs. From time to time a lark arose from among the corn, and ascending high in the air seemed as if floating above the summit of a pyramid of song.

Beholding this magnificent country the traveller exclaimed: "But there must be splendid shooting here, is there not?"

"Yes, but it is strictly preserved," replied the coachman.

"So much the better," said our friend, "there will be all the more game."

In fact, before they had gone quite a mile from the town, Frisk, who had given various signs of impatience, sprang out of the carriage, rushed into a field of clover, and pointed.

"Shall I go on or wait," enquired the driver, seeing the young man loading his gun.

"Go on a yard, or two," was the answer. "There, that will do; now, draw up as near to the field as you can."

The carriage, with the sportsman standing up in it, gun in hand, halted within thirty yards of the dog. The driver looked on with all the interest of his class, an interest which is always on the side of the sportsman and hostile to the landlord and the gamekeeper. "That is a clever dog," he remarked. "What is he pointing at?"

"It is a hare."

"How do you know?"

"Had it been a bird he would have wagged his tail. See."

A big leveret showed itself among the clover and fell a victim to the gun. It was promptly brought in by Frisk. Further on a covey of partridges was seen, but the dog was called off, and the young brood left in peace. They were already approaching Hanover when a startled hare was seen some sixty yards from the carriage.

"Ah!" said Lenhart, "this one wisely keeps his distance."

"It does not follow," replied the sportsman.

"You don't expect to hit at that distance, do you?"

"Have you still to learn, my friend, you who profess to be able to shoot, that to a good shot and a good gun distance is of small importance? Now, watch!"

Then, having altered the charges in his gun the young man enquired:

"Do you know all about the manners and customs of hares, Lenhart?"

"Why, yes, I think I know all any one can know who can't speak their language."

"Well, I can tell you this. A startled hare, if not pursued, will run about fifty paces and will then sit down to have a look round and perform his toilet. Look!"

And in fact, the hare, which had run towards the carriage, instead of away from it, suddenly stopped, sat down, and began to wash its face with its forepaws. This predicted toilet cost the poor animal its life. A prompt shot and the hare bounded upwards and fell back dead.

"Beg pardon, Excellency," said Lenhart, "but if we are going to war as it is said we are, on which side will you be?"

"As I am neither Austrian nor Prussian, but happen to be a Frenchman, you will probably find me fighting for France."

"So long as you do not fight for these Prussian beggars I am quite satisfied. If you will fight against them, however—donnerwetter—but I have something to say."

"Well? at is it?"

"I offer you the free use of my carriage to fight from."

"Thanks! my friend, 'tis an offer not to be despised. I always thought that if I had to fight, I should like to make the campaign in a carriage."

"Well, then, here is the very thing you want. I can't tell you how old my horse is, he wasn't young when I bought him ten years ago, but I know if I took him to a Thirty Years' War he would see me through it. As for the carriage, you can see it is as good as new. Those shafts were put on only three years ago, and last year it had new wheels and a new axle, and it is only six months since I provided it with a new body."

"You remind me of an anecdote we have in France," replied the other. "It is that of Simple Simon's knife, which had first a new blade and then a new handle, but was still the same knife."

"Ah, sir," said Lenhart, with the air of a philosopher, "every country has its Simple Simon's knife."

"And also its simpletons, my good friend."

"Well, if you put new barrels on your gun you might give me the old ones. Here comes your dog with the hare," lifting it by the ears. "You can join the other, you fool," he said. "See what comes of too much vanity! Ah, sir! don't fight against the Prussians if you don't want to, but, good heaven, don't fight for them!"

"Oh, as to that you may be quite easy. If I do fight, it will be against them, and perhaps I shall not wait for war to be declared."

"Bravo! Down with the Prussians!" cried Lenhart, touching up his horse with a sharp cut. The animal, as if to justify his praises, and excited by his master's voice and cracking whip, broke into a gallop, bolted through the suburban streets and only stopped at the Hôtel Royal.

# CHAPTER VI. BENEDICT TURPIN

Lenhart, in his double capacity of hackney coachman and purveyor of travellers and tourists for the Hôtel Royal, Hanover, was well known to Mr. Stephen, landlord thereof, who gave him a cordial reception. Anxious to magnify the importance of his present consignment, Lenhart hastened to inform him that the new arrival was a mortal enemy of the Prussians, that he never missed a shot, and that if war were declared, he would place himself and his deadly weapon at the disposal of the King of Hanover. To all of which Stephen lent an attentive ear.

"But where does your traveller come from," he at length enquired.

"He says he's a Frenchman, but I don't believe it. I've never once heard him boast about anything, besides, his German is too good. But there, he is calling you."

Stephen quickly answered the summons. The stranger was talking to an English officer of the Royal Household and his English appeared no less fluent than his German. Turning to Stephen he said in the latter language.

"I have asked a question of Colonel Anderson, who has kindly given me one-half of the answer, and tells me to apply to you for the rest. I asked for the title of the principal newspaper here, and the name of its editor. Colonel Anderson says the 'Hanoverian Gazette,' but does not know the editor's name."

"Wait a moment, Excellency. Yes, yes, let me see. He is Herr Bodemeyer, a tall, thin man with a beard, is he not?"

"Never mind his appearance. I want his name and address. I wish to send him my card."

"I only know the office address, Park Strasse. Do you dine at the table d'hôte? If so, Herr Bodemeyer is one of our regular guests. It is at five o'clock, he will be here in half-an-hour."

"All the more reason why he should have my card first," and producing a visiting-card bearing the legend "Benedict Turpin, Artist," he addressed it to Herr Bodemeyer, and handed it and a florin to the hotel messenger, who undertook to deliver it within ten minutes.

Stephen then ventured to suggest that if there were private matters to discuss a private room might be desirable.

"A good idea," said Benedict, and going to Colonel Anderson, "Sir," said he, "although we have never been formally introduced, I nevertheless hope you will waive etiquette and do me the honour of dining with me and Herr Bodemeyer, who I think will not refuse to join us. Our host promises an excellent dinner and good wine. It is six months since I left France, consequently six months since I had a chance of conversation. In England they talk, in Germany they dream, it is in France only that they converse. Let us have a nice little dinner at which we can do all three. Here is my card, that of an insignificant artist, devoid of armorial bearings or coronets, but with the simple Cross of the Légion d'Honneur. I would add, colonel," he continued seriously, "that in a day or two I may find myself obliged to ask a favour of you, and I should like to prove myself not unworthy of the consideration I hope you will show me."

The colonel accepted the card and bowed politely.

"Sir," said he with courteous English formality, "the hope you give me of being able to render you some service would certainly induce me to accept your hospitality. I have no reason whatever against dining with Herr Bodemeyer, and I have a thousand for wishing to dine with you, not the least being, if I may say so, that I find your person and manners exceedingly attractive."

Benedict bowed in his turn.

"Since you have done me the honour to accept," he said, "and I feel pretty sure of Herr Bodemeyer, it becomes my first duty to see that the dinner is a decent one. If you will excuse me I should like to interview the chef on the subject," and he departed kitchenwards while the colonel sought the hotel reading-room.

Left in possession of a fair income at an age when the usual idea is only how best to squander it, Benedict Turpin had shown practical sense as well as genius. A believer in the excellent proverb which says that a man doubles his opportunities in life when he learns a new language, he had quadrupled his by spending a year in England, another in Germany, a third in Spain, and a fourth in Italy. At eighteen he was a first-rate linguist, and he spent the next two years in completing his education by classical and scientific studies, not neglecting the use of weapons and the general practice of games, calculated to further his physical development. By the time he was twenty he had attained an all-round proficiency very unusual in youths of his age and promised much in the time to come.

He took part in the Chinese expedition, and being possessed of sufficient means to indulge his taste for travelling, spent several years in world-wide wandering, hunting wild beasts, traversing deserts, picking up tapestries, jewels, curiosities, etc., wherewith on his return he furnished one of the most artistic studios in Paris. At the time our story opens he had, in the course of a round of visits to celebrated German painters, arrived in Berlin, where he upheld the honour of France, with the insolent good luck which seemed never to desert him. When the attention of the mob was momentarily diverted by the attack on the Prime Minister, Benedict succeeded in escaping unnoticed, and took refuge at the French Embassy, where he was well known. Early in the following morning he left by train and finally arrived at Hanover without let or hindrance. He had just given his last instructions to the cook when he was warned that Herr Bodemeyer was already approaching the hotel.

Benedict hurried to the entrance, where he saw close at hand a gentleman drawing near, who held a visiting card in his hand, and seemed pondering much as to what the owner could possibly want with him.

It is said that the denizens of that ancient Gaul which gave Cæsar so much trouble have so marked a personality that, wherever one is seen, the passers-by immediately remark: "Look, that's a Frenchman!"

Herr Bodemeyer, at any rate, seemed to recognize Benedict's nationality at once. He advanced smiling, with extended hand. Benedict promptly descended the steps to meet him and the two exchanged the customary civilities. Hearing that the artist had come from Berlin, and being professionally eager for news, the editor at once demanded an account of the uproar of the previous evening, and of the attempted assassination of Count Bismarck.

As to the latter, Benedict could give little information. He had heard the shots, seen two men struggling, and one handed over to some officers, and then had hastily sprung into the café, left it by a door in another street, and found shelter at the Embassy. There he heard further that the young man was the stepson of a proscribed refugee of the '48, named Blind, and that he had made terrible accusations against the count, which, coming as they did from the relative of a banished rebel, were held to count for very little.

"Well, we know a little more than that," said Herr Bodemeyer, "we hear that the young man attempted to cut his throat with a penknife, but that the wounds were only slight and the doctor says are not dangerous. But the "Kreuz Zeitung" will be here directly and we shall know a little more."

Even as he spoke newsboys hurried down the street shouting "Kreuz Zeitung—Zeitung!" There was a rush for the paper. Hanover was nearly as excited as Berlin had been the night before. Did the poor little kingdom already feel itself in the crushing embrace of the Prussian boa-constrictor?

Benedict beckoned to one of the newsboys and bought a paper. Turning to the Hanoverian editor,

"I hope you will dine with me and Colonel Anderson," he said. "We have a private room, and can talk politics as much as we like. Besides, I have something to ask of you which I could hardly ask at a public table."

Just then Colonel Anderson approached. He and Bodemeyer knew each other by sight already. Benedict now formally introduced them. The colonel had already glanced at his newspaper.

"Do you know," said he, "that although the doctor pronounced the wound of no consequence, young Blind nevertheless died early this morning? A Hanoverian officer come from Berlin says that about four o'clock a man wrapped in a large cloak and wearing a large shady hat which concealed his face, arrived at the prison provided with a permission to see the prisoner, and was taken to his cell. Blind had been put into a strait waistcoat and no one knows what passed between them, but when his cell was inspected at eight o'clock he was dead. The doctor says he must have been dead nearly four hours, so that he must have died about the time this mysterious visitor left him."

"Is this official news?" enquired Bodemeyer. "As editor of a Government paper I am bound to accept only official information. Let us see what the 'Kreuz Zeitung' has to say."

They withdrew to the room assigned to them, and the Hanoverian editor proceeded to examine the Berlin newspaper. The first paragraph of consequence stated:

"We are assured that the king's warrant decreeing the dissolution of the Lower Chamber will be officially published to-morrow."

"Come," said the colonel, "that is of some importance."

"Wait a moment; there is something more."

"It is also announced that a decree ordering the mobilization of the Landwehr will be officially published the day after to-morrow."

"That is enough," observed the colonel, "we know now that the minister wins all along the line and that war will be declared in less than a fortnight. Let us have the general news. We know all we want to know of the political. Only, first, on which side will Hanover be?"

"There is no doubt about that," replied Bodemeyer. "Hanover is bound to adhere to the Confederation."

"And on which side is the Confederation," asked Benedict.

"On the side of Austria," answered the journalist promptly. "But listen, here is a fresh account of the scene in Unter den Linden."

"Oh! let us have that by all means," cried Benedict. "I was there, and I want to know if the account is correct.

"What! were you there?"

"Very much there," and he added laughing, "I might even say with Æneas, '*Et quorum pars magna fui.*' I was in the thick of it."

Herr Bodemeyer continued:

"We are now able to give fuller details concerning the demonstration in Unter den Linden which occurred yesterday after the report of the Emperor Louis Napoleon's speech had been received. It appears that just as our most distinguished vocalist finished singing 'The German Rhine,' which was received with tremendous enthusiasm, a loud hiss was heard. It was soon seen that the author of this insult was a foreigner, a French painter, evidently intoxicated, and who would probably have atoned for his folly with his life, had not some Prussian officers generously protected him from the infuriated populace. The young fool further defied the crowd by giving his name and address, but when enquiries were made at the Black Eagle this morning he had disappeared. We commend his prudence and wish him a pleasant journey."

"Is that paragraph signed," asked Benedict.

"No. Is it inaccurate?" returned the reader.

"May I be permitted to remark that the one thing I have everywhere observed in my wanderings over three of the four quarters of the world—I beg your pardon, there are five, if we count Oceania—is the extremely small regard for truth shown by the purveyors of this sort of news. Whether in the north or the south, St. Petersburg or Calcutta, Paris or Constantinople, they are all alike. Each journal is bound to give so many beats of its drum every day. Good or bad, false or true, it has to give them, and those who feel injured must obtain redress—if they can."

"Which means, I suppose," observed Colonel Anderson, "that this account is incorrect."

"Not only incorrect, but incomplete. The 'young fool' it speaks of, not only hissed, but cried, 'Vive la France!' Further, he drank to the health of

58

France, and also disposed satisfactorily of the four first who attacked, him. It is true that these three Prussian officers intervened. They wished him to cry 'Vive Guillaume I' and 'Vive la Prusse.' He mounted a table, and instead, gave them a recital of Alfred de Musset's 'Answer to the German Rhine' from end to end. It is also true that just then the reports of Blind's revolver attracted general attention, and, not proposing to fight all Berlin, he profited by the incident to escape, taking refuge in the French Embassy. He had challenged one, two, or four adversaries, but not the entire populace. He also left a message at the Black Eagle to be given to any enquirers to the effect that he could not remain in Berlin, but would wait in some neighbouring country in order to oblige any one demanding satisfaction. And, leaving Berlin by an early train he arrived at Hanover an hour ago and at once sent his card to Herr Bodemeyer, hoping that that gentleman will kindly announce in his Gazette both the town and the hotel where this 'young fool' may be found by any one unable to find him at the Black Eagle."

"Good heavens," exclaimed the editor, "then it was you who caused this mighty uproar at Berlin."

"Even I; small things make much noise, as you see." Turning to the Englishman, Benedict continued, "And now you also see why I warned Colonel Anderson that I had a favour to ask him. I want him to be my second in case, as is quite possible, some wrathful individual should arrive demanding why, being in a foreign country, I have dared to uphold the honour of my own."

His hearers, with one accord, immediately offered their hands. Benedict continued:

"And now, to show I am not absolutely unknown, here is a letter from the Head of our 'Department of Fine Arts' to Herr Kaulbach, Painter to the King of Hanover. He lives here, does he not?"

"Yes, the king had a charming house built on purpose for him."

At this moment the door communicating with the next room was thrown open, the rotund figure of the landlord appeared in the opening and a solemn and impressive voice announced:

"Their Excellencies are served."

Whether the chef had perceived that Benedict really understood what he was talking about, or else had had orders from his master to do what he was told, he had, at any rate, carried out his instructions to the very last letter, the result being neither French, English, nor German, but cosmopolitan, a banquet for a conference if not a congress. Nor was brilliant conversation lacking. Bodemeyer, like all German journalists, was a well-read man, but had never been outside Hanover. Anderson, on the contrary, had read little, but had travelled everywhere and seen much. He and Benedict had explored the same countries and encountered the same people. Both had been at the siege of Pekin; Anderson had followed Benedict in India, and preceded him in Russia. Both related their experiences, the one with English reserve and humour, the other with French vivacity and wit. The Englishman, a true modern Phœnician, saw everything from the industrial and commercial point of view, the Frenchman from that of intellectual progress. Their different ideas, brought forward with warmth and also with the courtesy of well-bred and distinguished men, crossed each other like foils in the hands of experienced fencers, emitting sparks, brilliant if transitory. Bodemeyer, unused to this style of discussion, endeavoured to give it a philosophical turn, in which he was met by Benedict, but which Anderson found difficult to follow. The journalist seemed unintelligible, but Benedict's theories he understood as he had never understood before.

The clock striking eight abruptly terminated the conversation. The editor sprang up.

"My paper!" he cried, "my 'Gazette'! It is not ready by half!" Never before had he succumbed to such an intellectual temptation. "Frenchmen are the very devil," he muttered, trying in vain to find a hat which would fit him. "They are the champagne of the earth, they are clear, strong, and sparkling. In vain did Benedict entreat him for five minutes in which to write his announcement. "You must let me have it before eleven o'clock," cried Bodemeyer, as, having discovered his own hat and cane he fled as if the enemy were behind him.

Next morning the following announcement might have been read in the "Hanoverian Gazette".

"On June 7th, 1866, in Unter den Linden at Berlin I had occasion to both give and receive several blows in an encounter with various excellent citizens who wished to tear me to pieces because I had publicly emptied my glass to the glory of France. I have not the honour of knowing who gave these blows, but, wishing to be known by those who received mine, I hereby announce that during the next eight days I may be found at the Hôtel Royal, Hanover, by any one wishing to criticize either my words or actions on the said occasion, and I particularly hope that the author of a certain article referring to me in yesterday's issue of the 'Kreuz Zeitung,' will accept this invitation. Being ignorant of his name, I have no other means of addressing him.

"I wish to thank the three Prussian officers who interfered to protect me from the amiable people of Berlin. But, should any of them consider himself offended by me, my gratitude will not extend to refusing him satisfaction.

"I said then and I repeat now, that I am familiar with the use of all weapons."

"BENEDICT TURPIN.

"*At the Hôtel Royal, Hanover.*"

# CHAPTER VII. KAULBACH'S STUDIO

Benedict lost no time in leaving his note at the "Gazette" office, and his letter of introduction at Kaulbach's studio, where he left also his card on which was written, "I hope to have the honour of calling on you to-morrow." He therefore ordered Lenhart to be ready a little before eleven, in order to pay his two visits, one of thanks to Herr Bodemeyer, and one to Kaulbach. As the latter lived at the extreme end of the town where the king had had a charming little house erected for him, he called at Herr Bodemeyer's office first. The last copies of the "Gazette" were just being struck off, and Benedict was able to convince himself that his letter was actually in print. As the "Gazette" had numerous subscribers in Berlin and would be on sale there at six that evening, there was no doubt but that his communication would be widely read. The dissolution of the Chamber was confirmed and it was certain that mobilization would be announced on the morrow. Benedict continued on his way to the studio.

Seen by daylight the house appeared to be a pretty villa in Italian style, standing in a garden enclosed with iron railings. The gate stood invitingly open. Benedict entered, rang, and was answered by a servant in livery, whose manner showed that the visit was expected. He at once led the way to the studio.

"The master is just finishing dinner," he said, "but he will be with you in a moment."

"Tell the master," replied Benedict, "that I am too delighted at being able to see the beautiful things here to wish to hurry him."

And, indeed, the studio, full of original pictures, sketches, and copies of some of the works of the greatest painters known, could not fail to be intensely interesting to an artist such as Benedict, who now suddenly found himself in the sanctuary of one of the greatest of German painters. Kaulbach is an artist who has adhered to his Christian faith, and everywhere one saw proofs of this. But among highly finished sketches for some of his world-famous pictures, such as "The Dispersion of Mankind," "The Taking of Jerusalem," etc., Benedict's attention was drawn to a modern portrait group of five persons. It represented an officer, evidently of high rank, holding a boy of about ten by the hand. His charger stood ready on the terrace below, and a lady in the prime of life sat near him with two little girls, one leaning against her knee, while the other sat at her feet and played with a small dog and some roses. The picture, apparently, was a work of love, for the artist had taken immense pains with it; too much so, in fact, for the elaborately finished details threw the faces into the background, and the general effect was too flat.

Absorbed in the study of this group, Benedict did not observe that Kaulbach had entered the room and was standing beside him, looking on with a smile. Presently he said:

"You are right, that picture is too flat, and I had it brought back, not to finish it still more, but to tone it down and soften some parts. Such as it is your public would never like it. Delacroix has spoilt you for 'clean' pictures."

Benedict laughed.

"Do you mean to imply that he painted dirty ones?" he enquired.

"Heaven forbid! His works are excellent, but your nation did not appreciate them."

"We do him justice now, however."

"Yes, now that he is dead," said Kaulbach smiling. "Is it not always so?"

"Not in your case. Admired in France, adored in Germany, happily you are yet with us."

Kaulbach at this time about fifty-two, slightly grey, sallow in complexion, having brilliant dark eyes and a highly nervous constitution. Tall and slight, he was at the zenith of his artistic powers and hardly past that of his physical ones. The two men studied each other critically, until at last Turpin began to laugh.

63

"Do you know what I am thinking?" asked the German. "I am wondering how you have managed to wander from Pekin to St. Petersburg, from Astrakhan to Algiers, and yet found time to produce the remarkable pictures you have painted. I know these only by report unfortunately, but I have heard a good deal. You are a pupil of Scheffer's?"

"Yes, I have also studied under Cabat."

"Great masters, both of them. And you are the hero of that unlucky business at Berlin. I have just read your letter in the 'Gazette.'"

"But why 'unlucky'?"

"Well, you will have two or three duels on your hands."

"So much the worse for my adversaries."

"Allow me to remark that you are not lacking in self-confidence."

"No, because I have the certainty of success. Look!" and Benedict held out his hand. "Observe that the line of life is double. There is not the slightest break anywhere—nothing to indicate accident, sickness, or even the slightest scratch. I might live to a hundred—but I won't say as much of those who quarrel with me."

Aulbach smiled.

"At the end of your letter of introduction," he said, "there was a postscript, which informed me that you were more deeply interested in studying occult science than in pursuing your own art."

"I don't know that I study either very much. I am rather a slave to temperament. If a thing amuses me, well, yes, I study it. If I think I have found a truth, I try to follow it out to the very end. And I do believe that chiromancy can give us a glance into the future, and that the hand is a page on which the lines of our fate have been traced by Destiny. If for five minutes only I could study the hand of either the King of Prussia or of Count Bismarck, I could give you some idea of what will happen."

"Meanwhile," said Kaulbach, "your science says you will escape scot-free from any duels arising out of this Berlin scrimmage?"

"Certainly I shall. But we were talking about your work, which is infinitely more interesting. I believe I know all your pictures, or nearly so."

"I would wager you don't know the best of them."

"Yes, I do. You mean 'Charlemagne visited in his Tomb by the Emperor Otho'? It is the masterpiece of modern German painting."

Kaulbach was evidently delighted.

"You have seen that!" he exclaimed, and he held out his hand to Benedict. "I don't think as much of it as you seem to do, but it is the best thing I have done. Oh! pardon me, but I see two visitors who come for a sitting. But wait, they are kind friends of mine, and may not object to your presence. I will tell them who you are, and then if they do not mind your being here you can please yourself as to whether you go or stay." So saying he hastily quitted the studio.

A carriage was at the garden gate, quite plain in appearance, with no arms emblazoned on the panels, yet Benedict's practised eye saw at once that the horses had cost at least £200 each. Two gentlemen were leaving it, the elder of the two, who seemed about forty-five, wore the epaulettes of a general with an undress uniform of dark green, the collar and facings being of black velvet. Kaulbach said a few words, upon which he took off an order he was wearing and also two crosses, retaining those of the Guelphic Order and of Ernest Augustus. Then, that he might cross the little garden and ascend the steps he took the arm of the younger man, who seemed to be his son, and who, tall and very slight, appeared to be about one-and-twenty, and wore a Hussar uniform of blue and silver.

Kaulbach opened the studio door and stood respectfully aside. Benedict, as he bowed, instantly recognized the central figure of Kaulbach's portrait group. He glanced quickly at the picture on which the missing decoration was depicted in all its glory. It was the Star of the Order of the Garter, worn by few except sovereign princes. He knew at once that the visitors must be the blind King of Hanover, one of the most cultivated and artistic sovereigns of Germany, and his son, the Crown Prince.

"Milords," said Kaulbach, "I have the honour to present a brother artist to you. He is young, but is already famous, and he brings a special introduction from the Minister of Fine Arts at Paris. May I add that his own personality is a better recommendation even than those."

The general bent his head graciously, the youth touched his cap. The elder man then addressed Benedict in English, regretting that his French was only indifferent. Benedict replied in the same language, saying that he was too great an admirer of Shakespeare, Scott, and Byron not to have made an effort to read these authors in their own tongue. The king, satisfied that he was unrecognized, discussed various subjects, and, knowing that Benedict had travelled much, asked many questions which were in themselves a compliment, for only men of superior intelligence could have asked and answered them. Kaulbach, meanwhile, rapidly worked at his picture softening down the too hard accessories. The young prince listened eagerly, and when Benedict offered to show him sketches made in India, he appealed anxiously to his father as to when and where he could see them.

"Better ask both these gentlemen to lunch in your own rooms," said the King, "and if they do you the honour to accept—"

"Oh! can you come to-morrow?" enquired the prince, delighted.

Benedict looked at Kaulbach in embarrassment.

"I fear I may have work of another kind to-morrow," he replied.

"Yes," said Kaulbach, "I fear my friend here is a trifle hot-headed. He only arrived yesterday and he has already written a letter for the 'Gazette,' which is now well on its way to Berlin."

"What! the letter I thought so amusing that I read it aloud to my father! Is that yours, monsieur? But, indeed, you will have duels without end."

"I count on two," said Benedict. "It is a lucky number."

"But suppose you are killed or wounded?"

"If I am killed, I will, with your permission, bequeath you my album. If I am badly hurt, I will ask Herr Kaulbach to show it you instead. If I am only scratched, I will bring it myself. But you need not be anxious on my account; I can assure you nothing unpleasant will happen to me."

"But how can you know that?"

"You know my friend's name, I think," said Kaulbach. "He is Benedict Turpin. Well, he descends in the direct line from the famous enchanter Turpin, the uncle of Charlemagne, and he has inherited the gifts of his ancestor!"

"Good heavens," said the prince, "are you spirit, magician, or what?"

"None of them. I simply amuse myself by reading the past, the present, and as much of the future as one's hand can reveal."

"Before you came," said Kaulbach, "he was deeply regretting not being able to see the hand of the King of Prussia. He would have told us what will happen in the war. My lord," he continued, emphasizing the title, "could we not find somewhere a royal hand for him to see?"

"Very easily," said the king, smiling, "only it should be that of a real king or a real emperor. Such as the Emperor of China, who is obeyed by millions of subjects, or Alexander, who reigns over the ninth part of the whole world. Do you not think so, M. Turpin?"

"I think, sir," replied Benedict, as he bent low before the king, "that it is not always great kingdoms which make great kings. Thessaly produced Achilles, and Macedonia gave birth to Alexander," and again bowing, even more deeply, he left the studio.

# CHAPTER VIII. THE CHALLENGE

Benedict's prediction was duly fulfilled. He had hardly opened his eyes the next morning when Lenhart, who had assumed the duties of valet, appeared, bearing a magnificent silver salver which he had borrowed from the landlord. On it were displayed two cards.

The cards bore the respective names of "Major Frederic von Bülow" and "Georges Kleist, Editor of the 'Kreuz Zeitung.'" Two different classes of Prussian society were therefore represented desiring satisfaction.

Benedict enquired where these gentlemen were to be found, and hearing that they were both at his own hotel, sent a hasty message to Colonel Anderson, begging him to come at once. When he appeared Benedict gave him the cards, requesting him to deal with the owners in due order of precedence, beginning with Major von Bülow, and to agree to whatever terms were proposed whether as to weapons, time, or place. The colonel would have protested, but Benedict declared he would have it his own way or not at all, and Anderson had no choice but to agree.

He returned at the end of half-an-hour. Von Bülow had chosen swords. But, having been sent officially to Frankfort, and having come out of his way in order to accept M. Turpin's challenge, he would be greatly obliged if the meeting might take place as soon as possible.

"The sooner the better," said Benedict. "It is the very least I can do to oblige a man who comes out of his way in order to oblige me."

"All he wants, seemingly, is to be able to continue his journey this evening," observed Anderson.

"Ah!" said Benedict. "But I cannot answer for his ability to do that, however early we meet!"

"That would be a pity," said the colonel. "Major von Bülow is very much a gentleman. It seems that three Prussian officers interfered to protect you from the mob on condition that you cried 'Vive King William!' 'Vive la Prusse!'"

"Pardon me, there were no conditions."

"Not on your side, but they undertook it for you."

"I did not prevent them from crying it as much as they liked."

"Doubtless, only, instead of doing it yourself—"

"I recited one of Alfred de Musset's finest poems; what more could they want?"

"They consider that you treated them with disrespect."

"Perhaps I did. Well, what next?"

"When they read your letter they decided that one of them must accept the challenge and the other two act as seconds. They drew lots, and the lot fell on von Bülow. That very moment he received orders to go on this mission to Frankfort. The others wished that one of them should take his place in the duel. But he refused, saying that if he were killed or badly wounded, one of them could take on the dispatches which would not be much delayed. So I then arranged the meeting for one o'clock."

"Very well. What about the other man?"

"Herr Georges Kleist is not remarkable in any way: he is a typical German journalist. He chooses pistols and wants to fire at close quarters on account of his defective eyesight. I believe it is quite good enough, but, however, he does wear glasses, so you are to be at forty-five paces—"

"Good gracious! Do you call that close quarters?"

"Have a little patience! You may each advance fifteen paces nearer, which reduces the ultimate distance to fifteen. But we had a discussion. His seconds say that he is the aggrieved party and has the right to fire first. I say, nothing of the kind; you ought to fire together, at a given signal. You must decide; it is a serious matter, and I decline the responsibility."

"It is soon decided; he must fire first. I hope you fixed an early time for him also? We could then kill two birds with one stone."

"That is just what I have done. At one o'clock you meet von Bülow with swords, and at a quarter-past, Herr Kleist, with pistols."

"Well then, my dear colonel, I will go and order breakfast, and will you be so good as to tell Herr Kleist that he can have first shot? And," he added, "let it be understood that I don't provide any arms myself; I will use the swords and pistols they bring with them."

It was then eleven o'clock. Benedict promptly ordered breakfast. Colonel Anderson returned in ten minutes and announced that all was settled. Whereupon they applied themselves to their repast until the clock struck twelve.

"Colonel," said Benedict, "do not let us be late."

"We have no great distance to go. It is a pretty place, as you will see. Are you influenced by surroundings?"

"I would rather fight on grass than on cultivated ground."

"We are going to Eilenriede; it is a sort of Hanoverian Bois de Boulogne. In the middle of the wood there is a little open glade with a spring in it, which might have been made for this sort of encounter. I have been there once or twice on my own account and three or four times on other people's. By the way, have you secured another second?"

"There are five on the other side, one of them will oblige me."

"But suppose they refused?"

"Not likely! But, even if they did, you alone would be sufficient. And, as they seem anxious to finish the affair one way or another, there will be no difficulties."

Lenhart had already announced the carriage. The colonel explained the way to him. In half-an-hour they arrived at the little glade, with ten minutes to spare.

"A lovely spot," said Benedict. "As the others are not yet here, I will sketch it."

And, producing a sketch-book from his pocket, he dashed off a very accurate view of the place with remarkable rapidity and skill.

Presently a carriage appeared in the distance. As they drew near Benedict rose and took off his hat. The three officers, the editor, and a surgeon they had brought, occupied it. In the officers, Benedict at once recognized his three protectors at Berlin.

His adversaries left their carriage at a little distance and courteously returned his salute. Colonel Anderson went to meet them and explained that his principal, being a stranger, had no second but himself, and asked if one of his opponents would supply the deficiency. They consulted a moment, then one of the officers crossed over and bowed to Benedict.

"I am much obliged by your courtesy, sir," said Benedict.

"We will agree to anything, sir—rather than lose time," replied the officer.

Benedict bit his lip.

"Will you at once select the weapons," he said to Colonel Anderson in English, "we must not keep these gentlemen waiting."

Von Bülow had already divested himself of helmet, coat, waistcoat, and cravat. Benedict studied him carefully as he did so. He appeared to be about thirty-three and to have lived in his uniform until he felt uncomfortable out of it. He was dark, with glossy black hair cut quite short, a straight nose, black moustache and very decided chin. Both courage and loyalty could be read in the frank and open glance of his dark eyes.

Von Bülow, having provided the swords, Benedict was offered his choice of them. He simply took the first that came, and immediately passed his left hand along the edge and felt the point. The edge was keen as a razor. The point sharp as a needle. The major's second observed his action, and, beckoning Colonel Anderson aside.

"Will you," he said, "kindly explain to your principal that in German duels we use only the edge of the sword? To thrust with the point is inadmissible."

"The devil!" said Benedict when this information was repeated to him, "it is well you told me. In France, where duels, especially military ones, are usually serious, we use every stroke we can, and our sword-play is actually called 'counterpoint.'"

"But indeed," exclaimed von Bülow, "I beg, sir, that you will use your sword in whatever way you find best."

Benedict bowed in acknowledgment. Having fought several duels at Heidelberg he was well acquainted with German methods of fencing and placed himself with apparent indifference. As the affronted person has the right of attack, and a challenge may be considered an affront, he waited, standing simply on guard.

# CHAPTER IX. THE TWO DUELS

"Engage, gentlemen!" cried the colonel.

Von Bülow's sword swept through the air with a flash like lightning. But, rapid though it was, it descended in empty space. Warned by the instinct of a true fencer, the blades had barely crossed when Benedict sprang swiftly aside and remained standing unguarded, his point lowered, and his mocking smile disclosing a fine set of teeth. His adversary paused, perplexed, then swung round so as to face him, but did not immediately advance. However, feeling that this duel must be no child's play, he stepped forward and instantly the point of Benedict's sword rose menacingly against him. Involuntarily he retreated a step. Benedict now fixed his eyes upon him, circling round him, now bending to the right, now again to the left, but always keeping his weapon low and ready to strike.

The major began to feel a kind of hypnotic influence overpowering him. Determined to fight against it, he boldly stepped forward, holding his sword aloft. Instantly he felt the touch of cold steel. Benedict thrust, his rapier pierced von Bülow's shirt and reappeared on the other side. Had not the major remained standing motionless opposite him, an onlooker would have supposed he had been run through the body.

The seconds hastened up, but:

"It is nothing, I assure you," said the major.

Then, perceiving that Benedict had only intended to pierce his shirt and not himself, he added:

"Come, sir, let us continue this game in earnest."

"Ah!" said Benedict, "but you see, had I played in earnest, you would now be a dead man!"

"On guard, sir," cried von Bülow, furious, "and remember this is a duel to the death."

Benedict stepped back and saluting with his sword:

"Pardon me, gentlemen," he said, "you see how unfortunate I am. Although fully intending not to use my point I have nevertheless made two holes in my opponent's shirt. My hand might again refuse to obey my will, and, as I do not visit a country merely to rebel against its customs— particularly when they happen to be philanthropic—so—"

He went up to a rock which rose out of the little valley and, placing the point of his rapier in a crevice, broke off a good inch of the blade.

His adversary wished to do likewise, but,

"It is quite unnecessary, sir," said Benedict, "you are not likely to use your point."

Being now reduced to ordinary sword-play, Benedict crossed swords with his opponent, which necessitated their keeping close together. But he continually retreated half a pace and advanced again, thanks to which incessant movement the major merely made cuts in the air. Becoming impatient, he endeavoured to reach Benedict, missed again, and involuntarily lowered his weapon. Benedict parried a back stroke and touched von Bülow's breast with the broken point. Said he:

"You see I was right in breaking the point of my sword. Otherwise, this time something besides your shirt would have been pierced."

The major remained silent, but quickly recovering himself again stood on guard. He now saw that his adversary was a most skilful swordsman, who united French celerity with determined coolness and who was fully conscious of his strength.

Benedict, seeing that an end must be made, now stood still, calm but menacing, with frowning brows and eyes fixed on his enemy, not attempting to strike but retaining a posture of defence. It seemed as if he awaited the attack, but suddenly with the unexpected celerity which characterized all his movements, he sprang forward with a bound like that of a jaguar, aimed a blow at his adversary's head, and as the latter raised his arm in defence, drew

74

a line with his blade right across his chest. Then, springing lightly back in the same instant he again lowered his sword as before.

Von Bülow's shirt, slashed as though cut by a razor, was instantly tinged with blood. The seconds moved forward.

"Do not stir, I beg," cried the major, "it is nothing but a scratch. I must confess the gentleman's hand is a light one."

And he again stood on guard.

Courageous though he was, he felt he was losing confidence, and, dumbfounded by his enemy's agility, a sense of great danger oppressed him. Evidently Benedict was keeping just out of reach, and was merely waiting until he should expose himself by an unwary advance. He understood that hitherto his opponent had simply played with him, but that now the duel was approaching an end and that his smallest mistake would be severely punished. His sword, never able to encounter Benedict's, seemed to become lifeless, and ceased to respond to his will.

His previous experience in fencing seemed useless here, and this flashing blade which he could never touch, but which rose constantly before him, alert, intelligent, as if endued with life, confused his senses. He dared not risk a movement before this enemy always just beyond his reach, so imperturbable and yet so alert, and who evidently intended, like the artist he was, either to finish with one brilliant stroke or else—which did not seem likely—to expire in a dignified pose like the "Dying Gladiator."

But, exasperated by his opponent's perfect bodily grace, by his elegant and masterly swordsmanship, and still more by the mocking smile which hovered on his lips, von Bülow felt the blood rise to his temples, and could not resist muttering between his teeth:

"This fellow is the very devil!"

And, springing forward, no longer fearing the broken point, he raised his sword and aimed a blow with all his might at his adversary, a blow which, had it reached its object, would have split his head as though it had been an apple. Again, the stroke only encountered empty air, for once more Benedict had effaced himself by a light, graceful spring, very familiar to Parisian fencing masters.

The major's raised sword had broken his guard. A flash, as of lightning, and his arm, streaming with blood, fell against his side. His sword dropped, but remained upright supported by the sword knot.

The seconds hurried to his side. Very pale, but with smiling lips, von Bülow bowed to Benedict and said:

"I thank you, sir. When you might have run me through the body you only wounded my shirt; when you might have cut me in two you let me off with the sort of cut one gets in shaving, and now, when you might have either cleft my head or maimed my arm, I escape with a ruined sleeve. I now ask you to extend your courtesy even further, and to complete the record like the gentleman you are by explaining why you have spared me thus?"

"Sir," said Benedict with a smile, "in the house of Herr Fellner, the Burgomaster of Frankfort, I was introduced to his god-daughter, a charming lady, who adores her husband. Her name was the Baroness von Bülow. When I saw your card it occurred to me that you might be related, and though, beautiful as she is, mourning could only add to her charm, it would grieve me to have been the cause of compelling her to wear it."

The major looked Benedict in the face and, stern soldier though he might be, there were tears in his eyes.

"Madame von Bülow is my wife," he said. "Believe me, sir, wherever she may meet you she will greet you thus: 'My husband foolishly quarrelled with you, sir; may you ever be blessed because for my sake you spared him!' and she will give you her hand with as much gratitude as I now offer you mine."

And he added smiling:

"Forgive me for only offering my left hand. It is entirely your own fault that I cannot give you the right."

And now, although the wound was not dangerous, von Bülow did not refuse to have it dressed. The surgeon promptly ripped up his sleeve, disclosing a wound, not very deep, but terrible to look at, which extended down the arm from the shoulder to the elbow. And one shuddered to think what such a wound would have been, had the swordsman struck with all his force instead of simply drawing his blade along the arm.

The surgeon dipped a cloth in the ice-cold spring which rose at the foot of the rock and wrapped it round the arm. He then drew the sides of the wound together and strapped them with plaster. He assured the major that he would be quite able to continue his journey to Frankfort in the evening.

Benedict offered his carriage to the major, who, however, declined, being curious to see what would happen to his successor. He excused himself on the score that courtesy required him to wait for Herr Georges Kleist.

Although Herr Kleist, having had time to see what sort of adversary he had to deal with, would willingly have been some leagues away, he put a brave face on the matter, and although he grew perceptibly pale during the first duel, and still paler when the wound was dressed, he was, nevertheless, the first to say.

"Excuse my interrupting you, gentlemen, but it is my turn now."

"I am quite at your service, sir," said Benedict.

"You are not properly dressed for a duel with pistols," interposed Colonel Anderson, glancing at Benedict's costume.

"Really," said Benedict, "I never thought about what clothes I was to fight in. I only wanted to do it with comfort to myself. That's all!"

"You can at least put on your tunic and button it!"

"Bah! It is much too hot."

"Perhaps we ought to have taken the pistols first. All this sword-play may have unsteadied your hand."

"My hand is my servant, dear colonel; it knows it has to obey me and you will see it does so."

"Do you wish to see the pistols you are to use?"

"You have seen them, have you not? Are they double barrelled or single?"

"Single barrelled duelling pistols. They were hired this morning from a gunsmith in the Grande Place."

"Then call my other second and see them properly loaded. Mind the shot is inside the barrels, and not dropped outside."

"I will load them myself."

"Colonel," asked the Prussian officers, "do you wish to see the pistols loaded?"

"Yes. I wish to do so. But how are we to arrange? Herr Kleist will only have one second."

"These two gentlemen may answer for Herr Kleist," said the major, "and I will go over to M. Turpin." And his wound being now bandaged, he went and sat down on the rock which gave its name to the glade.

Meanwhile the pistols were loaded, Colonel Anderson fulfilling his promise by putting in the balls himself. Benedict came up to him.

"Tell me," the Englishman asked gravely, "do you mean to kill him?"

"What do you expect? One can't exactly play with pistols as one can with swords or rapiers."

"Surely there is some way of disabling people with whom you have no serious quarrel without killing them outright?"

"I really cannot undertake to miss him just to oblige you! Think! He would naturally go and publish everywhere that I did not know how to shoot!"

"All right! I see I need not have spoken. I bet you have an idea of some sort."

"Frankly, I have. But then he must do his part."

"What must he do?"

"Just keep perfectly still, it ought not to be so very difficult. See, they are ready."

The seconds had just measured the forty-five paces. Colonel Anderson now measured off fifteen from each end, and to mark the exact limit which neither combatant was to pass, he laid two scabbards across and planted a sword upright in the ground at each end to decide the starting-point.

"To your places, gentlemen," cried the seconds.

Herr Kleist having selected his pistol, the colonel brought the other to Benedict, who was talking to the major, and who took the pistol without as much as looking at it, and still chatting with von Bülow, walked quietly to his place.

The duellists now stood at the extreme distance.

"Gentlemen!" said Colonel Anderson, "you are now forty-five paces apart. Each of you may either advance fifteen paces before firing, or may fire from where he now stands. Herr Georges Kleist has the first shot and may fire as soon as he pleases. Having fired, he may hold his pistol so as to protect any part of himself he wishes.

"Now, gentlemen!"

The two adversaries advanced towards each other. Having arrived at the mark, Benedict waited, standing, facing his opponent with folded arms. A light breeze ruffled his hair and blew his shirt open at the chest. He had walked at his ordinary pace.

Herr Kleist, dressed entirely in black, bare-headed, and with closely buttoned coat, had advanced slowly, by force of will overcoming physical disinclination. He halted at the limit.

"You are ready, sir?" he asked.

"Quite ready, sir."

"Will you not turn sideways?"

"I am not accustomed to do so."

Then, turning himself, Herr Kleist slowly raised his pistol, took aim, and fired.

Benedict heard the ball whiz close by his ear and felt the wind ruffle his hair; it had passed within an inch of his head.

His adversary instantly raised his pistol, holding it so as to protect his face, but was unable entirely to control a nervous movement of his hand.

"Sir," said Benedict, "you courteously asked just now if I would not stand sideways, which is unusual between combatants. Permit me in my turn to offer a piece of advice, or rather, make a request."

"What is it, sir?" asked the journalist, still protecting himself with his pistol.

"This; keep your hand steady, your pistol is moving. I wish to put my ball in the wood of your pistol, which will be very difficult unless you keep it quite still. Against my own will I might hit you, either in the cheek or the back of the head, whereas—if you keep your hand just as it is—"

He raised his pistol and fired instantly.

"There! it is done now!"

It was done so rapidly that no one could have supposed he had taken any aim at all. But, even as the report was heard, Herr Kleist's pistol was blown to pieces and he himself staggered and fell on one knee.

"Ah!" said Anderson, "you have killed him."

"I think not," replied Benedict. "I aimed between the two screws which hold the hammer. It is the shock of the concussion which has brought him down."

The surgeon and the two seconds hastened to the wounded man, who now held only the butt end of his pistol. There was a terrible bruise on his cheek, reaching from the eye to the jaw. Otherwise he was untouched, only the shock had knocked him down.

The barrel of the pistol was picked up on one side and the lock on the other. The ball had lodged exactly between the two screws. Had it continued its course unobstructed it would have broken the upper jaw and penetrated the brain.

The dressing was simple—the bruise was a very bad one, but the skin was only broken in two places, and the surgeon considered a cold-water bandage to be all that was required.

Benedict embraced the major, bowed to the journalist, shook hands with the seconds, put on his coat, and got into the carriage, looking less dishevelled than if he had come from a picnic.

"Well, my dear sponsor," he said to Colonel Anderson.

"Well, my dear godson," responded the latter, "I know at least ten men besides myself who would willingly have given a thousand pounds to see what I have seen to-day."

"Sir," said Lenhart, "if you would promise neither to hunt nor to fight unless I am there to see, I, my horse, and my carriage should be at your service for the rest of my life."

And indeed, Benedict returned as he had foretold, having fought his duels, vanquished his adversaries, and come off without a single scratch!

# CHAPTER X. "WHAT WAS WRITTEN IN A KING'S HAND"

When Benedict returned to his hotel he was met by Kaulbach's servant, sent by his master to learn what had happened. In the good town of Hanover it had speedily become known that in answer to Benedict's letter in the "Gazette" two challenges had been received that very morning, and that he, his challengers, and seconds, had all gone to Eilenriede, the usual place for settling affairs of this description. Benedict desired him to assure his master that all was well, adding that he would have come in person to acknowledge his courtesy, had he not feared to rouse the curiosity of the whole town.

Colonel Anderson had made an excuse for leaving Benedict as soon as they returned. Being an officer of the Royal Ordnance he had probably some report to make to the king.

The news of the result of this double combat spread as rapidly as had that of the challenges. Such an event as two duels successfully fought without a scratch being received was quite unheard of, and was considered so extraordinary that the young men of the town, who also had no love for the Prussians, sent a deputation to congratulate Benedict on his success. He received the deputies and replied in such excellent German that they retired marvelling more than ever.

The doors had scarcely closed on them when Stephen appeared, and announced that all his guests were so interested in the events of the day that they begged Benedict would honour them by dining at the table d'hôte, in order that they might all have the pleasure of personally congratulating him.

Benedict replied that he did not in the least understand so much admiration for his perfectly natural conduct, but that he was quite willing to do anything which might be agreeable to his fellow guests.

Stephen had time to let the news circulate in the town that the young Frenchman of whom every one was talking, would, for once only, consent to dine at the table d'hôte. Instead of twenty-five only, he had covers laid for two hundred guests. Every place was occupied.

The police feared disorder of some kind, and came to investigate. They were assured that it was only a family affair, a demonstration such as had been made three days before under the windows of Count von Bismarck—only it was the other way about! Now the Hanoverian police was an excellent body, which highly approved of family fêtes and patriotic demonstrations. Therefore, instead of objecting to this one they encouraged it with all their power, thanks to which all passed off in perfect order.

At midnight, Benedict was at length allowed to retire, but his admirers organized a serenade beneath his windows which lasted till two o'clock in the morning.

At nine Kaulbach entered his room. The Crown Prince invited Benedict to breakfast at the Palace of Herrenhausen, and requested him to bring his sketches. Kaulbach was commissioned to bring him back. The breakfast was at eleven, but the prince would be obliged if Benedict would come at ten in order to have some time for conversation both before and after.

Benedict lost no time in dressing, and although Kaulbach, intimate at the palace, assured him he could go in ordinary costume, he preferred to wear the naval uniform in which he had made the Chinese campaign. On his breast was the Cross of the Légion d'Honneur, of which the simple red ribbon means much more when worn by some than do the various grand crosses worn by others. He added a sabre, the gift of Said Pasha, took his sketches, and got into the carriage with Kaulbach.

Lenhart had a whole day's holiday.

Twenty-five minutes brought them to Herrenhausen, which is about a league from Hanover, and, the carriage being open, Benedict could see the young prince watching for him eagerly at a window. He was accompanied only by his aide-de-camp, an officer of Engineers, and consequently well able to draw. Also, which is more unusual, he did not disdain the picturesque.

The prince enquired courteously after Benedict's health, without making the smallest allusion to the duels of the day before. It was evident nevertheless that he knew all about them. Had there been any doubts on the subject they would have been dispelled by the appearance of Colonel Anderson as another invited guest.

But the prince's chief interest centred in the portfolio which Benedict carried under his arm.

Anticipating his wishes, Benedict observed;

"Your Highness wished to see some of my sketches. I have brought some representing hunting incidents, thinking that they might interest you most."

"Oh! let me see, let me see!" exclaimed the prince, extending his hand, and placing the portfolio on the piano, he began eagerly to examine the contents. After having turned over several, "Ah," said he, "but they are beautiful. Will you not tell me something of the adventures which I am sure they illustrate? They must be so interesting."

Benedict endeavoured to gratify the prince, and the time both before and after the breakfast passed rapidly in listening to accounts of elephant hunting, of encounters with pirates in the Straits of Malacca, of adventures in the Caucasus, and he had just finished an especially thrilling anecdote relating to the poisonous snakes of India when the king was seen approaching from the gallery. He held the arm of his aide-de-camp with whom he was conversing and walked firmly as if able to see. He entered the dining-room without being announced. The four guests rose immediately, but:

"Do not let me disturb you, gentlemen," said the king. "I merely came to visit the prince, to ask if he has all he wants, and if not, to convey his wishes to the persons concerned."

"No! thanks to Your Majesty's kindness, nothing is wanting here except yourself. Your knowledge of men has not deceived you, and Monsieur Benedict is the most delightful companion I ever met."

"The prince is imaginative, sire," said Benedict laughing. "He attributes to some very simple anecdotes and hasty sketches an excellence which they do not possess."

But the king replied as if answering his own thought, the thought which had led him to visit the young man.

"Yesterday," he said, addressing Benedict and turning towards him, as he always did in conversation, "you said something about a science which interested me in former days, namely, chiromancy. My thoughts carry me on towards the mysterious unexplored regions of the human mind, of nature, of creation. I should like to know they are based upon logic, on physiology, for instance."

"I know, sire," replied Benedict, smiling, "that is why I ventured yesterday to mention the occult sciences to Your Majesty."

"You know. But how?" demanded the king.

"I should be a poor student, sire, if I had limited my enquiries to the hands only, and had not united the study of Lavater and Gall to that of Arpentigny. I saw at once in the form of your hands and head those precious aptitudes which are shown in phrenology by the well-developed organs of the poetic faculty and of the love of harmony, which betoken the student of natural science. The protection accorded by Your Majesty to the poor herbalist, Lampe, arose not from benevolence only, but from the conviction that certain men are empowered to receive a revelation, and that it is not always the highly placed ones of earth to whom truth is thus manifested."

"It is true," said the king. "Other men may see the stars shining in the midnight silence, but it seems to me that I actually hear that 'music of the spheres' spoken of by Pythagoras. And I am proud to think that while I stand on the summit of earthly society, there are, immediately above me, intermediate angelic influences which carry on a boundless electric chain, linking us not merely with our own little planetary system, but with others— with the whole universe."

"I do not venture," the king continued with a smile, "to discourse openly on these beliefs. I should get the reputation of 'a king of dreams,' about the worst a king can have. But to you, who are a dreamer like myself, I do say— yes, I believe in these celestial influences, and I believe that each mortal has, in that precious casket which he calls his skull, the signs of his destiny. He may strive to alter or delay its course, but it will bear him on irresistibly to fortune, success, or misery, as the case may be.

"And I speak with conviction because I have had proofs. In early youth I once met a gipsy woman in the course of a solitary walk. She examined my hand and told me certain things which came to pass. I wish to believe you, but I must have proofs. Can you read the past in my hand even as the gipsy read the future. Can you, do you, sincerely believe you have this power?"

"I do, sire. And I think actual science will tell you what has before been perhaps merely guessed at by intuition or tradition."

"Well then," said the king, extending his hand, "now tell me what you read."

"Sire," replied Benedict, "I do not know how far I dare—"

"Dare what?" enquired the king.

"What if I read only a threatening future?"

"We live in days when no predictions, however terrible, can exceed the reality of the convulsions which are taking place around us. What can you predict for me that can be so terrible? Is it the loss of my kingdom? I lost more than a kingdom when I lost the vision of sun and sky, of earth and sea. Take my hand, and tell me what is written."

"Everything?"

"Everything. As for misfortunes, is it not better to know of them than to encounter them unforeseen?"

Benedict bowed so deeply over King George's hand that he almost touched it with his lips.

"A truly royal hand," he said, after having glanced over it, "a beneficent hand; an artistic hand."

"I did not ask for compliments, sir," said the king, smiling.

"See, my dear master," said Benedict, addressing Kaulbach, "how well the Mount of Apollo, there, under the ring-finger, is developed! Apollo bestows love of the arts; he is the giver of intelligence, of all that is brilliant and creates brilliance. It is he who gives the hope of an immortal name, calm of the soul, the sympathy that creates love. Look at the Mount of Mars, represented by the part opposite the thumb. This is what gives courage, both civil and military, calm, coolness in danger, resignation, pride, devotion, resolution, and the strength of resistance. Unfortunately, Saturn is against us. Saturn threatens. You know, sire, Saturn is Fate. Now, I ought to tell you, the lines of Saturn are not only unfavourable; they are calamitous."

And here Benedict raised his head and looking at the king with the utmost respect and sympathy:

"I might continue more intimately yet, sire," he said, "and reveal your whole character in its most secret recesses. I might sketch your inclinations one by one to you to their lightest shades; but I should prefer to pass at once to graver facts. At twelve years old, Your Majesty had a serious illness."

"It is true," said the king.

"At nineteen, a line extends both towards the brain and towards the Mount of the Sun—a nervous seizure on one side; on the other, something resembling death, but which is not death—an eclipse! And worse than that, an eclipse is momentary one night!"

"The gipsy told me literally the same as you—something that resembles death, but is not death! The fact is that at the age of nineteen I passed through great trouble."

"Stay! Here, sire, on Jupiter there is a marvellous gleam; one of the highest seats of human fortune—about the age of thirty-nine."

"Again the words of the gipsy. At thirty-nine I became king."

"I was ignorant of the precise dates," said Benedict, "but it might be supposed that I knew them. Let me look for a fact that I could not have known. Ah, I see it. Yes, it is certainly here. An agony of terror, an accident due to water. What is it? A boat in danger? A tempest watched from the shore? The imminent wreck of a vessel containing some one beloved? There is fearful terror, but terror only; for there is a rescue traced close to the line of fate. Your Majesty undoubtedly experienced terrible anxiety for the life of some one greatly beloved.'

"Do you hear this, Ernest?" said the king addressing his son.

"Oh, my father!" said the young prince, throwing his arms around his father's neck. Then, to Benedict: "Yes, indeed, my poor father was in terrible fear. I was bathing in the sea at Nordeney. I can swim fairly well; but without perceiving it I let myself be carried away on a current; and, upon my word, I was on the point of sinking when I grasped the arm of an honest fisherman who had come to my assistance. One second more, and all would have been over with me."

"And I was there," said the king. "I could hear his cries, I stretched my arms towards him—it was all I could do. Gloucester offered his kingdom for a horse: and I would gladly have given mine for a ray of light. Do not let us think of it. All the misfortunes of the future together are not more terrible than the shadow of that misfortune which did not happen."

"And so, sire?" said Benedict.

"And so I am convinced," said the king. "I have no need of further proofs. Let us pass on to the future."

Benedict looked with great attention at the king's hand. He hesitated a moment and asked for a magnifying glass, to see more distinctly. It was brought.

"Sire," he said, "you are about to be drawn into a great war. One of your nearest neighbours will not only betray, but will despoil you; and notwithstanding—look, monseigneur!" he said to the prince, "the line of the Sun shows victory: but an empty victory, useless, without fruit."

"And then?" asked the king.

"Oh, sire, what do I read in this hand!"

"Good tidings, or bad?"

"You told me to keep nothing from you, sire."

"And I repeat it. Tell me then; this victory—"

"This victory, as I have told Your Majesty, leads to nothing. Here is the Line of the Sun broken off above the Line of the Head by a line starting from Mars which also cuts the Mount of Jupiter."

"And that foretells?"

"A defeat. But however—No," said Benedict, seeking to read the most mysterious secrets from the royal hand; "moreover, it is not the last word of your destiny. Here is the Line of the Sun after its breakage starting afresh, reaching the ring-finger and stopping at its base. And there see further, above this line traversing Jupiter, a straight line like a furrow crowned with a star, as a sceptre is crowned with a diamond."

"And that prophesies?"

"Restoration."

"Then according to you, I shall lose the throne and reconquer it?"

Benedict turned towards the prince.

"Your hand, if you please, monseigneur."

The prince gave him his hand.

"After the age of forty, monseigneur, the Line of Life sends a branch towards the Line of the Sun. At that period you will ascend the throne. This is all that I can tell you. Now, if you ascend the throne, prince, it can only mean that your father has either recovered or has never lost it."

The king remained silent for a moment, resting his head on his left hand. He seemed gazing fixedly before him as if absorbed in some great idea. The most profound silence reigned in the apartment.

"I cannot tell you," he said at length, "how much this unknown science interests me. Does Providence permit each of us to recognize his destiny in advance, just as the wrestler of ancient Greece might calculate the strength of his adversary in the circus, and consider how best to avoid his grip and obtain the victory?"

He remained silent for a few moments, then continued:

"After all, it would seem only just, only reasonable, that Providence which announces a storm by gathering clouds and muttering thunder, should allow to man and especially to man placed on the highest point of earthly grandeur, some indication of the approach of the storms of life. Yes, this science should be true, if only for the reason that it is necessary, and has hitherto been a missing link—unknown as it was—in the harmony of creation and in the logic of the Divine Mercy."

At this moment an usher appeared and informed the king that the Minister of Foreign Affairs desired an audience on account of important business.

The king turned to Benedict:

"Sir," said he, "though your predictions are gloomy, you will always be welcome in the home of him to whom you have made them. You have foretold a victory; well, I to-day commission you to depict it. And if you remain with us, it only rests with you to share it. Ernest, give your Guelphic Cross to M. Benedict Turpin. I will tell my Minister of Foreign Affairs to have the patent ready for signature to-morrow."

The king embraced his son, gave his hand to Kaulbach, graciously saluted Anderson and Benedict, and taking the arm of his aide-de-camp left the apartment as he had entered it.

The young prince detached the cross and ribbon of the Guelphic Order which decorated his uniform, and fastened them on Benedict's coat with signs of the most livery pleasure. The latter thanked him and expressed his gratitude with evidently heartfelt warmth. Said the prince:

"Only promise me one thing, M. Benedict. If your predictions should be verified, and you should have nothing better to do, we will go on our travels together, and you will show me how to kill lions and elephants in these wonderful forests I have heard of to-day."

# CHAPTER XI. BARON FREDERIC VON BÜLOW

And now we will leave our friend Benedict Turpin in order to follow one of his adversaries who is destined to become an important character in our story. We mean Baron Frederic von Bülow, whom we left with Georges Kleist in the glade of Eilenriede.

Although his wound appeared at first sight the more serious of the two, it was not in reality so. Moreover, he was the most eager to leave the field. Entrusted as he was with a mission to Frankfort, he had turned aside from his road to call Benedict to account, and from the first moment that he was able to bear the fatigue of the journey he did not lose a moment in pursuing it.

Although untouched by the ball, the impact of the broken pistol with the right side of Kleist's face had had deplorable results. The blow was so violent that it had left a bruise of the exact shape of the muzzle of the pistol. His eyes were bloodshot and his cheek immoderately swollen. In short, Herr Kleist would be obliged for at least a fortnight to forgo the pleasures of society.

When the Baron Frederic von Bülow and Herr Kleist arrived at the Royal Hotel they found their misadventure and Benedict's triumph were already public property. The fact of their being Prussians was no recommendation, and they were received with an amount of derision which induced Herr Kleist, suffering though he was, to take the train immediately. As for the major, having already accomplished a third of his journey, he had only to continue on a branch line running direct from Hanover to Frankfort.

We have already given some account of the appearance and physique of the Baron Frederic von Bülow; we will now complete our description, first relating the romantic manner in which he entered the military career and the happy chance by which his undoubted merits found their due reward.

Frederic von Bülow came of a family belonging to Breslau. He had been a student at Jena. One fine day he resolved to make a tour which is frequently undertaken by German students along the banks of the Rhine. He set out alone; not that he was in the least misanthropical; but he was a poet. He loved to travel according to the inclination of the moment, to stop when it suited him, proceed when he pleased, and have no companion drawing him to the left when he wanted to follow a charming woman to the right.

He had reached the most picturesque part of the Rhine; the Seven Mountains. On the opposite bank, on the summit of a lofty hill there stood a fine Gothic castle, lately restored. It belonged to the brother of the King of Prussia, who was then only the Prince Royal. Not only had he rebuilt the castle on its ancient foundations, but he had furnished it throughout with appointments of the sixteenth century, collected in the neighbourhood from the peasantry and convents, and new pieces made by clever workmen from ancient models. Hangings, tapestries, mirrors, all were of the same period, and formed a charming miniature museum of arms, pictures, and valuable curiosities. When the prince was not in residence he allowed the castle to be shown to visitors of distinction.

How difficult it is to define the phrase "visitors of distinction." Frederic, whose family was of ancient nobility, considered that he had a right, though travelling on foot, to see the castle. Knapsack on shoulder, staff in hand, he climbed the steep path and knocked at the door of the keep. The sound of a horn was heard, and the door opened. A porter appeared and an officer in the costume of the sixteenth century, who asked what could be done for him. Frederic von Bülow explained his wish as an archæologist to see the Prince Regent's castle. The officer replied, regretting he was not able to gratify him; the prince's intendant had arrived the evening before, preceding his master only by twenty-four hours. Visitors could no longer be admitted. But the traveller was invited according to custom to inscribe his name, titles, and qualifications in the visitors' book. He took a pen and wrote Frederic von Bülow, student of the University of Jena. Then he took up his iron-shod stick, saluted the officer, and began to descend the path.

But he had not taken a hundred steps when he heard himself called. The officer beckoned and a page ran after him, saying the intendant begged him to return and would take upon himself to grant the desired permission to see the castle.

In the ante-room Frederic met, as if by chance, a man of about fifty-eight or sixty. It was the prince's intendant. He entered into conversation with the young man, appeared pleased with him, and offered to be his guide throughout the castle, an offer that Frederic took good care to accept. The intendant was very well informed; Frederic was a young man of ability, and three or four hours had passed without either being aware how the time was going, when a servant announced, dinner. Frederic gracefully expressed his concern at leaving his cicerone so soon; and his regret was evidently shared by his guide.

"See here," he said. "You are travelling as a student; I am here en garçon. Suppose you dine with me. You will not dine so well as you might with the king, but at any rate it will be better than hotel fare."

Frederic protested as far as he thought good breeding demanded, but as he was really longing to accept the invitation he ended by acceding with visible pleasure, and they consequently dined together. Frederic was a delightful companion, being both poet and philosopher, qualities one finds only united in Germany. He quite made a conquest of his host, who after dinner proposed a game of chess. Midnight struck, and each thought the evening barely begun. It was not possible to return to the village at such an hour. Frederic, after some modest reluctance, remained at the castle and slept in the Landgrave Philip's bed; and it was only the next day after lunch that he obtained his host's permission to resume his journey.

"I am not without some slight influence at court," said the intendant on taking leave of him, "and if I can ever be of any service to you, pray make use of me."

Frederic promised that he would.

"And whatever may happen," added his host, "I shall remember your name. You may forget me, but I shall not forget you."

Frederic finished his travels on the Rhine, returned to the University of Jena, concluded his studies there, entered the diplomatic service and was greatly astonished at being one day summoned to the cabinet of the grand

94

duke.

"Sir," said the great man, "I have selected you to convey my congratulations to William the First, King of Prussia, on his recent accession to the throne."

"But, Highness!" cried Frederic in astonishment, "who am I to be honoured with such a commission?"

"Really! are you not Baron Frederic von Bülow?"

"Highness! Baron? I? But since when have I become a baron?"

"Since I made you one. You will start at nine o'clock to-morrow; your letters of credit will be ready at eight."

Frederic could only bow and utter his thanks; he bowed deeply, gratefully thanked the grand duke and left the room.

The next morning at ten o'clock he was in the train and by the evening he was in Berlin. His arrival was immediately announced to the new king. The new king replied that he would receive him the following day at the castle Of Potsdam.

On the morrow Frederic, in his court suit, started for Potsdam and arrived at the castle. But to his great astonishment he learnt that the king had just gone away and had left only his intendant to represent him.

Frederic's first idea was to return to Berlin; but he remembered that it was this official who had entertained him so kindly and courteously two years before at the castle of Rheinstein. He did not want to appear ungrateful or offended, so had his name sent in accordingly. But while crossing the ante-room he observed a full-length portrait of the king. He stopped for an instant stupefied. His Majesty resembled his intendant as one drop of water resembles another. The truth now dawned on Frederic. It was the king's brother himself who, to-day reigning as King William I, had received him at the castle of Rheinstein, who had acted as his guide, had kept him to dinner, who had won three games of chess out of five, and had made him sleep in the Landgrave Philip's bed—who had offered his influence at court, and who on taking leave of him had promised not to forget him.

He understood now why he had been chosen by the Grand Duke of Weimar to carry his congratulations to the king; why the Grand Duke of Weimar had made him a baron, why the king had appointed a meeting at Potsdam, and why finally His Majesty had returned to Berlin, leaving his intendant only to represent him.

His Majesty wanted to enjoy another day like that they had passed together at Rheinstein. Frederic was a good courtier, and was ready to contribute all in his power to this caprice. He entered as if he had no suspicion, greeted his host like an old acquaintance, only showing the respect due to an older man, thus recalling the scene which had left such a pleasing influence on his mind.

The intendant made excuses for His Majesty, and invited Frederic to pass the day at the castle of Potsdam, an invitation which was accepted like the one at Rheinstein. He again offered his services as cicerone, took him into the mausoleum, and showed him the tomb and the sword of the Great Frederic.

A court carriage was ready waiting for them, and they went to see the castle of Sans-Souci, which is only two miles from Potsdam. It was here, it will be remembered, in the park of this château that the famous mill was situated which its owner refused to sell to Frederic II, and which caused the king to exclaim when the miller gained his lawsuit, "So there are still judges at Berlin!" In the sequel the descendants of the stubborn miller were softened and sold their mill to William I, who, wishing to preserve it as a monument of the occurrence, refused to allow it to be demolished.

But time, which cares nothing for the commands of kings, had in store for William and his guest an example of its disregard. An hour before the arrival of Frederic and the so-called agent, the four sails of the windmill had fallen, bringing down in their fall the balustrade which surrounded it. So that to day one must conclude that there are no longer judges in Berlin, as there is no longer a mill at Sans-Souci.

On their return to Potsdam, Frederic and his companion found a table ready laid for two. They dined alone together, played five games of chess out of which the agent won three, and it was only at midnight that they separated, when on the agent wishing Frederic a good night, the latter replied with a deep bow: "Sire, may God grant Your Majesty a good night."

The next day the fiction was abandoned. The king breakfasted with Frederic, gave him the Order of the Red Eagle, and with much pressing induced him to hand in his resignation and join the army. A week later he received his commission as lieutenant of the line, and came to pay his respects in his new character to the king, who undertook that the king would ever remember him whom the prince had promised not to forget.

Two years later, Frederic received a proof that the king indeed had not forgotten. His regiment was stationed in garrison at Frankfort, where at the house of Herr Fellner, the burgomaster, he made the acquaintance of a family of French descent exiled by the revocation of the Edict of Nantes, which had since its expatriation become Catholic. The family consisted of the mother, aged about thirty-eight, the grandmother, who was sixty-eight, and two girls of twenty and eighteen. Their family name was Chandroz.

The elder daughter, Emma, had black hair, black eyes, a pale clear skin, and well-marked eyebrows; her marvellously beautiful teeth showed like pearls against her vividly red lips. She had, in fact, that stately dark beauty which suggests the Roman matron, Lucretia and Cornelia in one.

Helen was worthy of her name. Her hair was of that exquisite blonde tint which can only be compared to the colour of ripe corn. Her complexion faintly tinted with rose had the freshness and delicacy of the camellia. And the effect was almost astonishing when under these fair locks, and upon that countenance of almost transparent pallor, she raised large dark eyes, eloquent of passion, overarched with dark eyebrows and fringed with lashes which gave to their sparkling orbs deep reflections like those of the black diamonds of Tripoli. And as one had only to look at Emma to see foreshadowed in her the calm and wisdom of those matrons among whom the Catholic religion finds its saints, so one could divine in Helen all that tempestuous future which the united passions of two races hold in store for the hybrids of their sex.

Whether it were that this strange manifestation of divine caprice dismayed him, or whether he felt himself drawn by irresistible sympathy to the elder of the two sisters—it was to her that the Baron von Bülow paid his homage. He was young, handsome, and rich. It was known that the King of Prussia held him in warm regard. He stated that if he were granted Emma's hand, his royal protector at the same time would make him a captain. The two young people were in love, and the family had no serious opposition to raise to their union. They said: "Obtain your promotion as captain, and we will see." He asked three days' leave, started for Berlin, and came back on the third day with his captain's commission.

All was arranged. But during his absence Emma's mother was slightly indisposed. Her illness increased, developed into disease of the lungs, and at the end of six months Emma was doubly orphaned.

It was a further reason for giving the family a protector. The grandmother, sixty-nine years of age, might die at any moment. They waited till the strict season of mourning dictated both by their hearts and by custom had elapsed, and at the end of six months they were married.

Three days after the birth of his first child, a boy, the Baron Frederic von Bülow received his commission as major. On this occasion the protection of the king was so obvious and so kindly intentioned that the baron resolved to make a second journey to Berlin, not on this occasion to ask for favours, but to return thanks for them. This journey was all the more opportune because a word dropped by His Majesty's secretary had warned him that there were great events on the horizon in which he might take part, and that he would do wisely to come to Berlin on any suitable pretext and see the king in person.

And in fact we have already said that Count von Bismarck had worked hard to bring great events to pass. The king had three times received Baron Frederic in private, and had freely discussed with him the probability of a terrible war. To crown all, he attached him to the staff, so that he might become aide-de-camp to any general whom he sent to any special place, or even at need to his son or his cousin.

This was how Baron Frederic chanced to find himself at Berlin on June 7th, that is, on the day of the attempted assassination of Bismarck. As we have seen, he, with two other officers rescued Benedict from the hands of the mob; but, having promised the crowd that the Frenchman should shout "Long live Prussia! Long live King William I!" he was confounded when, instead of adopting this prudent course, Benedict declaimed Alfred de Musset's verses on the Rhine, almost as well known in Prussia as the song to which they were an answer. He and his comrades took this affront, which the public had witnessed, as a deliberate insult. All three presented themselves at the Black Eagle, which Benedict as we know had given as his address, intending to demand immediate satisfaction.

But, as they met each other and learnt that their errands were all the same, they recognized that three men, who do not wish to gain their end by intimidation, cannot all demand satisfaction from a single opponent. For this reason they cast lots as to who should have the honour of fighting with Benedict, and the lot as we have seen fell upon Frederic.

# CHAPTER XII. HELEN

There stands in Frankfort-on-Main, at the corner of the Ross-market, opposite the Protestant Church of St. Catherine, a mansion, which, by its architecture, belongs to the transition period between Louis XIV and Louis XV. It is known as Passevent House. The ground-floor was occupied by a bookseller, and all the rest by the Chandroz family, already known to the reader by name.

A sort of uneasiness, not quite amounting to actual trouble, seemed to prevail in the house. The morning before a letter had been received by Baroness von Bülow, announcing her husband's return in the evening, and close upon that came a telegram, saying that he would not arrive before the following morning, and that she must not be anxious if there were a further delay. The fact was, that two hours after writing his letter, the baron saw Benedict's announcement in the "Gazette." Fearing that he might be delayed by a wound, he wished to spare his wife any possible anxiety, her infant being only just over a week old.

Although the train was not due until four in the morning, Hans, the confidential servant of the family, had already departed at three, taking the carriage to meet his master at the station and at least ten times during the interval Emma rang up her maid, wondering why the time passed so slowly.

At length the sound of a carriage was heard, followed by the creaking of the great gate, the carriage passed under the arch, the tread of spurred boots echoed on the staircase, Emma's door opened, and Emma's arms enfolded her husband.

It did not escape her notice that Frederic winced when she threw her arms round him. She asked the cause. Frederic replied with a cock-and-bull story of a cab accident in which he had slightly sprained his arm.

The sound of the carriage and the general movement in the house informed Helen of the baron's arrival. Hastily wrapping herself in a dressing-gown with her beautiful hair falling loosely over it, she hurried to greet her brother-in-law whom she loved tenderly. In order not to disturb the Countess de Chandroz, their grandmother, orders had been given to keep her wing of the house as quiet as possible.

Madame von Bülow, with the usual penetration of wives, soon guessed that Frederic's arm was more hurt than he chose to acknowledge. She insisted that the family doctor, Herr Bodemacker, should be sent for, and Frederic, who knew by the pain he suffered, that the bandage must have been displaced during his journey, made no objection. He only begged her to keep quiet while he went to his own room for the bath he had ordered, saying that it would be much better for the doctor to follow him there and decide which of his two hundred and eighty-two bones required attention.

The question of importance was to keep the baroness in ignorance as to the serious nature of the wound. With the help of Hans and the connivance of the doctor this would be easy. The bath was a marvellous help, and Emma allowed him to go to his room without suspecting the real cause of his requiring it.

When the doctor arrived, Frederic astonished Hans by explaining that the evening before he had received a sword wound which had laid open his arm, that the bandage must have slipped in the train, and that it, his coat, and his shirt were all soaked in blood.

The doctor slit the sleeve the whole way up, and then cut it clear at the top. Frederic then was told to plunge his arm into the warm water of the bath which enabled the doctor to remove the coat sleeve. He then loosened the shirt sleeve by sponging it with the warm water, and finally, cutting it away at the shoulder, was able to expose the wound.

The arm, compressed by the sleeves, was frightfully red and swollen, the plaster had given way, the wound was gaping widely through its whole length, and in the lower part the arm appeared cut to the bone. It was fortunate that there had been plenty of warm water at hand. The doctor brought the two sides of the cut together again, fixed them carefully, bandaged the whole arm and put it in splints as if it had been broken. But it was absolutely necessary that the baron should remain quite quiet for two or three days. The doctor undertook to find the general in command and to explain privately that Baron von Bülow was charged with a mission to him but could not possibly leave the house.

Hans quickly removed the water and stained bandages. Frederic went down, kissed his wife, and satisfied her by saying the doctor had merely ordered him to rest for a few days. The word dislocation spread through the house and accounted for the baron's indisposition. Returning to his own apartment he found the Prussian general awaiting him. He explained matters in two words; moreover, before long the story would be in all the papers. The important question was, to keep the baroness in ignorance. She would be uneasy about a dislocation, but in despair over a wound.

Frederic handed over his despatches to the general. They merely warned him to be ready for action at a moment's notice. It was evident that Count Bismarck, from whom the order came, wished to have a garrison at hand during the Diet, to overawe the assembly, if possible. Afterwards he would withdraw it or leave it, according to circumstances. This question would be put to the Diet. "In case of war between Austria and Prussia, on which side will you be?"

Frederic was extremely anxious to see his young sister Helen, having important communications to make. After he and Benedict had vowed eternal friendship on the field of battle, and Benedict had spoken of having met the baroness at the burgomaster's house, he had conceived an idea which he could not drive away, namely, to marry Benedict to his sister-in-law. From what he had seen and heard of the young man, he felt convinced that these two impetuous, imaginative, and artistic characters, always ready to pursue an idea suggested by a ray of sunlight or a scented breeze, were, out of the whole creation, the best suited to each other. Consequently he wished to ascertain if Helen had been attracted by his friend. Were this the case, he would find some pretext for bringing Benedict to Frankfort, and, little as Helen cared for admiration, he thought the acquaintance would soon assume the character he wished.

Moreover, he wished to warn Helen to keep newspapers away from her sister and grandmother, and on this account it was absolutely necessary to take her into his confidence. She anticipated his wishes, for scarcely had the general left him, when some one knocked softly at his door, such a knock as might have proceeded from a cat or a bird. He knew Helen's gentle manner of announcing herself.

"Come in, little sister, come in!" he cried, and Helen entered on tip-toe.

The baron was lying on his bed in his dressing-gown, lying on his left side, his wounded arm extended along his body.

"Ah! you good-for-nothing," said she, folding her arms and gazing at him, "so you have been and gone and done it, have you?"

"How? done what?" enquired Frederic, laughing.

"Well, now I have got you alone, we can talk."

"Exactly, dear Helen, now we are alone as you say. You are the strong-minded person of this house, although no one else knows it, not even yourself. So I want to discuss important matters with you—and they are not a few."

"So do I, and I shall begin by taking the bull by the horns. Your arm is not dislocated nor even sprained. You have fought a duel, like the hothead you are, and your arm is wounded by either a sabre or sword-cut."

"Well, my little sister, that is exactly what I wanted to tell you. I did fight a duel—for political reasons. And I did get a sabre cut in my arm, but it was a friendly sabre, very neatly and prettily applied. It is not dangerous, no artery or nerve severed. But the story will be in all the papers; it has made noise enough already. Now we must prevent both grandmamma and Emma from seeing the newspapers."

"The only paper taken here is the 'Kreuz Zeitung.'"

"Which is precisely the one that will say the most."

"What are you smiling at?"

"I can't help thinking of the face of the man who will have to supply the details!"

"What do you mean?"

"Nothing. I was only talking to myself, and when I say things to myself they are not worth repeating aloud. The question is—to keep an eye on the 'Kreuz Zeitung.'"

"Certainly I will keep an eye on it."

"Then I need not trouble any more about it?"

"When I tell you that I will see to it myself!"

"Very well! We will talk about something else."

"About anything you like."

"Do you recollect meeting a young Frenchman at Herr Fellner's, an artist, a painter?"

"Monsieur Benedict Turpin? I should think so! A charming man who makes the most rapid sketches, and though they are flattering, they are still likenesses."

"Oh! come, come! You are quite enthusiastic."

"I can show you one he did of me. He has given me a pair of wings, and I really look like an angel!"

"Then he is clever?"

"Enormously clever."

"And witty."

"He can certainly give you as good as you gave. You should have seen how he routed some of our bankers when they tried to chaff him. He spoke better German than they did."

"Is he rich as well?"

"So they say."

"It also seems as if there were remarkable affinities between his character and that of a little girl I know."

"But who? I don't understand."

"Nevertheless, it is some one you know. He appears to be capricious, imaginative, vivacious; he adores travelling, is an excellent rider, and a good sportsman, either on foot or horseback, all which coincides admirably with the tastes of a certain 'Diana Vernon.'"

"I thought that was what you always called me."

"So it is. Do you recognize my portrait?"

"Not at all, not in the least. I am gentle, calm, collected. I like travelling, yes. But where have I been? To Paris, Berlin, Vienna, London, and that is all, I love horses, but what do I ever ride except my poor little Gretchen?"

"She has nearly killed you twice over!"

"Poor thing! it was my own fault. As for shooting, I have never held a gun, and as for coursing, I have never started a hare."

"True, but why not? Only because the grandmother objected. If you could have had your own way—"

"Oh, yes! It would be glorious to rush against the wind, to feel it blowing through one's hair. There is great pleasure in rapid motion, a feeling of life which one finds in nothing else."

"So you would like to be able to do these things which you don't do."

"Yes, indeed."

"With Monsieur Benedict?"

"Why Monsieur Benedict more than any one else?"

"Because he is more charming than most."

"I do not think so."

"Really?"

"No."

"Then; supposing you were allowed to choose a husband out of all my friends, you would not choose M. Benedict?"

"I should never dream of doing so."

"Now, little sister, you know I am an obstinate man, who likes to understand, things. How is it that a man, young, handsome, rich, talented, courageous, and imaginative, fails to interest you, particularly when he has both the good qualities and the defects of your own character?"

"What am I to say? I do not know, I cannot analyse my feelings. Some people are sympathetic to me, some indifferent, some downright disagreeable!"

"Well, you don't class Monsieur Benedict among the disagreeable, I hope."

"No, but among the indifferents."

"And why among the indifferents?"

"Monsieur Benedict is of medium height, I like tall men: he is fair, I like dark men. He is volatile, I like serious people. He is bold, always rushing off to the ends of the world; he would be the husband of other men's wives, and not even the lover of his own."

"Let us resume. What sort of man, then, must he be that would please you?"

"Somebody just the opposite of M. Benedict."

"He must be tall."

"Yes."

"Dark?"

"Either dark or dark chestnut."

"Grave."

"Grave, or at least, serious. Also brave, steady, loyal, and—"

"Just so. Do you know that you have described, word for word, my friend, Karl von Freyberg?"

Helen blushed crimson, and moved quickly, as if to leave the room, but Frederic, disregarding his wound, caught her hand and made her sit down again. The light from between the curtains irradiated her face like the sunlight falling on a flower. He looked at her intently.

"Well, yes," she said, "but no one knows but you."

"Not Karl himself?"

"He may have some idea."

"Well, little sister," said Frederic, "I see no great harm in all this. Come and kiss me, and we will talk again another time."

"But how comes it," exclaimed Helen, with vexation, "that you know all you want to know, although I have told you nothing at all?"

"Because one can see through a crystal which is pure. Dear little Helen, Karl von Freyberg is my best friend, he has all I could wish in a brother-in-law, or that you could desire in a husband. If he loves you as much as you seem to love him, there should be no great difficulty about your becoming his wife."

"Ah! dear Frederic," said Helen, shaking her pretty head, "but I once heard a Frenchwoman say that the marriages which present no difficulties are just those which never come off!"

And she retired to her own room, wondering no doubt as to what difficulties Destiny could interpose to the completion of her own marriage.

# CHAPTER XIII. COUNT KARL VON FREYBERG

In the days of Charles V the Austrian Empire dominated for a period both Europe and America, both the East and the West Indies. From the summit of the Dalmatian mountains Austria beheld the rising of the sun, from the chain of the Andes she could watch his setting. When the last ray of sunset sank in the west, the first light of dawn was reappearing in the east. Her empire was greater than that of Alexander, of Augustus, of Charlemagne.

But this empire has been torn by the devouring hands of Time. And the champion by whom the armour of this colossus, piece by piece, has been rent away, is France.

France took—for herself—Flanders, the Duchy of Bar, Burgundy, Alsace, and Lorraine. For the grandson of Louis XIV she took Spain, the two Indies, and the islands. For the son of Philip V she took Naples and Sicily. She also took the Netherlands and made two separate kingdoms of them, Belgium and Holland, and, finally, she tore away Lombardy and Venetia, and gave them to Italy. And to-day the boundaries of this empire, upon which, three hundred years ago, the sun never set, are, in the west, Tyrol; in the east, Moldavia; to the north, Prussia; to the south, Turkey.

Every one knows that, strictly speaking, there is no Austria, properly so called, only a dukedom of Austria, with nine to ten millions of inhabitants, of which Vienna is the capital. And it was a duke of Austria who imprisoned Richard Cœur-de-Lion on his return from Palestine, and only released him on payment of a ransom of two hundred and fifty thousand gold crowns.

The map-space now occupied by Austria, outside the actual dukedom, its kernel, consists of Bohemia, Hungary, Illyria, the Tyrol, Moravia, Silesia, the Sclavonian district of Croatia, the Vaivody of Servia, the Banat, Transylvania, Galicia, Dalmatia, and Styria.

We do not count four to five millions of Roumanians scattered throughout Hungary, and on the banks of the Danube. Every one of the above districts has its own character, its own customs, language, costume, frontier. Especially the dwellers in Styria, composed of Norica and the ancient Pannonia, have retained their own language, costume, and primitive customs. Before it became included in Austria, Styria had its own separate history and nobility, dating from the time when it was known as the march of Styria, about 1030. And from that epoch Karl von Freyberg dated his ancestry, remaining a great noble at a time when great nobles are becoming rare.

He was a handsome young man of about twenty-seven, tall, straight, slight, flexible as a cane, and equally tough. His fine black hair was cut close, and he had beneath black eyebrows and eyelashes, those dark grey eyes which Homer attributes to Minerva and which shine like emeralds. His complexion was sunburnt, for he had hunted since childhood. He had small hands and feet, unwearied limbs, and prodigious strength. In his own mountains he had hunted bear, wild goat, and chamois. But he had never attacked the first of these animals with any weapon except lance or dagger.

He was now a captain in the Lichtenstein Hussars, and, even in barracks, was always followed by two Tyrolean chasseurs dressed in the national costume. While the one carried out an order the other remained at hand, so that there might be always some one to whom his master might say "Go and do this." Although they understood German he always spoke to them in their own tongue. They were serfs, understanding nothing about enfranchisement, who considered that he had absolute power of life and death over them, and although he had several times tried to explain matters, telling them they were free to go where they chose, they had simply refused either to believe or to listen.

Three years before, during a chamois hunt, one of his keepers lost his footing. He fell down a precipice, and was dashed to pieces. Karl ordered his steward to pay the widow an annuity. She thanked him, but was quite unable to understand that he owed her anything merely because her husband had been killed in his service.

When there was a hunt—and he who writes this had twice the honour to be of the party—whether in his own country or not, Karl always wore his national costume and very picturesque it was.

The count's two attendants never left him. They were loaders. When Karl had fired, he dropped his gun on the ground and another ready loaded was instantly slipped into his hand.

Whilst waiting for the beaters to be placed, which generally took half an hour, the two chasseurs drew from their game-bags small Tyrolean flutes made of reeds, on which they played, sometimes together, sometimes alone, but always joining again after a certain number of bars, Styrian airs, melancholy, but sweet and plaintive. This lasted some minutes, then, as if drawn by the music, the count in his turn produced a similar flute and put it to his lips. He now took up the melody, the others only played accompaniments, which I think must have been improvised—so original were they. It seemed as if the accompaniments pursued the air, overtook it, and then turned around it like creepers or tendrils. Then the air reappeared, charming, but always sad, and reaching notes so high that one would have thought only silver or glass could produce them. Then a gun was heard, that of the chief beater, announcing that all was ready. The three flutes vanished inside the game-bags, the musicians took their guns and again became hunters, ear and eye strained to the utmost.

Count Karl knocked at eleven o'clock at Baron von Bülow's door, having heard both of his return and his accident. Frederic received him with an unusually smiling countenance, but only offered his left hand.

"Ah! then, it is true, is it? I have just read the 'Kreuz Zeitung.'"

"What have you read, my dear Karl?"

"I read that you fought with a Frenchman and were wounded."

"Hush—not so loud. I am not wounded for the family, only dislocated."

"What does that mean?"

"It means, my dear fellow, that my wife won't think she need inspect a sprained arm, but she would positively insist on examining a wounded one. Now she would die of fright over this wound, while I believe you would

110

rather like to have it. Have you seen many wounds a foot long? I can show you one if you like."

"How so? A skilled fencer like you, who uses his sabre as if he had invented it!"

"None the less, I found my master."

"A Frenchman?"

"A Frenchman."

"Well, instead of hunting wild boar in the Taunus to-morrow, as I intended, I should like to go and hunt your Frenchman, and bring back one of his paws to replace your wounded one."

"Don't do anything of the kind, my dear friend, you might easily only bring back a nice little cut like this of mine. Besides, the Frenchman is now my friend, and I want him to be yours also."

"Never! A rascal who has cut your arm open—how far? A foot, did you say?"

"He might have killed me. He did not. He might have cut me in two, and he only gave me this wound. We embraced on the battlefield. Did you see the other details?"

"What other details?"

"Those concerning his other duel, with Herr George Kleist."

"Superficially. I don't know him, I only cared about you. I did see that your Frenchman had damaged the jaw of some man who writes articles in the 'Kreuz Zeitung.' He seems to have quarrelled with two professions, since he chooses to encounter an officer and a journalist on the same day."

"He did not choose us, we were foolish enough to choose him. We pursued him to Hanover, where he was very comfortable. Probably he was annoyed by being disturbed. So he sent me home with my arm in a sling, and dismissed Herr Kleist with a black eye."

"Is the fellow a Hercules?"

"Not at all, it is curious. He is a head shorter than you, but formed like Alfred de Musset's Hassan, whose mother made him small in order to turn him out perfect."

"And so you embraced on the battlefield?"

"Better still. I have an idea."

"What is it?"

"He is a Frenchman as you know."

"Of good family?"

"Dear friend, they are all of good family since the Revolution. But he is clever—very."

"As a fencing master?"

"Not at all, as an artist. Kaulbach says he is the hope of the present school. He is young."

"Young?"

"Yes, twenty-five or six at most, and handsome."

"Handsome as well?"

"Charming. An income of twelve thousand francs."

"A trifle."

"Not everybody has two hundred thousand, like you, my dear friend. Twelve thousand francs and a fine talent might mean fifty or sixty thousand."

"But why in the world do you consider all this?"

"I should like him to marry Helen."

The count nearly sprang out of his chair.

"What! Let him marry Helen! your sister-in-law! A Frenchman!"

"Well, is she not herself partly of French origin?"

"I am sure Mademoiselle Helen loves you too much to be willing to marry a man who has wounded you like this. I hope she refused?"

"She did."

The count breathed again.

"But what the deuce put such an idea into your head as to marry him to your sister?"

"She is only my sister-in-law."

"That does not matter. What an idea to think of marrying one's sister-in-law to the first person picked up on the high road!"

"I assure you this young man is not just—"

"Never mind! She refused, did she not? That is the chief thing."

"I hope to make her think better of it."

"You must be quite mad."

"But tell me, why should she refuse? Explain if you can! Unless, indeed, she cares for some one else."

The count blushed up to his eyes.

"Do you think that quite impossible?" he stammered.

"No, but then if she should love someone else, she must say so."

"Listen, Frederic, I cannot positively say that she loves some one else, but I can declare that some one else loves her."

"That is half the battle. Is it some one as good as my Frenchman?"

"Ah! Frederic, you are so prejudiced in favour of your Frenchman. I dare not say yes."

"Then tell me at once. You see what might have happened had my

Frenchman been here, and I had made any promise to him."

"Well, at any rate, you won't turn me out for saying it. The some one is myself."

"Always modest, loyal, and true, dear Karl but—"

"But? I will have no 'buts.'"

"It is not a very terrible 'but,' as you will see. You are a great noble, Karl, compared to my little sister Helen."

"I am the last of my race, there is no one to make objections."

"And you are very rich for a dowry of two hundred thousand francs."

"I can dispose of my own fortune as I choose."

"These are observations I felt bound to make to you."

"Do you consider them really serious?"

"I acknowledge objections to them would be much more so."

"Is it of no consequence to ascertain whether Helen loves me or not?"

"That can be decided at once."

"How?"

"I will send for her, the shortest explanations are always the best."

The count became as pale as he had been red the moment before. In a trembling voice he exclaimed:

"Not now, for Heaven's sake! not now!"

"But, my dear Karl!"

"Frederic!"

"Do you believe I am your friend?"

"Good heavens! yes."

"Well, do you suppose I would subject you to an interview which could only make you unhappy?

"You mean—"

"I mean that I believe—"

"Believe what?"

"I believe that she loves you as much as you love her."

"My friend, you will kill me with joy."

"Well, since you are so afraid of an interview with Helen, go and do your hunting in the Taunus, kill your wild boar and come back again, the thing will be done."

"Done, how?"

"I will undertake it."

"No, Frederic, I will not go."

"What, you will not go? Only think of your men waiting there with their flutes."

"They may wait."

At this moment the door opened, and Helen appeared on the threshold.

"Helen!" exclaimed Karl.

"You will be careful—you must not be too long with my brother," she said, remaining at the door.

"He is waiting for you," observed Frederic.

"For me?"

"Yes, come here."

"But I don't understand in the least."

"Never mind! Come here."

Karl offered his hand to Helen.

"Oh, mademoiselle," he said, "do what your brother asks, I entreat you."

"Well," she said, "what shall I do?"

"You can lend your hand to Karl; he will return it."

Karl seized her hand and pressed it to his heart. Helen uttered a cry. Timid as a child, Karl released the hand.

"You did not hurt me," said Helen.

Karl promptly repossessed himself of the released hand.

"Brother," said Frederic, "did you not say you had a secret you wished to confide to Helen?"

"Oh yes, yes," cried Karl.

"All right, I am not listening."

Karl bent towards Helen's ear, and the sweet words "I love you" fell from his lips with a whisper as of a moth's wings, which flitting by your ear on a spring evening breathes the eternal secret of Nature.

"Oh! Frederic, Frederic!" cried Helen, hiding her forehead on his couch, "I was not mistaken!"

Then raising her head and languidly opening her beautiful eyes.

"And I," she said, "I love you."

# CHAPTER XIV. THE GRANDMOTHER

For a few moments Frederic left the lovers to themselves and their happiness. Then, as both raised their eyes to his, as if enquiring what next should be done:

"The little sister," said he, "must go and tell all this to her big sister, the big sister will relate it to the grandmother, and the grandmother, who believes in me, will come and talk it over and we will arrange things together."

"And when must I go and tell all this to the big sister?" enquired Helen.

"At once, if you will."

"I will go now! You will wait for me, Karl?"

Karl's smile and gesture answered her. Helen glided out of his embrace and vanished like a bird.

"Now for our own affairs!" said Frederic.

"How! what affairs?"

"I have something to tell you."

"Anything important?"

"Very serious."

"Anything about our marriage? You alarm me!"

"Suppose this morning when you doubted the possibility of Helen's love I had answered, 'Do not be afraid, Helen loves and will marry you, but there is an obstacle, and the marriage cannot possibly take place in less than a year?'"

"What would you have? I should have been in despair at the delay, but transported by the news."

"Well, my friend, I tell you now what I should have told you this morning. Helen loves you. She did not ask me to tell you this; she has told it herself, but at this moment there is an insurmountable obstacle."

"At least you will explain what the obstacle is?"

"I am going to tell you what is yet a secret, Karl. In a week, or at most, a fortnight, Prussia will declare war against Austria."

"Ah! I feared it. Bismarck is Germany's evil genius."

"Well, now you will understand. As friends we can serve on opposite sides, that happens every day. But—as brothers-in-law—we could not. You can hardly become my brother-in-law at the very moment of unsheathing your sword against me."

"You are quite sure of your information?"

"Most certainly I am. Bismarck now occupies such a position in regard to the Chambers, and has forced the king into such a position with regard to the other German princes, that, either he must embroil Germany from Berlin to Pest and even to Innspruck, or he will be tried for high treason, and end his days in a fortress! Now, Bismarck is a power—a power of darkness if you will—he will not be tried for high treason, and he will embroil Germany—for this reason: Prussia has nothing to gain by upsetting him, whereas by upsetting Germany she can annex two or three little kingdoms or duchies, which will round off her borders very comfortably."

"But the Confederation will be against him."

"Little will he care for that, so long as he himself remains indispensable. And, listen to what I tell you; the more enemies Prussia has, the more she will beat them. Our army is organized as no other European army is organized—at the present moment."

"You say our army, then you have become a Prussian. I thought you were a German."

"I am a Silesian, Prussian since the days of Frederic II. All I have I owe to King William, and I would willingly die for him, while regretting it should

118

be in a bad cause."

"What do you advise in my case?"

"You are a Styrian, therefore an Austrian. Fight for your emperor like a lion, and if by ill luck we meet in a cavalry charge you turn your horse to the right, I also turn mine; we salute and pass on. Don't yourself get killed, that is all, and we will sign the marriage contract the day peace is declared."

"Unhappily, I see no other way out of it, unless by good luck we could both remain at Frankfort, a free and neutral town. I have no wish to fight with Germans. It will be an iniquitous war. If it had been Turks, French, or Russians, it would be all right, but between children of the same country, speaking the same language! My patriotism ends there, I confess."

That last hope must be given up. I myself brought orders to the Prussian general here to be ready to leave, Austria will certainly withdraw her troops also. Frankfort may have a Bavarian garrison or be left with one of her own, but most certainly we, to the last man, shall have to rejoin the army."

"Poor dear Helen! What are we to say when she comes back?"

"We will say the marriage is decided on, that the betrothal will take place; but the marriage must be delayed for a year. If, in spite of my prophecy, war should not be declared, you can marry at once. If this war does take place, it is not a war which will last. It will be a tempest, a hurricane, passing over and destroying everything, then it will be peace. If I fix a date, it is because I am sure not to have to ask for further delay. Helen is eighteen, she will then be nineteen, you are now twenty-six, you will then be twenty-seven. This delay is not caused by circumstances of our making. Circumstances impose it on us. We must give way to them."

"You will promise not to let anything change your opinion of me, and that from to-day, June 12th, you count yourself my brother-in-law—on parole?"

"The honour is too dear for me ever to think of repudiating it. From to-day, June 12th, I am your brother-in-law—on parole."

"Madame von Beling!"

This exclamation was drawn from Karl by the unexpected appearance of an elderly lady dressed entirely in black. She had splendid hair, white as snow, and must in youth have been very beautiful. Her whole appearance betokened distinction and benevolence.

"How is this, my dear Frederic?" said she, entering the room. "You have been here since five o'clock this morning and I only hear of your arrival from your wife at two in the afternoon; also, that you are in pain."

"Dear grandmamma," answered Frederic, "but do I not also know that you do not awake before eleven, and only rise at noon?"

"True, but they tell me you have a sprained arm. I have three excellent remedies for sprains, one, which is perfect, came from my old friend Goethe, one from another old friend, Madame Schröder, and the third from Baron von Humboldt. You see the origin of all three is unimpeachable."

Turning to Karl, who, bowing, brought forward an armchair for her, she said:

"You, Herr von Freyberg, have evidently no sprains, for you are in hunting costume. Ah! you do not know how your Styrian dress recalls a happy memory of my youth. The first time I saw my husband, Herr von Beling it is now something like fifty-two years ago, for it was in 1814—at a carnival masked ball, he wore a similar costume to the one you are now wearing. He was about your age. In the middle of the ball—I remember as if it were yesterday—we heard of the landing of that accursed Napoleon. The dancers vowed that if he again ascended the throne they would go to fight him. The ladies each chose a cavalier, who should be entitled to wear her colours in the coming campaign. I did like the rest, and I chose Herr von Beling, although in my heart of hearts—for I have remained French in heart—I could not be very angry with the man who had made France so great.

"This fanciful nomination of Herr von Beling as a champion wearing my colours opened my parents' house to him. He could not, he said, be my knight without their permission. They gave their permission. Napoleon again became emperor. Herr von Beling rejoined his regiment, but he first asked my hand from my mother. My mother consulted me, I loved him. It was agreed that we should marry when the war was over. The campaign was not long, and when Herr von Beling returned we were married; I, at the bottom of my heart feeling a little vexed that he had contributed the three hundred millionth part towards the dethronement of my hero. But I never confessed this small infidelity of enthusiasm, and our life was no less happy on that account."

"Dear grandmamma," enquired Frederic, "did Herr von Beling—he must have been very handsome in Styrian garb, I have seen his portrait—did Herr von Beling kneel before you when he asked the favour of being your knight?"

"Certainly, and very gracefully he did it too," returned the old lady.

"Did he do it better than my friend Karl?"

"Better than your friend Karl? But is your friend Karl likely to kneel before me by any chance?"

"Just look at him."

Madame von Beling turned round and saw indeed Karl kneeling on the ground before her.

"Good gracious!" said she laughing, "have I suddenly grown fifty years younger?"

"My dear grandmother," said Frederic, while Karl took possession of the old lady's hand. "No, you have still your threescore and ten years, which become you so well that I will not let you off a single one of them; but here is Karl, who also is going to the war, and who asks to be called the knight of your granddaughter Helen."

"Really! and is my little granddaughter Helen actually old enough to have a knight of her very own?"

"She is eighteen, grandmother."

121

"Eighteen! My age when I married Herr von Beling! It is the age when leaves forsake the tree and are borne away by the wind. If Helen's hour has struck," she continued with a mournful smile, "she must go like the rest."

"Never, never, dear grandmother," cried the young girl who had entered unperceived, "never so far but that I can every day kiss the dear hand which gives life to all of us."

And she knelt down beside Karl and took the other hand.

"Ah!" said Madame von Beling, nodding her head, "so that is why I was invited to come upstairs. I was to be caught in a trap. Well, what am I to do now? How defend myself? To surrender at once is stupid; it is like a scene from Molière."

"Very well, grandmamma, don't surrender, or at least not without conditions."

"And what are they to be?"

"That these young people can be betrothed as soon as they like, but that the marriage, like your own, can only be celebrated when the war is over."

"What war?" asked Helen, in anxiety.

"We will tell you about it later. Meanwhile, if Karl is your knight, he must wear your colours. What are they?"

"I have only one," replied Helen. "It is green."

"Then he is wearing them now," said Frederic indicating his friend's coat with green facings, and the hat with its wide band of green velvet.

"And in honour of my lady love," said Karl, rising, "a hundred men shall also wear them, with me, and like me."

Everything was now settled, and the whole party, Frederic leading the way, Madame von Beling on Karl's arm, went downstairs to convey the good news to the dear invalid.

That same evening it was known that the Diet was convoked at Frankfort for June 15th.

# CHAPTER XV. FRANKFORT-ON-MAIN

It is time to give some information concerning the town in which the chief events of our history will take place.

Frankfort ranks as one of the most important towns in Germany, not merely on account of the number of its inhabitants, nor because of its commercial standing, but by reason of the political position which it occupies as being the seat of the Imperial Diet.

One continually hears phrases repeated until they become familiar without the person precisely understanding the exact meaning. Let us in a few words explain what the functions of the Imperial Diet really are.

It is the duty of the Diet to watch over the affairs of Germany in general and to smooth down disagreements between the confederate States. The president is always a representative of Austria. The decisions of the assembly are called Recesses. The Diet, which has existed since very remote ages, had at first no fixed seat, but was held sometimes at Nuremberg, sometimes at Ratisbon, or at Augsbourg. Finally, June 9th, 1815, the Congress of Vienna established Frankfort as the permanent seat of the Diet of the Germanic Confederation.

Thanks to the new constitution Frankfort has a quarter vote at the Diet, the other three-quarters belonging to the three free towns of Hamburg, Bremen, and Lubeck. In return for this honour, Frankfort was to raise seven hundred and fifty men for the Germanic Confederation and fire a salute on the anniversary of the battle of Leipzig. The execution of this latter obligation was at first a trifle difficult, for the reason that since 1803 Frankfort had ceased to possess ramparts, and since 1813 had owned no cannon. But in the first moments of enthusiasm a subscription was opened which allowed the purchase of two four-pounders, so that since 1814, on the proper day, Frankfort has duly paid the debt of fire and smoke owed to the Holy Alliance.

As to the ramparts, they exist no longer. Instead of old walls and muddy ditches, Frankfort has seen the gradual formation of a charming English garden, a gracious and perfumed enclosure, which enables one to make the circuit of the town, while walking on the smoothest of paths and under magnificent trees. So that, with its houses painted white, green, and pink, Frankfort looks like a bouquet of camellias set in a border of heather. The tomb of the mayor to whom this improvement is due stands in the midst of a delightful labyrinth of walks, much frequented by the burghers and their families about four or five o'clock in the afternoon.

The Teuton name Frankfort means a free ford, and the town owes its origin to an imperial castle built by Charlemagne at a point where the Namur is fordable. The first historical notice of it is the date of the Council held there in 794, in which was discussed the question of image worship. As to Charlemagne's palace, no trace of it can be found, but antiquaries say that it stood where now is the Church of St. Leonard.

It must have been about 796 that Charlemagne founded the colony of Sachsenhausen peopled by the Saxons whom he had conquered and baptized. In 822 Louis le Debonnaire built the Sala on the site of the present Saalhof, and in 838 Frankfort had already a court of justice and walls of defence.

In 853 Louis the German raised it to the rank of capital of the eastern portion of the French empire; extended its borders, and built the church of St. Saviour close to where the autumn fair was held, in accordance with the traders' custom of setting up their booths under the walls of churches and temples.

The custom of electing the emperor at Frankfort was begun by that great Swabian house whose name alone calls up a host of terrible and melancholy recollections. In 1240 Frederic II granted letters of safe conduct to all going to the market of Frankfort; and the Emperor Louis of Bavaria, wishing to show gratitude for his election, proved his attachment to the town by granting great advantages, among others the right of holding a fair for fifteen days during Lent, which was known as the Easter fair.

The Emperor Charles IV confirmed the right of the Imperial Election to Frankfort by the famous Golden Bull issued in 1356. This Bull provided the Emperor Napoleon with an opportunity for displaying his excellent memory. Dining one day with half a score of sovereign princes, at the meeting of Erfurth, the conversation chanced to turn on the Golden Bull, which, until the Confederation of the Rhine, had laid down the rules for Imperial elections. The Prince Primate, being on his own ground, gave some details concerning the Bull, fixing the date for 1409.

"I think you are mistaken, prince," said Napoleon. "If my memory is correct, the Bull was published in 1356 in the reign of the Emperor Charles IV."

"Your Majesty is right," said the primate, reconsidering, "but how is it you remember the date of a bull so exactly? Had it been a battle it would be less wonderful."

"Shall I tell you the secret of this wonderful memory, prince?" enquired Napoleon.

"Your Majesty would give us all much pleasure."

"Well," continued the emperor, "you must know that when I was a sub-lieutenant in the Artillery—"

Whereupon there was so decided a movement of surprise and curiosity among the illustrious guests that Napoleon paused an instant, but seeing that all were waiting for him to continue, he resumed with a smile:

"I was saying that when I had the honour of being a sub-lieutenant of Artillery I was in garrison at Valence for three years. I did not care for society, and lived very quietly. By a lucky chance I had rooms opposite a well-read and obliging bookseller, whose name was Marcus Aurelius, and who gave me the run of his library. I read and re-read everything in his shop two or three times during my stay in the capital of the Drôme, and I remember everything I then read—even to the date of the Golden Bull."

Frankfort continued to govern itself as a free imperial town until, after having been bombarded by the French in the wars of the Revolution, it was one fine day handed over by Napoleon to the Prince Primate Charles of

Dalberg, when it became the capital of the Grand Duchy of Frankfort.

The most interesting building in Frankfort is undoubtedly the Römer, a huge building which contains the Hall of the Electors, now used for the sittings of the Upper Senate of Frankfort, and the Hall of the Emperors in which the latter were proclaimed. A peculiarity of this hall, which contains the portraits of all the emperors from Conrad to Leopold II, is that the architect who built it made exactly as many niches as there have been sovereigns wearing the Imperial crown. So that when Francis II was elected, all the niches were already filled, and there was no space found for the new Cæsar. There was much discussion as to where his portrait could be placed, when in 1805 the ancient German empire crumbled into dust at the noise of the cannon of Austerlitz, and the courtiers were relieved from their difficulty. The architect had exactly foreseen the number of emperors to come. Nostradamus himself could not have done better.

After the town hall the most interesting place is the street of the Jews. When the writer of these lines visited Frankfort for the first time, some thirty years ago, there were still Jews and Austrians there—real Jews, who hated Christians even as Shylock hated them, and real Christians who hated Jews as did Torquemada.

This street consisted of two long rows of tall houses, black, gloomy, sinister in aspect, closely crowded, looking as if they clung to each other in terror. It was Saturday, which no doubt added to the gloom of the street. Every door was closed, bastard little doors made to allow only one person to pass at once. All the iron shutters were also closed. No sound of voice, or step, or movement was heard; a look of anguish and terror seemed spread over all these houses. Occasionally an old woman with a hooked nose like an owl glided past and disappeared in a sort of cellar or basement in this strange street. To-day all this is more civilized and the houses have a more active and lively appearance.

The population of Frankfort consists of a historic bourgeoisie forming the aristocracy of the Imperial town, the coronation town by right of the Golden Bull. The chief families are those of the old nobility; those of French

126

extraction expatriated by the revocation of the Edict of Nantes, and who by their intelligence and industry stand in the first rank of society; thirdly, Italian families, in whom the feelings of race have been stronger than religious differences, and who, although Catholics by profession, have mingled with the French Protestants. Finally the Jewish bankers, who naturally group themselves around the house of Rothschild as being incontestably members of the same clan. All are devoted to Austria, because to Austria the town owes its peculiar position, the source of its wealth and independence, and all these classes, though divided by race, language, and religion, are united by their common affection for the House of Hapsburg—a love which perhaps hardly attains to devotion, but which, in words at least, amounts to fanaticism.

One must not omit the suburb of Sachsenhausen, situated on the other side of the Main, the colony founded by Charlemagne. Its inhabitants, living closely together and only marrying among themselves, have retained some of the roughness of the old Saxon character. This roughness, contrasted with the growing politeness among other nations, now seems to be absolute rudeness, but rudeness which is not intentional. They are said to be ready in the use of the somewhat harsh, but occasionally witty retorts, wherewith the weak sometimes retaliate upon the strong. We can give two specimens of the rough speech of the people of Sachsenhausen.

As is usual in the month of May, owing to the melting of the snow, the Main was in flood. The Great Elector himself came to judge of the rise of the water, and the damage it would probably cause. Meeting a man from Sachsenhausen:

"Well," he asked, "is the Main still rising?"

"Well, idiot that you are!" replied the individual addressed, "can't you see that for yourself?"

And the old Saxon went on, shrugging his shoulders. One of his comrades ran after him:

"Do you know to whom it was you spoke?" he asked.

"No, I don't."

"Well, it was the Elector of Hesse himself."

"Thunder and lightning!" exclaimed the old man, "how glad I am I answered him civilly!"

At the play one of these honest people leaned against the man sitting in front of him; the latter moved away:

"Am I annoying you?" demanded the aggressor, "because if it were you who annoyed me, I should give you a punch you would remember the rest of your life!"

Since 1815 Frankfort has been garrisoned by two detachments of fifteen hundred to two thousand each, one Austrian, the other Prussian; the former were much beloved; the latter equally, or even more, hated. A Prussian officer was taking some friends to see the curiosities of Frankfort. They arrived at the Dôme. There, among other votive offerings, representations of hearts, hands, or feet, the sacristan exhibited a mouse, made of silver.

"What was that for?" some one asked.

"Through the divine wrath," answered the sacristan, "a whole quarter of Frankfort once found itself eaten up by swarms of mice. In vain they fetched all the cats of the other quarters, all the terriers, bulldogs, every sort of animal that can kill a mouse; the plague increased. At last a devout lady thought of having a silver mouse made and dedicated to the Virgin as a votive gift. At the end of a week not a mouse was to be seen!"

And as the listeners were somewhat astonished when they heard this legend:

"What fools these Frankforters are!" said the Prussian, "to tell tales of that kind and believe them!"

"We tell them," said the sacristan, "but we do not believe them. If we did we should have made a silver Prussian and offered him to the Virgin long ago."

It is to be remembered that our friend Lenhart, Benedict's coachman, was a citizen of the Sachsenhausen colony.

# CHAPTER XVI. THE DEPARTURE

Since the Schleswig-Holstein troubles, the Diet had always assembled at Frankfort on June 9th, this year that date was the day after the attempted assassination of Bismarck on which Benedict drank to the health of France. The Diet, knowing of the mobilization of the Landwehr and the dissolution of the Chamber, decreed that, if Frankfort were not to be compromised in its position as a free and imperial town in the various events which would necessarily follow a war between Prussia and Austria, the Prussian and Austrian garrisons must be withdrawn, and replaced by a Bavarian garrison.

It was agreed that Bavaria should appoint the commander-in-chief, and Frankfort the governor of the town. The Bavarian Colonel Lessel, who had been for many years member of the federated military commission for Bavaria, was appointed commander-in-chief, and the lieutenant-colonel of the Frankfort battalion became governor of the town.

The departure of the Prussian and Austrian troops was fixed for June 12th, and it was decided that the Prussians should leave by two special trains on the Main-Weser line, at six and eight in the morning, for Wetzlar, and the Austrians at three in the afternoon of the same day.

This arrangement was known in Frankfort on the 9th, and as may be understood, filled the Chandroz house with despair. Emma would be separated from her husband and Helen from her lover.

We have said that the Prussians were to leave first. At five in the morning Frederic said farewell to his wife, his child, his dear sister Helen, and the grandmother. It was too early for Karl von Freyberg to be in the house at that hour; but he waited for his friend on the Zeil. He and Helen had agreed the evening before that after having seen Frederic off Karl should come back and wait for her in the little Catholic church of Notre Dame de la Croix.

The harmony between the two young people was perfect. Helen and Karl, though born in two different countries hundreds of leagues apart, were both Catholics. Doubtless they had selected this early hour, because they knew the little liking the people of Frankfort had for the Prussians. No manifestation of regret was shown on the departure of the latter, perhaps they were watched through the closed shutters, but not a window or blind opened for a flower to fall which might say "Au revoir," no waving handkerchief said "Farewell!"

One would have sworn it was a troop of the enemy leaving a town, and the town itself seemed only to wait for their departure in order to wake up and rejoice. Only the officers of the city battalion came to the station courteously to see them off, wishing nothing better than soon to fight them with deadly hate.

Frederic left by the second train at eight o'clock in the morning, consequently Karl was late and it was Helen who waited for him. She was standing by the holy water stoup leaning against a white pillar. She smiled sadly when she saw Karl, gently dipped two fingers in the holy water and held them towards him. Karl took her whole hand, and made the sign of the cross with it.

Never had the beautiful girl looked so lovely as at this moment when Karl was going to be parted from her. She had scarcely slept all night; all the rest of the time she had wept and prayed. She was dressed in white like a bride, with a wreath of little white roses on her head. They went together, Karl with Helen's hand in his, to kneel in one of the side chapels where Helen was accustomed to pray. Almost all the ornaments in the chapel, from the altar cloth to the Virgin's dress, were the work of her hand alone, and the Madonna's gold and pearl crown had been her gift. They prayed together; then Karl said:

"We are going to part, Helen; what vows shall I make you? and in what words shall they be made?"

"Karl," replied Helen, "tell me again before the beloved Madonna who has watched over me in childhood and youth, tell me again that you will love me always, and that you will have no other wife but me."

Karl quickly extended his hand.

"Ah! yes," he said, "and willingly! for I have always loved you. I love you now, and I shall love you always. Yes, you shall be my wife in this world and in the next, here and above!"

"Thank you," said Helen; "I have given you my heart, and with my heart, my life. You are the tree, and I am the creeper; you are the trunk and I am the ivy which covers you with its verdure. At the moment when I first saw you, I said with Juliet: 'I will belong to you or to the tomb.'"

"Helen," cried the young man, "why link that dismal word with such a sweet promise?"

But she, not listening, continued her thought:

"I ask no other vow than that which you have sworn, Karl; it is the repetition of mine; keep yours as it is; but when I have said that I will love you always, that I will never love any one but you, and that I will never be another's, let me add: and, if you die, I will die with you!"

"Helen, my love, what are you saying?" exclaimed the young man.

"I say, my Karl, that since my heart has left my bosom, to dwell in yours, you have become all that I think of, all I live for; and that if anything happened to you, I should not need to kill myself, I should only have to let myself die. I know nothing of these royal quarrels, which seem to me wicked, because they cost the blood of men and tears of women. I only know that it matters not to me whether Francis Joseph or William I is victorious. I live, if you live I die, if you die."

"Helen, do you wish to drive me mad, that you say these terrible things?"

"No, I only wish you to know, when you are absent, what is happening to me, and if, when far from me, you are mortally wounded, instead of saying: 'I shall never see her again!' you must simply say: 'I am going to meet her!' And I say this as truly and sincerely as I lay this wreath at the feet of my beloved Virgin."

And she took her wreath of white roses and laid it at the Virgin's feet.

"And now," she continued, "my vow is made, I have said what I had to

131

say. To stay here now, to speak longer of love would be sacrilege. Come, Karl; you go this afternoon at two o'clock, but my sister, my grandmother, and Frederic will permit you to remain with me till then."

They rose again, offered each other the holy water and left the church. The young girl took Karl's arm for from that moment she considered herself as his wife. But with the same feeling of respect which made him take off his kolbach when he entered the church, he only allowed her hand to lie lightly on his arm all the way from Nôtre Dame de la Croix until they reached the house.

The day was passed in intimate conversation. On the day when he had asked Helen which were her favourite colours and she had answered green, he had made a resolution which he now explained to her. This was what he wished to do.

He would ask his colonel for eight days' leave; surely fighting would not begin for eight days. It would take him scarcely twenty hours to reach his mountains, where he was king. There, besides the twenty-two rangers always in his service he would select seventy-eight chosen men from the best Styrian hunters. They should wear the uniform he himself wore when hunting, he would arm them with the best rifles he could find, then he would give in his resignation as captain in the Lichtenstein Light Infantry, and ask the emperor to appoint him captain of his free company. An excellent shot himself, at the head of a hundred men renowned for their smartness, he could hope for results which, when buried in a regiment under the orders of a colonel there would be no possibility of his attaining.

There would also be another advantage in this arrangement. As the head of a free regiment, Karl would have liberty of movement. In such a case he would not be attached to any special regiment. He would be able to fight on his own account, doing all possible harm to the enemy, but only answerable to the emperor. He would thus be able to remain near Frankfort, the only town which now existed for him in the world, since in this town lived Helen. The heart exists not where it beats, but where it loves.

According to the Prussian plan of campaign which was to envelop

Germany as in a half-circle, hurling king, grand-dukes, princes, and peoples one on the top of another while marching from west to east, there would certainly be fighting in Hesse, in the duchy of Baden, and in Bavaria, all near Frankfort. It was there that Karl would fight; and with good spies he could always ascertain where his brother-in-law was likely to be and so avoid the risk of meeting him.

In the midst of all these plans, for which unfortunately they could not enlist the aid of Fortune, time was flying. The clock struck two.

At two o'clock the Austrian officers and soldiers were to assemble in the courtyard of the Carmelite barracks. Karl kissed the baroness and the child lying in its cradle beside her; then he went with Helen to kneel before her grandmother and ask her blessing.

The dear old lady wept to see them so sad; she laid her hands upon their heads wishing to bless them, but her voice broke. They both rose, and stood mute before her; silent tears flowed down their cheeks. She pitied them.

"Helen," she said, "I kissed your grandfather when I bade him farewell, and I see no reason against your granting poor Karl the same favour."

The young people threw themselves into each other's arms, and their grandmother, under pretext of wiping away a tear, turned away, leaving them free for their last kiss.

Helen had long sought for some means of seeing Karl again, after leaving the house where he had been permitted to take his last farewell. She had not succeeded, when suddenly she remembered that the burgomaster Fellner, her sister's godfather, had windows overlooking the station.

She asked her good grandmother to come with her to ask her old friend for a place in his window. Women who remain beautiful when growing old generally keep a young heart: the kind grandmother consented. So it was only a goodbye of the lips which the young people had already said; there remained a last adieu of the eyes and heart.

Hans was ordered to bring round the carriage without delay; while Karl went to the Carmelite barracks. Helen would have time on her part to go to the burgomaster Fellner. Helen made a sign to Hans to hurry, but he replied with another that it was unnecessary. She then glanced again at Karl, he had never seemed so handsome as at this moment when about to leave her. She came down leaning on his arm, in order not to leave him until they reached the threshold, the last moment possible. Once there, a last kiss sealed their separation and pledged their vows.

A hussar waited for his captain at the door, holding his horse; Karl saluted Helen once again, then galloped off, sparks flying from under his horse's hoofs: he was more than a quarter of an hour late.

The instant he had gone, Hans came with the carriage; in another moment they were at Herr Fellner's.

Frankfort was now a very different town to what it had been in the morning. We have told of the sombre and sad departure of the Prussians, who were detested there. The citizens now wished to give a friendly farewell to the Austrians, who were adored.

Therefore, although the departure was a separation, and each separation may hide the invisible and hide also a coming grief, this departure was to be made a farewell fête. The windows were all draped with Austrian flags, and at each window where floated a flag might be seen the prettiest women of Frankfort with bouquets in their hands. The streets which led to the station were crammed with people until one asked how the regiment could pass. In the street leading to the station, the Frankfort regiment stood at attention, each soldier with the stock of his rifle between his feet, and a bouquet in the muzzle of it.

The crowd was so great that Helen was obliged to get out of the carriage. At last she reached the house of Herr Fellner, who, although not formally advised of the engagement of his young friend, had noticed that Captain Freyberg was not indifferent to her. His two daughters and his wife received Helen and her grandmother at the door of their apartments. They formed a charming family, living with Herr Fellner's sister and brother-in-law, who had no children.

134

In the days of peace and happiness at Frankfort, Herr Fellner and his brother-in-law received their friends twice every week. Any strangers of distinction passing through were sure to be made welcome by Herr Fellner. It was at his house that Benedict Turpin had met the Baroness Frederic von Bülow, a meeting which as we have seen he did not forget.

At three o'clock precisely, they heard in the midst of cries, hurrahs, and acclamations, the trumpets of the regiment, which was coming to the station by the Zeil and the street of All Saints, playing Radetzky's March.

It might have been said that the whole population of Frankfort was following the splendid regiment. Men waved flags from the windows above them; women threw them their bouquets, and then waved their handkerchiefs with those cries of enthusiasm which women only know how to utter on such occasions.

Helen had recognized Karl, as soon as he turned the corner, and Karl had answered her waving handkerchief by saluting with his sabre. When he passed under the window she threw him a scabious bound up with forget-me-nots. The scabious meant "sorrow and desolation," and the forget-me-not "Do not forget me."

Karl caught the flowers in his kolbach and fastened them on his breast. Still turning to look back, his eyes never left Helen until the moment when he entered the station. At length he disappeared.

Helen leaned far out of the window. Herr Fellner put his arm round her waist and drew her back within the room. Seeing the tears that flowed from her eyes and divining their cause:

"With the help of God, dear child," he said, "he will return."

Helen escaped from his arms, and threw herself on a sofa, endeavouring to hide her tears in the cushions.

# CHAPTER XVII. AUSTRIANS AND PRUSSIANS

Desbarolles says in his book on Germany:

"It is impossible to talk for three minutes with an Austrian without wishing to shake hands with him. It is impossible to talk for three minutes with a Prussian without longing to quarrel with him."

Does this difference in the two organizations spring from temperament, education, or the degree of latitude? We cannot say; but it is a fact that along the whole way from Ostrow to Oderburg, we know when we have left Austria and entered Prussia by the way in which the porters bang the carriage doors. This double impression is particularly evident at Frankfort, a town of gentle manners, cultivated habits, and amateur bankers; the country of Goethe has appreciated this difference between the extreme civilization of Vienna and the rough Protestant shell of Berlin.

We have seen the different demonstrations of feeling at the departure of the two garrisons; the people of Frankfort not having the least doubt of the result of the war, and believing, after the conclusions of the Diet, in the superiority of the Austrian arms, which would be aided by all the little States of the Confederation. They had not cared to put the least restraint on the manifestation of their feelings; they allowed the Prussians to depart like vanquished enemies whom they would never see again, and they had, on the contrary, fêted the Austrians like victorious brothers, for whom if they had had the time, they would have made triumphal arches.

The good burgomaster's drawing-room, where we have introduced our readers, was at noon on June 12th an exact and complete specimen of all the other drawing-rooms of the town, whatever the origin, country or religion of the inhabitants might chance to be.

Thus, while Helen, with whose grief all sympathized, wept, keeping her face buried in the cushions, and her good grandmother left the window to sit beside her and hide her somewhat from view, Councillor Fischer, editor of the "Post Zeitung," was writing on a corner of the table, an article in which he compared with undisguised antipathy and sympathy, the departure of the Prussians to a nocturnal flight, and that of the Austrians to a triumphal leave-taking.

In front of the fireplace, the Senator von Bernus, one of the most distinguished men in Frankfort, by ability, education, and birth, was talking with his colleague, Doctor Speltz, Chief of Police, who, owing to the position which he held, was always well informed. A slight difference rather than a discussion had arisen between them. Herr Doctor Speltz did not completely agree with the opinion of the majority of the town's people as to the certain victory of the Austrians. His private information, as Chief of Police, was of the kind which may be relied on, and which is obtained, not to help the opinions of others, but to form one's own, and it represented the Prussian troops as full of enthusiasm, admirably armed, and burning with desire for battle. Their two generals, Frederick Charles of Prussia and the Crown Prince, were both able to command and to execute, and their rapidity and courage no one could doubt.

"But," observed Herr von Bernus, "Austria has an excellent army which is animated with an equal spirit; it was beaten at Palestro, at Magenta, and at Solferino, it is true, but by the French, who also beat the Prussians at Jena."

"My dear von Bernus," replied Speltz, "it is a far cry from the Prussians of Jena to the Prussians of to-day; the miserable state into which the Emperor Napoleon reduced them, by only allowing them to put forty thousand men under arms for six years, was the providential cause of their strength; for with this reduced army the officers and administrators could superintend the smallest details and bring them as near as possible to perfection. From this has grown the Landwehr."

"Well," said von Bernus, "if the Prussians have the Landwehr, the Austrians have the Landsturm; all the Austrian population will rise in arms."

"Yes, if the first battles are unsuccessful; yes, if there is a chance that by rising they can repel the Prussians. But three-quarters of the Prussian army are armed with needle guns which fire eight or ten shots a minute. The time is past

137

when, as said Marshal Saxe, the rifle is only the handle of the bayonet; and of whom did he say that? Was it not the French, a fiery and warlike nation, not methodical and military like the Austrians. You know, mein Gott, victory is an entirely moral question; to inspire the enemy with an unaccountable fear is the secret. Generally, when two regiments meet, one of them runs without having ever come to grips with the enemy. If the new guns, with which the Prussians are armed, do their work, I am very much afraid that the terror in Austria will be so great that the Landsturm, from Königsgrätz to Trieste, from Salzburg to Pest, will not raise a man."

"Psst!... my dear friend, you have named the real stumbling block; if the Hungarians were with us, my hope would be a conviction. The Hungarians are the nerve of the Austrian army, and one can say of them what the ancient Romans said of the Marsi; 'What are we to do, either against the Marsi or without the Marsi?' But the Hungarians will not fight until they have their separate government, their constitution, and their three ministers, and they are right. For one hundred and fifty years Hungary has been promised that constitution, it has been given and withdrawn again, and now Hungary is angry; but the emperor has only one word to say, one signature to write, and the whole nation would rise for him. Then the Szozat would be heard, and in three days they would have a hundred thousand men under arms."

"What is the Szozat?" asked a big man, who kept a whole window to himself, and whose expansive face testified to great commercial prosperity. He was, indeed, the first wine merchant of Frankfort, Hermann Mumm.

"The Szozat," said Fischer, still writing his article, "is the Hungarian Marseillaise by the poet Vœrœsmarti. What the deuce are you doing there, Fellner?" he added, lifting his glasses to his forehead and looking at the burgomaster, who was playing with his two youngest children.

"I am doing something much more important than your article, councillor, I am making a village, of which Master Edward is to be the baron, with some houses I got in a box from Nuremburg."

"What does baron mean?" asked the child.

"That is a difficult question. To be a baron is much and it is nothing.

It is much if you are called 'Montmorency.' It is nothing if you are called 'Rothschild.'" And he went back seriously to his village.

"It is said," went on von Bernus to Doctor Speltz, taking up the conversation where they had left it before Hermann Mumm's interruption, "that the Emperor of Austria has named General Benedek as General in Chief with all powers."

"The nomination was discussed in the council and signed yesterday."

"Do you know him?"

"Yes."

"It seems to me a good choice."

"May God grant it."

"Benedek is a self-made man, he has won every step sword in hand. The army will love him better than it would love an archduke made field-marshal by right of birth."

"You will laugh at me, von Bernus, and will say I am a bad republican. Very well, I would rather have an archduke than this self-made man as you call him. Yes, if all our officers were self-made men, it would be admirable, because, if none knew how to command, they would at least know how to obey: as it is, our officers are nobles, who are officers by position or by favour. They will not obey, or will only obey such a commander unwillingly. Further, you know, I have the misfortune to be a fatalist, and to believe in the influence of the stars. General Benedek is a Saturnian. May Austria escape his fatal influence! He may have patience in a first loss, resolution against a second perhaps; but in a third he will lose his head and be good for nothing.

"Also, do you not see that there cannot be two equally Great Powers in Germany. Germany, with Prussia in the north, and Austria in the south, has two heads like the Imperial Eagle. Now, he who has two heads has not even one. Last winter I was at Vienna on New Year's Day. Always, on January 1st a new standard is raised on the fortress. The Standard for 1866 was displayed at six in the morning. A moment afterwards a furious storm, such as I have seldom seen, came from the north, the Standard was torn, and the rent cut off the two heads of the Eagle. Austria will lose her supremacy both in Italy and Germany."

A profound gloom as of painful foreboding seemed to have spread over the company. The only person unaffected was "Baron" Edward, who, while anxiously considering as to in which corner of his village he should put the belfry, had fallen fast asleep.

Herr Fellner rang three times, and a beautiful peasant from Baden, answering the signal, came in and took the child. She was carrying him away asleep in her arms, when Herr Fellner, wishing to change the subject, motioned to the company.

"Listen!" he said, and putting his hand on the nurse's shoulder. "Linda," he said, "sing us that song with which the Baden mothers sing their children to sleep." Then, turning to the others he said: "Gentlemen, listen to this song, which is still sung low in the Duchy of Baden. Perhaps, in a few days, the time may have come to sing it aloud. Linda learnt it from her mother, who sang it over her brother's cradle. Their father was shot by the Prussians in 1848. Now Linda, sing as your mother sang."

Linda put her foot on a chair, holding the child in her arms as if she were pressing it to her breast and covering it with her body. Then, with anxious eyes, in a low and trembling voice, she sang:

> Sleep soft, my child, without a cry,
>
> For hark! the Prussian passeth by.
>
> The Prussian slew thy father dear
>
> And robbed thy mother of gold and gear
>
> The Prussian he will close thine eye.
>
> Sleep soft, my child, without a cry,
>
> For hark! the Prussian passeth by.

All bloody is the Prussian's hand

It closes on our dying land.

So must we all lie still and dumb

As doth thy father in his tomb.

> Sleep soft, my child, without a cry,
>
> For hark! the Prussian passeth by.

God knows how many a weary day

We wait the dawning of that ray

Those blessed radiance shall restore

Our liberty to us once more.

> Sleep soft, my child, without a cry,
>
> For hark! the Prussian passeth by.

But when that longed for hour shall come,

However narrow be his tomb,

His foes within that grave so deep

Shall share for aye thy father's sleep.

> Then shout, my child, shout loud and high,
>
> The Prussian in his grave doth lie.

The nurse had sung this song with such expression, that a shudder passed over the hearts of those who listened, and none thought of applauding. She went out with the child in a profound silence.

Only Helen murmured in her grandmother's ear: "Alas! alas! Prussia means Frederic, and Austria means Karl!"

141

# CHAPTER XVIII. THE DECLARATION OF WAR

On June 15th, at eleven in the morning, Count Platen of Hallermund, presented himself to the King of Hanover. They had conversed for some minutes when the king said:

"I must tell this news to the queen. Wait for me here; I will come back in a quarter of an hour."

Within the palace King George required no guide. Queen Mary was engaged upon a piece of wool work with the young princesses. Seeing her husband she went to him and offered him her forehead to kiss. The princesses took possession of their father's hands.

"See," said the king, "this is what our cousin the King of Prussia does us the honour to communicate through his First Minister." The queen took the paper and began to read. "Stay," said the king, "I want to call Prince Ernest."

One of the princesses hurried to the door.

"Prince Ernest," she cried to the usher.

Five minutes after the prince came in, embraced his father and sisters, and kissed his mother's hand.

"Listen to what your mother is going to read," said the usher to him.

The Minister Bismarck in the name of his master offered to Hanover an offensive and defensive alliance, on the condition that Hanover should support Prussia to the utmost of its power with men and soldiers and should give the command of its army to King William. The dispatch added that if this pacific proposal were not immediately accepted the King of Prussia would consider himself as in a state of war with Hanover.

"Well?" asked the king of his wife.

"No doubt," she replied, "the king has already decided in his wisdom what is best to do; but, if he has not finally decided and such a feature as the opinion of a woman is considered to be as a weight in the balance, I would say to you, refuse, sire!"

"Oh yes, yes, sire!" cried the young prince, "refuse!"

"I thought it right to consult you both," replied the king, "partly because of your upright and loyal natures, partly because your interests are one with mine."

"Refuse, father: the prediction must be fulfilled to the end."

"What prediction?" asked the king.

"You forget, sire, that the first word which Benedict said to you was this: 'You will be betrayed by your near relation.' You are betrayed by your German cousin; why should he be wrong about the rest since he was right at the beginning?"

"You know that he has predicted our downfall?"

"Yes, but after a great victory. We are little kings, it is true; but we are, on the English side, great princes, let us act greatly."

"That is your opinion, Ernest?"

"That is my prayer, sire," said the young prince, bowing.

The king turned to his wife and interrogated her by a movement of his head.

"Go, my dear," said she, "and follow your own thought, which is ours also."

"But," said the king, "if we are obliged to leave Hanover, what will happen to you and the two princesses?"

"We will stay where we are, sire, in our castle of Herrenhausen. After all, the King of Prussia is my cousin, and if our crown is in danger through him, our lives are not. Summon your council, sire, and take with you the two voices which say to you: 'Not only no treason against others, but above all no treason against our honour!'"

The king called a council of his ministers, who unanimously voted for refusal.

At midnight Count Platen replied verbally to the Prince of Issemburg, who had brought the proposal.

"His Majesty the King of Hanover declines the proposals of His Majesty the King of Prussia; as he is constrained to do by the laws of the Confederation."

This reply was instantly telegraphed to Berlin.

Immediately upon the receipt of the reply, another telegram from Berlin ordered the troops concentrated at Minden to enter Hanover. A quarter-of-an-hour later, the Prussian troops set foot over the borders of Hanover.

A quarter-of-an-hour had sufficed for Prussia to receive the reply and to order the opening of the campaign. Already the Prussian troops from Holstein, who had obtained permission from His Majesty the King of Hanover to cross his territory in order to get to Minden, had stationed themselves at Marbourg, and were thus in occupation, within the kingdom, as enemies, even before the king's decision.

Moreover, King George had only held back his answer until the evening in order to secure time for taking measures himself. Orders had been given to the different regiments of the Hanoverian army to mobilize and assemble at Göttingen. The intention of the king was to manœuvre so as to obtain the assistance of the Bavarian army.

Towards eleven at night, Prince Ernest had asked permission of Queen Mary to take leave of her and at the same time to present to her his friend Benedict. The real object of the young prince was to get his mother to entrust her hand to the palmist, and to be reassured by him as to the dangers which might encompass the queen.

The queen received her son with a kiss, and the Frenchman with a smile. Prince Ernest explained his wish to her. She readily granted his request and held out her hand. Benedict knelt on one knee and respectfully put his lips to the tips of her fingers.

"Sir," she said, "in the circumstances in which we are placed, it is not my good- but my ill-fortune that I wish you to tell me."

"If you see misfortunes before you, madam, I may be permitted to seek in yourself the powers which Providence has given you to resist them. Let us hope that the resistance will be stronger than the strife."

"A woman's hand is feeble, sir, when it has to struggle against that of destiny.

"The hand of destiny is brute force, madam; your hand is intelligent force. Look, here is a very long first joint to the thumb."

"What does that mean?" asked, the queen.

"Will power, Majesty. Your resolution once taken, reason alone can conquer you and make you change—danger, accident, persecution, never."

The queen smiled and nodded approvingly.

"Also, you can bear to hear the truth, madam. Yes, a great misfortune menaces you."

The queen started. Benedict went on quickly.

"But, calm yourself, it is neither the death of the king, nor of the prince: the line of life is magnificently marked, on their hands. No, the danger is entirely political. Look at the line of fate: it is broken here, above the line of Mars, which shows from what direction the storm will come; then this line of fate, which might dominate again if it stopped at the circle of the middle finger, that is, at the circle of Saturn, goes on, on the contrary, to the base of the first finger, a sign of ill-fortune."

"God tries every one according to the rank he holds. We will endeavour to bear our ill-fortune like Christians if we cannot bear it like kings."

"Your hand has answered me before you, madam; the Mount of Mars is smooth and without lines, the Mount of the Moon is smooth and even;

145

it means resignation, madam, the first of all the virtues. With this power Diogenes broke his porringer; with this, Socrates smiled at death; with this, the poor man is a king, the king is a god! With resignation and calm any strong feeling shown in the hand, worthily developed may replace the line of Saturn and create a new good fortune. But there will be a long struggle first. That struggle presents strange signs. I see in your hand, madam, auguries opposed to each other; a prisoner without a prison, wealth without riches: an unhappy queen, a happy wife, and a happy mother. The Lord will try you, madam, but as a daughter whom He loves. For the rest, you will have every kind of resource, madam; first music, next painting; the pointed and slim fingers show that; religion, poetry, invention, two princesses who love you at your side, a king and a prince who love you from a distance. God tempers the wind to the freshly shorn lamb."

"Yes, sir, shorn to the quick," murmured the queen, raising her eyes to heaven. "After all, perhaps the misfortunes of this world will secure the joys of another. In this case, I shall be not only resigned, but consoled."

Benedict bowed like a man who, having accomplished what was required of him, only awaits his dismissal.

"Have you a sister, sir?" asked the queen of Benedict, as she toyed with a string of pearls, fastened by a clasp of diamonds, which evidently belonged to one of the young princesses.

"No, madam," replied Benedict, "I am alone in the world."

"Then do me the pleasure to accept this turquoise for yourself. I am not making you a present; under that guise it would be worthless. No! it is an amulet which I offer you. You know that we people of the north have a superstition that turquoises bring good luck. Keep this as a remembrance of me."

Benedict bowed, received the turquoise ring and put it on the little finger of his left hand. While he did this the queen called Prince Ernest to her, and took up a satchel of perfumed leather.

"My son," said she, "we know the place which the exile's first step leaves, but not that at which his last will pause. This satchel contains 500,000 francs worth of pearls and diamonds. If I wished to give them to the king, he would refuse to take them."

"Oh! mother!"

"But to you, Ernest, I have the right to say I wish it! I wish you, dear child, to take this satchel as a last resource, to bribe a gaoler if you are made prisoner; to reward devotion—who knows—perhaps for the personal needs of the king or yourself. Hang it round your neck, put it in your belt; but in all cases, keep it always upon you. I embroidered it with my own hands; it bears your own monogram. Hush! here is your father!"

At this moment the king came in.

"There is not a minute to spare, we must be off," said, he, "Ten minutes ago the Prussians entered Hanover."

The king embraced the queen and his daughters; and Prince Ernest, his mother and sisters. Then, clinging together, king, queen, prince, princesses, went down the steps before which the horses were waiting. There took place the last adieus: there, tears flowed from the eyes of the most valiant, as well as from those of the most resigned. The king set an example by mounting his horse first.

The prince and Benedict rode two horses exactly alike, which were of the beautiful Hanoverian race, crossed with an English strain. An English carbine, which would send a pointed bullet four thousand yards, hung at the saddle-bow; and a pair of double-barrelled pistols, as true as duelling pistols, rested in the holsters.

A last farewell passed between the riders already in the saddle and the queen and princesses on the steps. Then the cavalcade, preceded by two scouts bearing torches, started at a quick trot.

A quarter-of-an-hour later they were in Hanover. Benedict proceeded to the Royal Hotel to settle his account with Mr. Stephen. Every one was up, for the news of the invasion of the Prussians and the departure of the king had already spread. As for Lenhart, he was invited to join the main body of the army with his vehicle. The rendezvous, as we know, was at Göttingen. As Lenhart was greatly attached to the dog Frisk, Benedict did not hesitate to entrust it to his care.

A deputation of the notabilities of the town, with the burgomaster at their head, waited on the king to bid him farewell. The king, his voice full of emotion, commended his wife and daughters to their care. There was but one voice in assuring him of their devotion. The whole town was abroad notwithstanding the hour of the night, and accompanied him, shouting 'Long live the king! Long live George V! May he return victorious!' Again the king commended the queen and the princesses, not now to the deputation, but to the whole population. The king entered the royal carriage amid a concert of tears and sobs. One would have said that every daughter had just lost a father, every mother a son, every sister a brother. Women crowded to the door of his carriage to kiss his hand. The locomotive had to whistle five or six times, and the signal had five or six times to be repeated, before the crowd could be detached from the carriage doors. At last the train had to be put into motion so as to shake off gently and almost imperceptibly the clusters of men and women who clung to it.

Two hours later Göttingen was reached.

# CHAPTER XIX. THE BATTLE OF LANGENSALZA

Two days after, the army, drawn from all parts of the kingdom, was assembled round the king.

Among others the regiment of the Queen's Hussars commanded by Colonel Hallelt, had remained thirty-six hours on horseback, and had been marching for thirty-six hours.

The king was lodged at the Crown Inn. This inn was on the line of march, and as each regiment of cavalry or infantry arrived, the king, warned by the music, went to the balcony and passed it in review. They filed one after another past the inn, flowers on their helmets, and cries of enthusiasm on their lips. Göttingen, the town of study, shuddered every instant, roused by the cheering warriors.

All the old soldiers on leave, whom there had not been time to recall, came of their own accord to rejoin their flag. All of them felt joyously, bringing with them from their villages and all along their routes a large number of recruits. Lads of fifteen gave their ages as sixteen in order to be enlisted.

On the third day they started. During this time the Prussians, on their side, had manœuvred. General Manteuffel from Hamburg, General von Rabenhorst from Minden, and General Beyer from Wetzlar were approaching Göttingen and enclosing the Hanoverian army in a triangle.

The simplest rules of strategy prescribed the union of the Hanoverian army, sixteen thousand strong, with the Bavarian, eighty thousand strong. The king, in consequence, had sent out couriers to Charles of Bavaria, brother of the old King Louis, who ought to have been in the valley of the Werra, to warn him, in entering Prussia and crossing Mulhausen, that he should proceed towards Eisenach. He added that he was followed closely by three or four Prussian regiments, who, united, would make twenty or twenty-five thousand men.

They arrived at Eisenach, by way of Verkirchen. Eisenach, defended by only two Prussian battalions, was about to be carried at the point of the bayonet, when a courier arrived from the Duke of Gotha, on whose territory they were, bringing a dispatch from the duke.

The dispatch announced that an armistice was arranged. The duke, in consequence, summoned the Hanoverians to retire. Unfortunately, as it came from a prince, the message was received without suspicion. The vanguard halted and took up its quarters where it was.

Next day, Eisenach was occupied by a regiment of the Prussian army. A great deal of time and many men had been lost in taking Eisenach, a useless manœuvre: and they resolved to leave Eisenach on the right and to proceed to Gotha. In order to put this project into execution, the army concentrated on Langensalza.

In the morning the king left, having on his left Major Schweppe, who held the sovereign's horse by invisible reins. The Prince Royal was on his right, having with him Count Platen, the first minister, and in the various uniforms of their regiments or of their calling, Count Wedel, Major von Kohlrausch, Herr von Klenck, Captain von Einem, various cuirassiers of the Guard, and Herr Meding. The cortège left Langensalza very early, and went to Thannesbruck.

Benedict rode near the prince, fulfilling the functions of a staff officer.

The army had left its cantonments in order to proceed to Gotha: but at ten in the morning, the vanguard, as it arrived on the banks of the Unstrut, was attacked by two Prussian regiments, commanded by the Generals Flies and Seckendorff. They were able to mount nearly a thousand men, both troops of the guard and landwehr.

Among these regiments of the guard was that of Queen Augusta, one of the élite. The rapidity of the Prussian fire showed at once that they must be armed, at least the greater part of them, with quick-firing rifles.

The king put his horse to the gallop in order to arrive as soon as possible on the spot where the battle had begun. The little village of Merscleben was on a hill to the left: behind the village, on higher ground than the Prussian artillery posts, they placed four batteries which at once opened fire.

The king desired to be informed of the disposition of the field. In front of him, running to the right and left was the Unstrut and its marshes; then a great thicket, or rather, a wood called Badenwaeldschen; and behind the Unstrut, upon the steep slope of the mountain, the Prussian masses advancing, preceded by formidable artillery which fired as it came.

"Is there a higher point whence I can direct the battle?" asked the king.

"There is a hill half a kilometre from the Unstrut, but it is under the fire of the enemy."

"That is the place for me," said the king. "Come, gentlemen."

"Pardon, sire," said the prince, "but half a gun-shot away from the hill where Your Majesty wishes to establish your camp, there is a sort of wood of alders and aspens stretching to the river. We must search that wood."

"Order fifty skirmishers to go down to the river."

"That will be unnecessary, sire," said Benedict, "there is no need for more than one man for that."

And he went off at a gallop, crossed the wood in every direction and reappeared.

"There is no one there, sire," said he, saluting.

The king put his horse to the gallop and posted himself on the top of the little hill. His horse was the only white one, and served as a target for bullets and balls. The king wore his uniform as general of the forces, blue, turned up with red; the prince his uniform of the hussars of the guard.

Battle was joined. The Prussians had driven back the Hanoverian outposts, who had recrossed the river, and a hot cannonade was exchanged between the Hanoverian artillery before Merscleben, and Prussians on the other side of the Unstrut.

"Sire," said Benedict, "don't you fear that the Prussians will send men

151

to hold the wood which I searched just now, and will fire on the king as at a target from its outskirts, only three hundred metres away?"

"What would you suggest?" asked the prince.

"I propose, monseigneur, to take fifty men and go to guard the wood. Our fire will protect you as the enemy approach."

The prince exchanged a few words with the king, who nodded approvingly.

"Go," said Prince Ernest; "but for heaven's sake don't get killed."

Benedict showed the palm of his hand.

"Can a man be killed, who has a double line of life on his hand?"

And he galloped to the infantry of the line.

"Fifty good marksmen for me," said he in German.

A hundred presented themselves.

"Come," said Benedict, "we shall not be too many."

He left his horse with a hussar of the prince's regiment, and threw himself into the underwood at the head of his men, who scattered. They had scarcely disappeared among the trees, when a terrible fusillade burst forth. Two hundred men had just passed the Unstrut; but, as they were ignorant of the number of men following Benedict, they retreated fighting, supposing him to have superior forces, and leaving a dozen dead in the wood. Benedict guarded the bank of the Unstrut, and by a well-sustained fire, kept off all approach.

The king had been recognized, the bullets whistled around him and even between his horse's legs.

"Sire," said Major Schweppe, "perhaps it would be well to seek a place a little further from the field of battle."

"Why so?" asked the king.

"The bullets may reach Your Majesty!"

"What does it matter! Am I not in the hands of the Lord?"

The prince came up to his father.

"Sire," said he, "the Prussians are advancing by great masses towards Unstrut, despite our fire."

"What are the infantry doing?"

"They are marching to take the offensive."

"And—they march well?"

"As on parade, sire."

"The Hanoverian troops were once excellent troops; in Spain they held the élite of the French troops in check. To-day, when they fight before their king they will prove worthy of themselves, I trust."

And, in fact, all the Hanoverian infantry, formed in column, advanced with the calm of veterans under the fire of the Prussian batteries. After having been a moment astounded at the hail of bullets which the muskets rained upon them, they continued their march, crossed the marshes of Unstrut, took the thicket of Badenwaeldschen by bayonet and struggled hand to hand with the enemy.

For a moment smoke and the unevenness of the ground hid the general aspect of the battle. But at that moment a horseman was seen to emerge from the smoke and to move towards the hill where the king was stationed, riding in hot haste and mounted on the horse of a Prussian officer. It was Benedict, who had killed the rider in order to take his horse, and who was coming to say that the Prussians had commenced the attack.

"Einem! Einem!" cried the king, "haste, order the cavalry to charge."

The captain hastened. He was a giant of over six feet, the most vigorous and handsomest man in the army. He put his horse to the gallop, crying, "Hurrah!" A minute afterwards, a sound like a hurricane was heard. It was the cuirassiers of the guard charging.

It would be impossible to describe the enthusiasm of the men as they passed the base of the hill, where stood the heroic king who wished to be at the most dangerous post. Cries of "Long live the king! long live George V! long live Hanover!" made the air tremble as in a tempest. The horses tore up the earth like an earthquake.

Benedict could not restrain himself. He put his spurs to his horse and disappeared in the ranks of the cuirassiers. Seeing the storm which was bursting upon them, the Prussians formed into squares. The first which encountered the Hanoverian cavalry disappeared under their horses' feet; then, whilst the infantry fired in their faces, the cuirassiers took the Prussian army on the flank, which, after a desperate struggle, tried to retreat in order, but, ferociously pursued, found themselves routed.

The prince followed these movements with an excellent pair of field glasses and described everything to the king, his father. But soon his glasses followed only a group of fifty men, at the head of whom was Captain Einem, whom he recognized by his great stature, and of whom Benedict, recognizable by his blue uniform among the white cuirassiers, was one. The squadron passed on by Nagelstadt and proceeded towards the last Prussian battery which still held out. The battery fired on the squadron from a distance of thirty yards. Everything vanished in the smoke. Twelve or fifteen men alone remained; Captain Einem was lying under his horse.

"Oh! poor Einem!" cried the prince.

"What has happened to him?" asked the king.

"I think he is dead," said the young man; "but no, he is not dead. There is Benedict helping to drag him from under his horse. He is only wounded. He is not even wounded! Oh, father, father! There are only seven left out of fifty; only one artilleryman is left; he is aiming at Einem, he is firing.... Oh, father! you are losing a brave officer, and King William a brave soldier; the artilleryman has killed Einem with a shot from his carbine, and Benedict has cut him down at his gun with his sabre."

The Prussian army was in full flight, the victory was with the Hanoverians!...

The Prussians retired to Gotha. The rapidity of the march to the field of battle had so fatigued the Hanoverian cavalry that they could not pursue the fugitives. In this respect the advantages of the battle were lost.

The results were: eight hundred prisoners, two thousand dead or wounded, two cannon taken.

The king rode round the field of battle to complete his task by showing himself to the unhappy wounded.

Benedict had become an artist once more, and was dreaming of his picture. He was seated on the first piece of cannon which had been taken, and was sketching a general view of the battlefield. He saw that the prince was searching among the killed and wounded officers of the cuirassiers.

"Pardon, monseigneur," said he, "you are looking for the brave Captain Einem, are you not?"

"Yes," said the prince.

"There, monseigneur, there, on your left, in the midst of that heap of dead."

"Oh," said the prince, "I saw him doing miracles."

"Can you believe that after I had drawn him from under his horse, he stabbed six with his sabre? Then he was hit for the first time and fell. They thought he was dead, and threw themselves upon him. He raised himself on one knee and killed two, who cried to him to surrender. Then he stood upright and it was at that moment that the last surviving artilleryman sent a ball into his forehead, which killed him. As I was not able to save him, being too much occupied myself, I avenged him!"

Then, presenting his sketch to the prince as calmly as if in the studio:

"Do you think that is right?" he asked.

# CHAPTER XX. IN WHICH BENEDICT'S PREDICTION CONTINUES TO BE FULFILLED

The visit to the field of battle having been paid, the king followed the highway and entered the town of Langensalza. He established his headquarters in the sharpshooters' barracks. The major-general had given orders that all should remain quiet during the night.

His Majesty's first care was to send by three different routes despatches to the queen to tell her of the day's victory and to ask for reinforcements, if not for the next day for the day after. And, as it turned out, he had nothing to fear from the Prussians: they were too thoroughly beaten not to wish for a day's rest.

The night was gay; money had been given to the soldiers, and they were told to pay for everything they had. The bands played "God save the King," and the soldiers sang in chorus,—a song by a Hanoverian volunteer, to the Polish tune:

"A thousand soldiers swear on bended knee."

The next day was spent in waiting for news of the Bavarian army, and in sending out couriers. The first came back with promises which were never kept.

A truce until morning had been offered to the Prussians so that the dead might be buried. The Prussians refused, and the Hanoverians alone proceeded with this pious work. The soldiers dug great trenches 25 feet long and 8 feet wide. The dead were placed in these in two rows. Four thousand armed men led by the king and prince stood bare-headed while Beethoven's funeral march was played. Over each grave a squadron passed and fired a salute by way of military mourning. The municipal officers who had come to thank the king for his orders to the soldiers, which had been strictly carried out, were present at the ceremony.

At eleven in the evening the men who were on guard towards the north announced that a large Prussian army was arriving by way of Mulhausen. It proved to be General Manteuffel's.

The third day after the battle, the Hanoverian army had received no news of the Bavarian army, and was surrounded by 30,000 men.

Towards midday, a lieutenant-colonel came with a flag of truce, from General Manteuffel, to propose that the king should surrender.

The king replied that he knew perfectly well that he was hemmed in on all sides, but that he, his son, his major-general, his officers, and soldiers, from the highest to the lowest, preferred to die, unless an honourable capitulation were offered them.

At the same time he called a council of war which declared unanimously for a capitulation, as long as it was honourable. There was, indeed, no choice. The army had only three hundred shells left, and rations for one night and day. The whole court, the king included, had dined on a piece of boiled beef and potatoes; the soup was given to the wounded. Every man was allowed but one glass of bad beer.

Each article of the capitulation was discussed, so as to spin out the delay as long as possible. The speedy arrival of the Bavarians was still hoped for.

At length, during the night, the following conditions were drawn up, between General Manteuffel for the King of Prussia, and General von Arentschild for the King of Hanover.

The Hanoverian army was to be disbanded and the soldiers sent back to their homes. All the officers and non-commissioned officers were to go free. They were to retain their arms and equipments. The King of Prussia was to guarantee their pay. The king, the prince, and their suite were to be free to go wherever they wished. The king's private fortune was to be intact and inviolable.

The capitulation being signed, General Manteuffel went to the king's quarters. Entering his cabinet he said to him:

"I am sorry, sire, to present myself before Your Majesty in such sad circumstances. We understand all that Your Majesty suffers, we Prussians who have known Jena. I beg Your Majesty to tell me to what place you wish to retire, and to give me my orders. It shall be my duty to see that you suffer no inconvenience on your journey."

"Sir," replied the king coldly, "I do not know where I shall await the finding of the congress which has to decide whether I shall remain king, or become once more a simple English prince. Probably with my father-in-law, the Duke of Saxe-Altenburg, or with His Majesty the Emperor of Austria. In either case I have no need of your protection, for which I thank you."

The same day the king's aide-de-camp left for Vienna, to ask permission for his master to retire through the Austrian states. As soon as this request reached Vienna, one of the emperor's aides-de-camp left to serve as guide and escort to the king. This officer was the bearer of the Marie-Thérèse medal for the king, and the order of knighthood for the prince.

On the same day, the king sent, as messengers to announce his arrival to His Majesty the Emperor of Austria; Herr Meding, representing the regency, the Minister of Foreign Affairs, Herr von Platen, and the Minister of War, Herr von Brandis.

The prince asked Benedict to accompany him. As Benedict had never seen Vienna, he assented. But upon conditions. His life, as at Hanover, was to be entirely independent of the court. He still had to arrange Lenhart's business, which, as we know, had been left to Benedict's discretion. Benedict had kept Lenhart for seventeen days. He now gave him four hundred francs and one hundred more as a gratuity—an unexampled generosity to which Lenhart replied by declaring his attachment to the House of Hanover to be such that he would never return to Brunswick from the moment when Brunswick became Prussian. This declaration was worth two hundred francs to him from the King of Hanover, and one hundred francs from the prince.

After this Lenhart's resolution was fixed. He sold, or had sold, all the carriages and horses which he had at Brunswick and with the proceeds he meant to set up a livery stable in Frankfort, a free town, where you seldom see any Prussians. At Frankfort, his brother Hans was in service with one of the best families in the town, that of Chandroz. Madame Chandroz' daughter, the Baroness von Bülow, was the burgomaster's goddaughter. With such connections he could be sure of prospering, and Benedict promised him his custom in case he returned to Frankfort.

The adieux between Benedict and Lenhart were most affecting, and still more so between Lenhart and Frisk, but they were forced to part. Lenhart set out for Frankfort. The king, the prince, Benedict, and Frisk, on their arrival at Vienna, took up their residence in the little château of Frœhliche Wiederkehr, which means Happy Return.

In this way Benedict's prediction to the king was realized—of victory, overthrow, exile.

# CHAPTER XXI. WHAT PASSED AT FRANKFORT BETWEEN THE BATTLES OF LANGENSALZA AND SADOWA

Frankfort followed from afar and with anxiety the struggle which went on in the other parts of Germany. But she did not believe that that struggle could reach even her. By June 29th Prince Charles of Bavaria had been appointed general of the Federated Troops. On the same day Frankfort heard the news of the victory of Langensalza. This caused great joy throughout the town, though no one dared to show it. On June 30th Rudolfstadt and the Hanseatic towns declared that they withdrew from the Confederation. The Würtemberg and Baden regiments were in the town; the soldiers, in groups of four and five, went gaily about the streets in hackney carriages. On July 1st, news came of the capitulation of the Hanoverian Army. On July 3rd Mecklenburg, Gotha, and the younger branch of Reuss declared that they withdrew from the Confederation. On July 4th the Prussian papers accused the people of Frankfort of having turned all Prussian subjects out of the town, even those who had been established there for ten years, and of having illuminated their streets on the news of the victory of Langensalza. They had not done so; but the falser the charge, the more it frightened the people of Frankfort. Evidently the Prussians were trying to pick a quarrel with them. On July 5th the gloom increased; news came of the defeat of the Austrians between Königsgrätz and Josephstadt. On July 8th the first news of the battle of Sadowa arrived in Frankfort.

Everything that that fatalist, Dr. Speltz, had said with regard to Marshal Benedek came true. After two checks he lost his head; to speak in the language of Herr Speltz, Saturn ruled above Mars and Jupiter. What he had foreseen in another direction, about the superior equipment of the Prussians—in conjunction with their natural courage—also came true. In no single encounter had the Austrians the advantage. The only victory gained over the Prussians was that when the King of Hanover had been in command.

But what particularly terrified Frankfort was the order given by the commanding officers of the Allies' Army to make entrenchments in the neighbourhood of the town. On this occasion, the Senate awoke from its inactivity, it arose and protested to the Diet that Frankfort was an unfortified town which was not able, and did not wish to be defended. But, in spite of the protestations of the Senate, the troops came to Frankfort.

On July 12th a fresh regiment was announced. It was the 8th regiment of the Federated Army, under the orders of Prince Alexander of Hesse, composed of men from Würtemberg, Baden, and Hesse, and an Austrian Brigade commanded by Count Monte Nuovo. They had scarcely entered Frankfort, when Count Monte Nuovo enquired for the house of the Chandroz family, and got himself billeted upon the widowed Madame von Beling who resided there.

Count Monte Nuovo, which title disguised the celebrated name of Neuburg, was the son of Marie Louise. He was a handsome, tall, fashionable general of forty-eight or fifty, who presented himself to Madame von Beling with all the Austrian grace and courtesy, and who, in saluting Helen, let fall from his lips the name of Karl von Freyberg.

Helen started. Emma had excused herself, as the wife of a Prussian, from doing the honours of her house to a man with whom her husband might be fighting on the morrow. This absence gave Count Monte Nuovo the opportunity of being alone with Helen. Helen, it is hardly necessary to say, awaited this moment with impatience.

"Count," said she, as soon as they were alone, "you mentioned a certain name."

"The name of a man who adores you, Fräulein."

"The name of my fiancé," said Helen, rising.

Count Monte Nuovo bowed and signed to her to reseat herself.

"I know it, Fräulein," he said; "Count Karl is my friend. He has bidden me hand you this letter and to give you news of him with my own lips."

Helen took the letter.

"Thank you, sir," she said, and, eager to read it. "You will allow me, won't you?"

"Certainly," said the count bowing, and he appeared to become absorbed in a portrait of Herr von Beling in his uniform.

The letter was all vows of love and protestations of tenderness such as lovers write to each other. Old phrases always new; flowers plucked on the day of creation, and, after six thousand years, as sweet as on the first day.

Having finished the letter, as Count Monte Nuovo still looked straight at the portrait:

"Sir," said Helen, in a low voice.

"Fräulein?" answered the count, approaching her; "Karl lets me hope that you will give me some details yourself," and he adds: 'Before coming to grips with the Prussians, he will, or indeed we shall perhaps, have the pleasure of seeing you again.'"

"It is possible, Fräulein, especially if we meet the Prussians in three or four days."

"Where did you leave him?"

"At Vienna, where he was organizing his volunteer regiment. We arranged a meeting-place at Frankfort, my friend Karl von Freyberg having done me the honour of wishing to serve under my orders."

"He tells me that he has as his lieutenant a Frenchman whom I know. Do you know of whom he is speaking?"

"Yes; he met him at the King of Hanover's, where he went to pay his respects; a young Frenchman called Benedict Turpin."

"Ah! yes," said Helen smiling, "he whom my brother-in-law wished me to marry in gratitude for the sabre-cut he received from him."

"Fräulein," said Count Monte Nuovo, "these things are riddles to me."

"And a little to me also," said Helen; "I will explain to you." And she told him what she knew of Frederic's duel with Benedict. She had scarcely finished when some one simultaneously knocked and rang at the door. Hans went to open it, and a voice asking for Madame von Beling, and reaching her ears through all the closed doors between, made her start.

"What is the matter, Fräulein?" asked Count Monte Nuovo. "You are quite pale!"

"I recognize that voice!" exclaimed Helen.

At the same moment the door opened, and Hans appeared.

"Fräulein," said he, "it is Count Karl von Freyberg."

"Ah!" cried Helen, "I knew it! Where is he? What is he doing?"

"He is below in the dining-room, where he is asking Madame von Beling's permission to pay his respects, to you."

"Do you recognize the gentleman in that?" asked Count Monte Nuovo. "Another man would not even have asked for your grandmother, but have flown straight to you."

"And I could have pardoned him." Then, in a louder voice. "Karl, dear Karl!" she said. "This way!"

Karl came in and threw himself into Helen's arms, who pressed him to her breast. Then, looking round him, he saw Count Monte Nuovo, and held out his hand to him.

"Excuse me, count," said he, "for not having seen you before; but you will readily understand that I had eyes for none but her. Is not Helen as beautiful as I told you, count?"

"More beautiful," replied he.

"Oh! dear, dear Helen," cried Karl, falling on his knees and kissing her hands.

Count Monte Nuovo began to laugh.

"My dear Karl," said he, "I arrived here an hour ago; I asked to be quartered at Madame von Beling's, in order to be able to carry out my commission. It was done as you knocked. I have nothing more to do here. If I have forgotten anything, here you are, and you can supply it. Fräulein, may I have the honour of kissing your hand?"

Helen held out her hand, looking at Karl as if for his permission, which he gave with a nod. The count kissed Helen's hand, then that of his friend, and went out.

The lovers gave a sigh of relief. Fate gave them, amid all the reverses of their political fortunes, one of those rare moments which she grants to those whom she favours most.

The news from the north was only too true. But all hope was not lost in Vienna. The emperor, the Imperial Family, and the Treasury had retired to Pest, and a desperate resistance was being prepared. On the other hand, the cession of Venice to Italy gave liberty to a hundred and sixty thousand men, as a reinforcement to the army in the north. It only remained to revive the spirits of the soldiers by a victory, and it was hoped that Count Alexander of Hesse would gain that victory. The battle would take place in all probability in the outskirts of Frankfort. This is why Karl had chosen to serve in the Prince of Hesse's army, and in Count Monte Nuovo's brigade. There at least, he was sure that he should see fighting. A second cousin of the Emperor Francis Joseph, brave and courageous, he had every interest in risking his life for the House of Austria, to which he belonged.

Helen devoured Karl with her eyes. His dress was that which she had seen him wear every day when she met him going or returning from the hunt; but, without one being able to be precise about it, there was something more warlike about him; his expression was—somewhat more severe. One felt that he was conscious of danger at hand, and in meeting it like a man he met it as one who clung to life, yet who above his life put honour.

During this time, Earl's little troop, whose second in command was Benedict, bivouacked a hundred paces from the railway station, just under the Burgomaster Fellner's windows. Not that they had anything to complain of from the authorities. Karl had sold one of his estates, and each of his men received a shilling every day for food. Each man was armed with a good carbine, rifle-barrelled and able, like a quick-firing gun, to fire eight or ten shots a minute. Each man also carried a hundred cartridges, and, in consequence, the hundred men could fire ten thousand shots. The two leaders carried double-barrelled carbines.

The burgomaster returning to the Hôtel de Ville, found in front of his door the little detachment dressed in an unknown uniform. He stopped with that naïve bourgeois curiosity which we call flânerie. After staring at the soldiers he went on to their leader before whom he stopped, not only with simple curiosity but astonishment. It seemed to him that the face of the leader was not entirely unknown to him.

And in fact, the officer, smiling, asked in excellent German:

"May I enquire after Burgomaster Fellner's health?"

"Ah! heavens and earth!" cried the burgomaster, "I was not mistaken. It is M. Benedict Turpin!"

"Bravo! I told you that your memory was unusually well developed. It must be so to recognize me in this costume."

"But you have become a soldier?"

"An officer."

"An officer! I beg your pardon."

"Yes, an amateur officer."

"Come up to my house; you must be in need of refreshment, and your men are thirsty. Aren't you, my friends?"

The men laughed.

"We are always more or less thirsty," one of them replied.

"Very well, I will send twenty-five bottles of wine and beer down to you," said the burgomaster. "Come in, M. Benedict!"

"Remember that my eye is upon you from the window," said Benedict, "and be careful."

"Be easy in your mind, captain," replied he who had spoken before.

"Madame Fellner," said the burgomaster on entering, "here is a captain of volunteers who is quartered on us. We must give him a worthy reception."

Madame Fellner, who was doing worsted work, raised her head and looked at her guest. An expression resembling her husband's passed over her face.

"Oh! it is surprising, my dear!" she cried, "how like this gentleman is to a young French painter...."

"There!" said Fellner, "there is no need to keep your incognito. Pay your respects to my wife, my dear Benedict; you are recognized."

Benedict held out his hand to Madame Fellner. As for the burgomaster, a slave to his promise, he looked out amongst a bunch of keys that of the cellar, and went down to choose the wine in which he wished Benedict's men to drink his health. A few minutes after, shouts of "Long live the burgomaster!" told that his wine was found to be of good quality.

# CHAPTER XXII. THE FREE MEAL

The burgomaster was uneasy, and did not try to hide it. The Prussians had marched on Frankfort by way of Vogeberg: a combat was bound to take place on the frontiers of Bavaria, and, if the Allies' army was beaten, the Prussians would occupy Frankfort on the following day. Orders had been given of which no one knew, but which could not be kept from him, as burgomaster. On July 14th, that is to say on the third day, the Federated Assembly, the Military Commission, and the Chancellor's Office, had received orders to go to Augsburg, a proof that Frankfort was not sure of being able to preserve her neutrality. The conviction, held by every one in Frankfort, that this was the moment of supreme crisis, had raised the sympathy of the inhabitants for the defenders of the cause dear to all, that is to say the cause of Austria, to the highest pitch. So, when the dinner hour came, the great houses of Frankfort invited the officers, while the bourgeois and working people invited the privates. Some took dinner to them, others laid tables before their doors.

Hermann Mumm, the famous wine merchant, had invited a hundred privates, corporals, and sergeants, and had laid an immense table before his door, where each man had his bottle of wine.

Burgomaster Fellner, his brother-in-law, Doctor Kugler, and the other inhabitants of the road abutting on the railway station, took care of Karl's hundred men. He himself dined with Madame von Beling and Count Monte Nuovo. Benedict, whom good Madame Fellner would not suffer to depart, could not refuse her invitation. They had invited Senators von Bernus and Speltz, but they had each their own guests, and only M. Fischer, the journalist, who lived a bachelor life, could come. Prince Alexander of Hesse dined with the Austrian consul.

The diners in the street formed strange contrasts with those inside. The soldiers, drinking together, careless of the morrow, looked for nothing but death; but death to a soldier is only a vivandière in black, who pours him the last glass of brandy at the end of the last day. The soldier only fears to lose his life, because in losing his life, he loses all with it, and at one blow; while the merchant, the banker, even the bourgeois, before losing life, may lose fortune, credit, and position. He may see his coffers pillaged, his house ransacked, his wife and daughters dishonoured, his children calling him, impotent to help them. He may be tortured through his family, his money, his flesh, and his honour. It was of these things that the citizens of the free town of Frankfort thought, and these things prevented them from being as gay as they would have wished with their guests.

As for Karl and Helen, they thought of nothing but their happiness. For them, the present was everything. They wished to forget: and, by force not of wishing, but of love, they did forget.

But the saddest of these gatherings, despite Benedict's efforts, was certainly that which took place at the burgomaster's. Herr Fellner was, in his administrative capacity, one of the most intelligent burgomasters that Frankfort had ever possessed. Furthermore, he was an excellent father to his family, adoring his children, and adored by them. During fourteen years of married life not the smallest cloud had passed across his union. During the whole dinner, in spite of the weighty political preoccupation which absorbed him, he attempted, with the help of his brother-in-law the councillor, and his friend Fischer, to throw a little gaiety over the solemnity of the conversation. At dessert a servant entered and informed Benedict that his travelling companion, Lenhart, asked leave to offer him his services again. The burgomaster enquired who Lenhart was, and, at the moment when Benedict smilingly asked permission to go and shake his hand in the vestibule, the ex-livery stable keeper slapped the servant on the shoulder to make him give way, and came in saying:

"Don't give yourself the trouble, M. Benedict; I'll come right into his worship the burgomaster's dining-room. I am not proud. Good day, your worship, and ladies and gentlemen."

"Ah!" said the burgomaster, recognizing the old Saxon accent, "you are from Sachsenhausen?"

"Yes, and my name is Lenhart, at your service; I am brother to Hans, who is in service with Madame von Beling."

"Well then, my friend," said the burgomaster, "drink a glass of wine to the health of M. Benedict, whom you wish to see."

"Two, if you like; he well deserves them! Ah! there's no stand-offishness with regard to the Prussians about him. Thunder and lightning! how he went at them at the battle of Langensalza!"

"What! you were there?" asked the burgomaster of Lenhart.

"On! yes, that I was, and now mad I was at not getting a slap at those cuckoos myself!"

"Why do you call them cuckoos?" asked the journalist.

"Because they take other people's nests to lay their eggs in."

"But how did you know I was here?" asked Benedict, a little embarrassed by this unceremonious visit.

"Oh!" said Lenhart, "I was walking peacefully along the road, when a dog came and jumped at my neck. 'There,' I said, 'it is Frisk, M. Benedict's dog.' Your men looked at me as if I were a curiosity, because I mentioned your name. 'Is M. Benedict here?' I asked them. They answered me: 'Yes, he is there, he is dining with your burgomaster, Herr Fellner, a good man, who has good wine.' 'Herr Fellner's good health,' I said to myself: 'Here, it's true! he is my burgomaster, because ever since yesterday I've been established in Frankfort, and as he is my burgomaster, I can go in And call on him, to say good-morning to M. Benedict.'"

"Well now that you have said good-morning to me, my good Lenhart, and drunk the health of his worship the burgomaster," said Benedict—

"Yes, but I haven't drunk yours, my young master, my benefactor, my idol! for you are my idol, M. Benedict. When I speak of you, when I talk about your duel, where you overcame those two men, one with a sabre cut, and what a one it was! M. Frederic de ——, you know the one I mean, don't you? Another with a pistol shot, that was a journalist, a great tall, ungainly fellow, like you, Herr Fischer."

"Thanks, my friend."

"I haven't said any harm, I hope."

"No, but leave these gentlemen in peace," said Benedict.

"They are very peaceful, M. Benedict; look how they are listening."

"Let him go on," said the doctor.

"I'd go on all the same, even if you wouldn't let me. Ah! when I'm on the subject of M. Benedict, I never run dry. Don't shrug your shoulders, M. Benedict; if you'd wanted to kill the baron, you'd have killed him, and if you'd wanted to kill the journalist, you'd only yourself to please."

"As a matter of fact," said the burgomaster, "we have seen that story in the 'Kreuz Zeitung.' My word! I read it without ever thinking that it was to you it happened."

"And the pretty thing is that it was he who told it you!" continued Lenhart. "He is as learned as a sorcerer! Only glanced at the poor King of Hanover's hand, and he foretold everything that's happened to him. First, the victory, then the pill."

At the moment, when they were going from the dining-room to the drawing-room, the sound of trumpets and drums was heard; the trumpet sounded "to horse," the drum beat "the alert." Madame Fellner waited impatiently; but her husband, smiling, signed to her to be patient. For the moment, a more lively and more general preoccupation was started by the sound of the alarm.

"This tells me, madam," said Benedict, pointing towards the street, "I have only time to drink your husband's health, and to the long and happy life you and your beautiful family will have with him."

The toast was repeated by all, and even by Lenhart, who thus drank twice, as he had said, to the health of the burgomaster. After which, grasping the hands of Herr Fellner, his brother-in-law, and the journalist, and kissing that of Madame Fellner, Benedict ran downstairs and out, crying: "To arms!"

The same warlike sound had surprised Karl and Helen at the end of dinner. Karl felt a terrible blow at his heart. Helen grew pale, although she did not know the meaning of the beating of the drums nor of the sounding of the trumpets; yet she felt it to be sinister. Then, at the glance exchanged between Count Monte Nuovo and Karl, she understood that the moment of separation had come. The count had pity on the two young lovers, and, to give them a minute for their last adieux, he took leave of Madame von Beling, and said to his young friend:

"Karl, you have a quarter-of-an-hour."

Karl threw a rapid glance at the clock. It was half-past four.

"Thank you, general," he answered. "I will be at my post at the time you mention."

Madame von Beling had gone to see Count Monte Nuovo off, and in order to be alone, the young people went into the garden, where a thick arbour of vines hid their adieux. One might as well try to write down the melancholy song of the nightingale, which burst forth a few paces from them, as to describe the dialogue interspersed with sighs and tears, with vows, with sobs, with promises of love, with passionate outbursts, and with tender cries. What had they said at the end of a quarter-of-an-hour? Nothing, and everything. The parting was inevitable.

As on the first occasion, Karl's horse was waiting at the door. He dragged himself away, leading Helen with him, encircled by his arms, there he covered her face with a rain of kisses.

The door was open. The two Styrians beckoned him. A quarter to five was striking. He threw himself upon his horse, driving the spurs into him. The two Styrians ran beside him, following the galloping horse. The last words which Karl heard were these: "Thine, in this world or in the next!" and with the ardour of a lover and the faith of a Christian, he replied: "So be it."

## CHAPTER XXIII. THE BATTLE OF ASCHAFFENBURG

During his dinner, Prince Alexander of Hesse had received this dispatch:

"The Prussian vanguard has appeared at the end of the Vogelsburg pass!"

This news very much astonished the commander-in-chief, who was expecting the enemy to come by the pass through the Thuringian Forest. He had, in consequence, immediately sent a telegram to Darmstadt to order a detachment of three thousand men to come by rail to Aschaffenburg and seize the bridge. Then he had immediately sounded the bugle-call and the signal to saddle.

Two steamboats were waiting at Hackenhausen. A hundred railway carriages were waiting at the station, capable of holding a hundred men each.

We have already mentioned the effect produced by the double trumpet call.

There was a moment of confusion: for a moment every one ran to and fro, uniforms were confused, cavalry and infantry were mixed, then as if a clever hand had put each man in his place, at the end of five minutes the cavalry were mounted and the infantry had their proper weapons. Everything was ready for a start.

Again, Frankfort showed its sympathy, not exactly to the Austrians, but to the defenders of Austria. Beer was handed round in half-pints and wine in jugfuls. Gentlemen of the first houses in the town shook hands with the officers. Fashionable ladies spoke cheeringly to the soldiers. A hitherto unknown brotherhood, born of the common danger, reigned over the free town.

People called from windows: "Courage! victory! long live Austria! long live the Allies! long live Prince Alexander of Hesse!"

Marie Louise's son was greeted for his part with cries of "Long live the Count of Monte Nuovo!" But it must be said that, as they came for the most part from ladies, they were due rather to his fine figure and military bearing than to his royal birth.

Karl's Styrian sharpshooters received orders to take their places in the first carriages. It was they who were to attack the Prussians. They went gaily into the station with no other music than the count's two flute players. After them came Count Monte Nuovo's Austrian brigade and lastly the Allies of Hesse and Würtemberg. The Italian brigade had left by the steamboats, protesting against what they had to do, and declaring they would never fire on their friends the Prussians for their enemies the Austrians.

The train went off, carrying men, rifles, guns, ammunition, horses, and ambulances. An hour and a half afterwards they were at Aschaffenburg. Night was beginning to fall. They had not seen the Prussians.

Prince Alexander of Hesse sent a party out to reconnoitre. The party came back towards eleven at night, after having fired a few shots at the Prussians at two hours' journey from Aschaffenburg.

A peasant who had crossed the pass at the same time as the Prussians, said that they were nearly five or six thousand strong, and that they had stopped because they were waiting for a body of seven or eight thousand men which was late. The numbers promised to be nearly equal.

It was found necessary to defend the passage of the Main and to protect Frankfort and Darmstadt by gaining the victory. The Styrian sharpshooters were placed on the road. Their mission was to do the greatest amount of damage possible to the enemy and retire, leaving the infantry and cavalry to work in their turn, and to rally at the head of the bridge, the allies only means of retreat, and to defend that bridge to the last.

During the night each man took up his position for the next day, and supped and slept in the open. A reserve of eight hundred men had been lodged in Aschaffenburg to defend the town if it were attacked. The night passed without disturbance.

At ten o'clock, Karl, growing impatient, mounted his horse and leaving the command of his men to Benedict galloped off towards the Prussians who at last were beginning to march.

In the course of his gallop Karl went up to Count Monte Nuovo and brought back the guns, which were put in position across the road. Four felled trees made a sort of entrenchment for the artillery. Karl got on to this entrenchment with his two Styrians, who took their flutes from their pockets, as if on parade, and began to play their sweetest and most charming airs. Karl could resist no longer. In a minute he took his pipe from his waistcoat pocket and sent on the wind a last message to his country.

The Prussians were advancing all this time. At half-range the booming of the two Austrian guns interrupted our three musicians, who put their flutes back into their pockets, and took up their rifles. The two volleys were well aimed, they killed or wounded a score of men. Again an explosion was heard, and a second messenger of death swept through the Prussian ranks.

"They are going to try and carry the guns by assault," said Karl to Benedict. "Take fifty men, and I'll take fifty; we will creep through the little wood on each side of the road. We have time for two shots each. We must kill a hundred men and fifty horses. Let ten of your men fire at the horses and the rest at the men."

Benedict took fifty men and crept along the right of the road. Karl did the same and crept along the left. The count was not mistaken; cavalry advanced from the middle on the first rank, and the gleam of the sabres was soon visible in the sunshine. Then was heard the thunder of three hundred horses, galloping forward.

Now began a fusillade, on both sides of the road, which would have seemed a game, if, at the first two shots, the colonel and the lieutenant had not been shot down from their horses, and if at each shot that followed those two a man or a horse had not fallen. Soon the road was strewn with dead men and horses. The first ranks could not advance. The charge stopped a hundred paces from the two guns, which kept up their fire and completed the confusion in the column.

Behind them the Prussians had brought forward the artillery, and had placed in position six guns to silence the two Austrian guns.

But our sharpshooters had advanced to about three hundred paces from the battery, and, when the six artillerymen had raised the match to fire with the regularity of a Prussian manœuvre, six shots were fired, three to the right and three to the left of the road, and the six artillerymen fell dead.

Six others took the burning match and fell beside their comrades. Meanwhile the two Austrian guns had fired and demolished one of the Prussian guns.

The Prussians did what they ought to have done at first; that is, they attacked the Styrian sharpshooters. They sent out five hundred Prussian sharpshooters with fixed bayonets.

Then, on both sides of the plain began a terrible fusillade, while along the road the infantry advanced in columns, firing on the battery as they came. The artillerymen harnessed horses to the guns and retreated. The two guns, by retiring, left the Neuberg brigade uncovered.

A hillock a little distance from Aschaffenburg was then crowned by a battery of six guns, the fire of which raked the Prussian masses.

The count himself seeing that in spite of the fire along the whole line, the Prussians were advancing, put himself at the head of a regiment of cuirassiers and charged. Prince Alexander ordered all the Baden army to support him. Unfortunately, he placed the Italian regiment on his left wing and for the second time the Italians told him that they would remain neutral, exposed to the shots of both sides, but would not fire themselves.

Whether by chance, or because they had been warned of this neutrality, the Prussians brought their principal effort to bear upon this left wing, which, by standing still, allowed the enemy to unhorse Count Monte Nuovo.

The Styrian sharpshooters had done marvels. They had lost thirty men, and had killed more than three hundred of the enemy. Then, according to their orders, they had rallied at the head of the Aschaffenburg bridge.

From that spot, Karl and Benedict heard a quick fusillade at the other

175

end of the town. It was the Prussian right wing which had overthrown Prince Alexander's left wing and was attacking the suburbs of the town.

"Listen," said Karl to Benedict, "the day is lost! Fate has overtaken the 'house of Austria.' I am going to kill myself, because it is my duty; but you, who are not tied to our fortune; you, who are fighting as an amateur; you, who are French when all is said and done, it would be folly for you to kill yourself for a cause which is not your own, and not even that with which you agree. Right to the last moment; then, when you know that all resistance is useless, get back to Frankfort, go to Helen; tell her that I am dead, if you have seen me die, or that I am in retreat on Darmstadt or Würtzburg with the remains of the army. If I live, I will write to her. If I die, I die thinking of her. This is my heart's testament, I confide it to you."

Benedict pressed Karl's hand.

"Now," proceeded Karl, "it seems to me that it is a soldier's duty to give the most service possible, to the last moment; we have a hundred and seventy men left. I am going to take some, I will take half to support the defenders of the town. You stay with the others at the bridge. Do your best here. I will do my best wherever I am. Do you hear the fusillade coming nearer? We have no time to lose. We must say farewell."

The two young men threw themselves into each other's arms. Then Karl hurried into the streets and disappeared in the smoke. Benedict went to a little hill covered with a thicket, where he could defend himself and protect the bridge.

He was scarcely there when he saw a cloud of dust rapidly approaching. It was the Baden cavalry, which had been driven back by the Prussian cuirassiers. The first fugitives crossed the bridge without difficulty; but soon the passage was obstructed with men and horses, and the first ranks were forced to return upon those who followed them.

At that moment, a volley from Benedict and his men felled fifty men and twenty horses. The cuirassiers stopped astonished, and courage returned to the Baden infantry. A second volley followed the first, and the click of the balls on the cuirasses could be heard like the sound of hail on a roof. Thirty men and horses fell. The cuirassiers became disordered, but in retiring they encountered a square broken by the lancers, which fled before them. The square found itself between the spears of the lancers and the sabres of the cuirassiers. Benedict saw them coming mixed pell-mell with the lancers and cuirassiers.

"Aim at the officers," cried Benedict, and he himself picked out a captain of cuirassiers and fired. The captain fell. The others had each chosen officers, but found it more convenient to choose the officers of the lancers. Death thus offered a larger target. Almost all the officers fell, and the horses bounding riderless joined the squadron. Men were still continuing to crowd the bridge.

Suddenly the greater part of the allies' army arrived almost upon the heels of the enemy. At the same time, in the street of the burning town, Karl was retreating with his usual calm. He killed a man at each shot. He was bare-headed. A ball had carried away his Styrian cap. A trickle of blood was running down his cheek.

The two young men greeted each other from afar. Frisk, recognizing Karl, whom he considered an admirable hunter, ran towards him, all delight at seeing him again.

At that moment, a heavy gallop made the earth shake. It was the Prussian cuirassiers returning to the charge. Through the dust of the road and the smoke of the firing could be seen the glitter of their breastplates, helmets, and sword blades. They made a hole in the centre of the Baden and Hessian fugitives, and penetrated a third of the way over the bridge.

With a last glance, Benedict saw his friend fighting against a captain, into whose throat he twice thrust his bayonet. The captain fell, but only to be succeeded by two cuirassiers who attacked Karl, sword in hand. Two shots from Benedict's rifle killed one and wounded the other.

Then he saw Karl carried away among the fugitives crossing the bridge, in spite of his efforts to rally them. Enclosed on all sides, his sole path to hope of safety was the bridge. He threw himself upon it with the sixty or sixty-five men who were left. It was a terrible struggle; the dead were trodden under foot, the cuirassiers, like giants on their great horses, stabbed the fugitives with their shortened swords.

"Fire on them!" cried Benedict.

Those of his men who had their rifles loaded fired; seven or eight cuirassiers fell; the bullets rattled on the breastplates of the rest.

A fresh charge brought the cuirassiers into the midst of the Styrian infantry. Pressed by two horsemen, Benedict killed one with his bayonet, the other tried to crush him with his horse against the parapet of the bridge. He drew his short hunting knife and thrust it up to the hilt in the horse's chest, the horse reared with a scream of dismay. Benedict left his knife with its living sheath, ran between the horse's legs, leapt over the parapet of the bridge and sprang, armed as he was, into the Main. As he fell, he cast a last look at the spot where Karl had disappeared, but his gaze sought his friend in vain.

It was about five o'clock in the evening.

# CHAPTER XXIV. THE EXECUTOR

Benedict had jumped into the Main on the left side of the bridge; the current carried him towards the arches. When he came to the surface he looked round him and saw a boat moored to one of them. A man was lying in the boat. Benedict swam towards him with one hand, holding his rifle above the water with the other. The boatman seeing him coming raised his oar.

"Prussian or Austrian?" asked he.

"French," answered Benedict. The boatman held out his hand.

Benedict, dripping as he was, jumped into the boat.

"Twenty florins," he said, "if we are in Dettingen in an hour. We have the current with us and I will row with you."

"That will be easy," said the boatman, "if you are sure you will keep your word."

"Wait a minute," said Benedict; throwing down his Styrian tunic and cap, and feeling in his pocket, "here are ten."

"Then, come on," said the boatman.

He took one oar, Benedict took the other: the boat impelled by four vigorous arms went rapidly down the river.

The struggle was still continuing; men and horses fell from the bridge into the stream. Benedict would have liked to stop and watch the spectacle, but time did not allow.

No one paid any attention to the little boat flying down stream. In five minutes the oarsmen were out of range and out of danger.

While passing a little wood on the edge of the river, called Joli-Buisson, he thought he saw Karl fighting desperately in the middle of a group of Prussians. But as the uniform of all the Styrians was alike, it might have been one of the infantry. Then Benedict fancied he saw a dog like Frisk in the throng, and he remembered that Frisk had followed Karl.

At the first bend of the river, they ceased to see anything of the battle. Further on, they saw the smoke of the burning houses in Aschaffenburg. Then at the little village of Lieder, everything disappeared. The boat flew down the river and quickly they passed Menaschoft, Stockstadt, Kleim, and Ostheim. After that the banks of the Main were deserted down to Mainflig. On the other bank, almost opposite, stood Dettingen.

It was a quarter-past six, the boatman had earned his twenty florins. Benedict gave them to him; but before parting from him he considered for a moment.

"Would you like to earn twenty florins more?" he asked.

"I should just think so!" replied the boatman. Benedict looked at his watch.

"The train does not go until a quarter-past seven, we have more than an hour before us."

"Besides which the trouble at Aschaffenburg will make the train another quarter of an hour late, if it does not stop it altogether."

"The deuce it will!"

"Will what I tell you fly away with my twenty florins?"

"No; but go into Dettingen first of all. You are just my height, go and buy me a boatman's dress like yours. Complete, you know. Then come back, and I will tell you what remains to be done."

The boatman jumped out of the boat and ran down the road to Dettingen. A quarter-of-an-hour later, he came back with the complete costume, which had cost ten florins. Benedict gave him that amount.

"And now," asked the boatman, "what is to be done?"

"Can you wait for me here three days with my uniform, my rifle, and my pistols? I will give you twenty florins."

"Yes; but if at the end of three days you do not come back?"

"The rifle, the pistols, and the uniform will be yours."

"I will wait here eight days. Gentlemen must have time to settle their affairs."

"You are a good fellow. What is your name?"

"Fritz."

"Very well, Fritz, goodbye!"

In a few moments Benedict had put on the coat and trousers and covered his head with the boatman's cap. He walked a few steps and then stopped suddenly:

"By the way, where will you stay at Dettingen?" he asked.

"A boatman is like a snail, he carries his house on his back. You will find me in my boat."

"Night and day?"

"Night and day."

"All is well then."

And in his turn Benedict went towards Dettingen.

Fritz had prophesied truly, the train was half an hour late. Indeed it was the last train which went through; hussars were sent to take up the rails; lest troops should be sent to Frankfort to help the allies.

Benedict took a third-class ticket, as befitted his humble costume. The train only stopped at Manau for a few minutes, and arrived at Frankfort at a quarter to nine, scarcely ten minutes late.

The station was full of people who had come to get news. Benedict passed through the crowd as quickly as possible, recognized M. Fellner, whispered in

181

his ear "beaten," and went off in the direction of the Chandroz' house.

He knocked at the door. Hans opened it. Helen was not in the house, but he went and asked for Emma. Helen was at the Church of Notre Dame de la Croix. Benedict asked the way there, and Hans, who thought he brought news of Karl, offered to show him. In five minutes they were there: Hans wished to go back, but Benedict kept him, in case there might be some order to be given. He left him in the porch and went in. One chapel was hit by the trembling light of a lamp. A woman was kneeling before the altar, or rather, crouching on the steps. This woman was Helen.

The eleven o'clock train had brought the news that a battle would take place that day. At twelve o'clock Helen and her maid had taken a carriage, and driven by Hans had gone down the Aschaffenburg road as far as the Dornighem wood. There, in the country silence they had heard the sound of cannon. It is unnecessary to say that each shot had had an echo in her heart. Soon she could listen no longer to the sound which grew louder and louder. She went back to Frankfort, and got down at the Church of Notre Dame de la Croix, sending back Hans to ease the minds of her mother and sister. Hans had not dared to say where Helen was without the permission of the baroness.

Helen had been praying since three o'clock. At the sound of Benedict's approach she turned. At first sight, and in his disguise, she did not recognize the young painter whom Frederic had wished her to marry, and took him for a Sachsenhausen fisherman.

"Are you looking for me, my good man?" she said.

"Yes," answered Benedict.

"Then you are bringing me news of Karl?"

"I was his companion in the fight."

"He is dead!" cried Helen, wringing her hands with a sob, and glancing reproachfully at the statue of the Madonna. "He is dead! he is dead!"

"I cannot tell you for certain that he is alive and not wounded. But I can tell you I do not know that he is dead."

"You don't know?"

"No, on my honour, I don't know."

"Did he give you a message for me before you left him?"

"Yes, these are his very words."

"Oh, speak, speak!" And Helen clasped her hands and sank on a chair in front of Benedict as though before a sacred messenger. A message from those whom we love is always sacred.

"Listen; he said to me: 'The day is lost. Fate has overtaken the house of Austria. I am going to kill myself because it is my duty.'"

Helen groaned.

"And I!" she murmured. "He did not think of me."

"Wait." He went on, "But you who are not tied to our fortune; you, who are fighting as an amateur; you, who are French when all is said, and done, it would be folly for you to kill yourself for a cause which is not your own. Fight to the last moment, then when you know that all resistance is vain, get back to Frankfort, go to Helen, tell her that I am dead, if you have seen me die, or that I am in retreat for Darmstadt or Würtzburg with the remains of the army. If I live, I will write to her if I die, I die thinking of her. This is my heart's testament, I confide it to you.'"

"Dear Karl! and then...?"

"Twice we saw each other in the fray. On the bridge at Aschaffenburg, where he was slightly wounded in the forehead, then a quarter-of-an-hour later, between a little wood called Joli-Buisson and the village of Lieder."

"And there?"

"There he was surrounded by enemies, but he was still fighting."

"My God!"

"Then I thought of you.... The war is over. We were the last of Austria's vital powers, her last hope. Dead or alive, Karl is yours from this hour. Shall I go back to the battlefield? I will search until I get news of him. If he is dead, I will bring him back."

Helen let a sob escape her.

"If he is wounded, I will bring him back to you, recovered I assure you."

Helen had seized Benedict by the arm, and looked fixedly at him.

"You will go on to the battlefield?" she said.

"Yes."

"And you will seek for him among the dead?"

"Yes," said he, "until I find him."

"I will go with you," said Helen.

"You?" cried Benedict.

"It is my duty. I recognize you now. You are Benedict Turpin, the French painter who fought with Frederic, and who spared his life."

"Yes."

"Then you are a friend and a man of honour. I can trust in you. Let us go."

"Is that settled?"

"It is settled."

"Do you seriously wish it?"

"I do wish it."

"Very well, then, there is not an instant to lose."

"How shall we go?"

"The railways have been destroyed."

"Hans will take us."

"I have a better plan than that. Carriages can be broken, drivers can be forced. I have the right man, a man who would break all his carriages and lame all his horses for me."

Benedict called, and Hans appeared.

"Run to your brother Lenhart. Tell him to be here within ten minutes with his best carriage and horses, and wine and bread. As you pass the chemist's tell him to get bandages, lint, and strapping."

"Oh, sir," said Hans, "I must write that down."

"Very well, a carriage, two horses, bread and wine; you mustn't forget that. I will see to the rest. Go." Then, turning to Helen, "Will you tell your relatives?" asked Benedict.

"Oh no!" she cried. "They would wish to prevent me from going. I am under the protection of the Virgin."

"Pray then. I will come back here for you."

Helen threw herself on her knees. Benedict went quickly out of the church. Ten minutes later he came back with all the necessary things for the dressing of wounds, and four torches.

"Shall we take Hans?" asked Helen.

"No, it must not be known where you are. If we bring back Karl wounded, a room must be ready for him, and a surgeon ready. Also, his arrival would cause agitation to your sister, scarcely well again, or to your grandmother, whose age must be taken into consideration."

"What time shall we get back?"

"I don't know, but we may be expected at four in the morning. You hear, Hans? And if they fear for your young mistress—"

"You will answer," said Lenhart, "that they may be easy, because Benedict Turpin is with her."

"You hear, dear Helen. I am ready when you are."

185

"Let us go," she said, "and not lose a minute. My God! when I think that he may be there, perhaps lying on the earth under some tree or bush, bleeding from two or three wounds, and calling on me with his dying voice for help!" and in high agitation she went on: "I am coming, dear Karl, I am coming!"

Lenhart whipped up his horses, and the carriage went off as quickly as the wind and as noisily as thunder.

# CHAPTER XXV. FRISK

In less than an hour and a half they were in sight of Dettingen, which was the more easy to see because it appeared from afar as the centre of a vast fire. As they drew nearer, Benedict said that the light came from the camp fires. After the victory, the Prussians had pressed their outposts beyond the little town.

Helen feared that they would not be allowed to continue their journey, but Benedict reassured her. The pity shown to the wounded, and the respect for the dead in all civilized countries, when once the battle is over, left him no doubt that Helen would be allowed to seek for her fiancé, dead or living, and that he would be allowed to aid her.

In fact, the carriage was stopped at the outposts, and the chiefs of the watch could not take it upon themselves to let them pass, but said they must refer to General Sturm, who commanded the outposts.

General Sturm had his quarters in the little village of Horstein, rather further on than Dettingen. Benedict was told where the house was, and went off at a gallop to make up for lost time. When he reached the house indicated, he found that General Sturm was away and that he would have to speak to the major.

He went in, and an impatient voice called out, "wait a minute."

Benedict had heard that voice before.

"Frederic!" he cried.

It was Baron Frederic von Bülow, whom the King of Prussia had made Staff-major to General Sturm. This rank was an advancement from brigade-general. Benedict explained that he was searching for Karl, who was dead or wounded on the field. Frederic would have liked to go with him, but he had work that must be done. He gave Benedict a permit to search the battlefield, and to take with him two Prussian soldiers as guards, and a surgeon.

Benedict promised to send back the surgeon with news of the expedition, and went out to the carriage where Helen was waiting impatiently.

"Well?" asked she.

"I have got what we want," answered Benedict. Then in an undertone he said to Lenhart, "Go on twenty paces, then stop."

He told Helen what had happened, and that if she wished to see her brother-in-law it would be easy to go back.

Helen chafed at the very idea of seeing her brother-in-law. He would be sure to keep her from going among the dead and wounded, and the thieves who were on the battlefield to rob the dead.

She thanked Benedict, and cried to Lenhart:

"Drive on, please!"

Lenhart whipped up his horses. They got back to Dettingen. Eleven o'clock struck as they entered the town. An immense fire was burning in the principal square. Benedict got down and went towards it. He went up to a captain who was walking up and down.

"Excuse me, captain," he said, "but do you know Baron Frederic von Bülow?"

The captain looked him up and down. It must be remembered that Benedict was still in his boatman's dress.

"Yes," he answered, "I know him, and what then?"

"Will you do him a great service?"

"Willingly; he is my friend; but how came he to make you his messenger?"

"He is at Horstein, and obliged to stay there by order of General Sturm."

"He is very uneasy about a friend of his, who was killed or wounded on the field. He sent me and a comrade to search for this friend, the fiancé of the lady whom you see in the carriage, and said: 'Take this note to the first

188

Prussian officer you see. Tell him to read it, and I am sure he will have the kindness to give you what you ask for.'"

The officer went to the fire, and read what follows:

"Order to the first Prussian officer whom my messenger meets, to put at the disposal of the bearer two soldiers and a surgeon. The two soldiers and the surgeon will follow the bearer wherever he leads them.

"From the quarters of General Horstein, eleven at night:

"By order, General Sturm.

"Principal staff officer,

"BARON FREDERIC VON BÜLOW."

Discipline and obedience are the two chief virtues of the Prussian army. These are what have made it the first army in Germany. The captain had hardly read his superior's order when he dropped the haughty look which he had assumed for the poor devil of a boatman.

"Hullo," he called to the soldiers round the fire. "Two volunteers to serve the principal staff officer, Frederic von Bülow."

Six men presented themselves.

"That's good, you and you," said the captain, choosing two men.

"Now who is the regiment's surgeon?"

"Herr Ludwig Wiederschall," answered a voice.

"Where is he billeted?"

"Here in the square," answered the same voice.

"Tell him he is to go on an expedition to Aschaffenburg to-night, by order of the staff officer."

A soldier got up, went across the square and knocked at the door; a moment after he came back with the surgeon-major.

Benedict thanked the captain. He answered that he was very happy to do anything for the Baron von Bülow.

The surgeon was in a bad temper, because he had been roused out of his first sleep. But when he found himself face to face with a young lady, beautiful and in tears, he made his excuses for having kept her waiting, and was the first to hasten the departure.

The carriage reached the bank of the river by a gentle slope. Several boats were anchored there. Benedict called in a loud voice:

"Fritz!"

At the second call a man stood up in a boat and said:

"Here I am!"

Benedict issued his orders.

Every one took their places in the boat; the two soldiers in the prow, Fritz and Benedict at the oars, and the surgeon and Helen in the stern. A vigorous stroke sent the boat into the middle of the stream. It was less easy travelling now, they had to go against the current; but Benedict and Fritz were good and strong rowers. The boat went slowly over the surface of the water.

They were far from Dettingen when they heard the clock strike midnight. They passed Kleim, Ostheim, Menaschoft, then Lieder, then Aschaffenburg.

Benedict stopped a little below the bridge, it was there that he wished to begin his search. The torches were lit and carried by the soldiers.

The battle had not been finished until dark; the wounded alone had been carried away, and the bridge was still strewn with dead, against whom one stumbled in the dark corners, and who could be seen by their white coats in the light ones.

Karl, with his grey tunic, would have been easily recognized, if among Prussians and Austrians; but Benedict was too sure of having seen him below the bridge to waste time in seeking for him where he was not. They went down to the fields, strewn with clumps of trees, and at the end of which was

190

the little wood called Joli-Buisson. The night was dark, with no moon, there were no stars, one would have said that the dust and smoke of battle was hanging between the earth and the sky. From time to time silent flashes of lightning lifted the horizon like an immense eyelid: a ray of wan light leapt out and lighted up the landscape for a second with bluish light. Suddenly all became dark again. Between the flashes, the only light which appeared on the left bank of the Main was that of the two torches carried by the Prussian soldiers, which made a circle of light a dozen paces across.

Helen, white as a ghost, and gliding like a ghost over the unevennesses of the ground as if they were non-existent, walked in the middle of the circle with arms outstretched, saying, "There, there, there!" wherever she thought she saw motionless corpses lying. When they came near they found them to be corpses indeed, but recognized Prussians or Austrians by their uniforms.

From time to time also, they saw something gliding between the trees, and heard steps hastening away; these were of some of the miserable robbers of the dead who follow a modern army as wolves used to follow ancient armies, and whom they disturbed in their infamous work.

From time to time Benedict stopped the group with a gesture; a profound silence fell, and in this silence he cried: "Karl! Karl!"

Helen with staring eyes and holding her breath, seemed like a statue of suspense. Nothing replied, and the little troop moved on.

From time to time Helen also stopped, and automatically, under her breath, as if she was afraid of her own voice, called in her turn, "Karl! Karl! Karl!"

They drew near the little wood and the corpses became fewer. Benedict made one of these pauses, followed by silence, and for the fifth or sixth time cried:

"Karl!"

This time, a lugubrious and prolonged cry replied, which sent a shudder through the heart of the bravest.

"What is that cry?" asked the surgeon.

"It is a dog, howling for some one's death," answered Fritz.

"Can it be?" murmured Benedict. Then he went on, "Over here! over here!" directing them towards the voice of the dog.

"My God!" cried Helen, "have you any hope?"

"Perhaps, come, come!" and without waiting for the torches he ran ahead. When he came to the edge of the wood, he cried again:

"Karl!"

The same lugubrious, lamentable cry was heard, but nearer.

"Come," said Benedict, "it is here!"

Helen leapt over the ditch, entered the wood, and without thinking of her muslin dress which was being torn to rags, she pushed on through the bushes and thorns. The torch-bearers had been thoughtful enough to follow. There in the wood they heard the sound of the robbers fleeing. Benedict signed a halt in order to give them time to escape. Then all was silent again he called a third time:

"Karl!"

This time a howl, as lamentable as the two first, answered, but so close to them that all hearts beat quickly. The men recoiled a step. The boatman pointed.

"A wolf!" said he.

"Where?" asked Benedict.

"There," said Fritz pointing. "Don't you see his eyes shining in the dark like two coals?"

At that moment a flash of lightning penetrated the trees, and showed distinctly a dog sitting beside a motionless body.

"Here, Frisk!" cried Benedict.

The dog made one bound to his master's neck and licked his face; then again, taking his place beside the corpse, he howled more lamentably than ever.

"Karl is there!" said Benedict.

Helen sprang forward, for she understood it all.

"But he is dead!" continued Benedict.

Helen cried out and fell on Karl's body.

# CHAPTER XXVI. THE WOUNDED MAN

The torchbearers had come up and a group, picturesque and terrible, was formed, by the bright light of the burning resin. Karl had not been plundered like the other corpses, the dog had guarded his body and prevented this. Helen was stretched upon him, her lips to his, weeping and groaning. Benedict was on his knees beside her, with the dog's paws on his shoulders. The surgeon stood, his arms folded, like a man accustomed to death and its sadness. Fritz had thrust his head through the leaves of a thorn-tree. Every one was silent and motionless for a moment.

Suddenly Helen cried out, she sprang up, covered with Karl's blood, her face haggard and her hair wild. They all looked at her.

"Ah!" she cried. "I am going mad." Then, falling on her knees, "Karl! Karl! Karl!" she cried.

"What is it?" asked Benedict.

"Oh! have pity on me," said Helen. "But I thought I felt a breath on my face. Did he wait for me, to give his last sigh?"

"Excuse me, madam," said the surgeon, "but if he whom you call Karl is not dead, there is no time to be lost in looking to him."

"Oh! come and look, sir," said Helen, moving quickly to one side.

The surgeon knelt down, the soldiers brought the torches near, and Karl's pale, but still handsome face was seen. A wound in his head had covered his left cheek with blood, and he would have been unrecognizable if the dog had not licked the blood away from his face as it flowed.

The surgeon loosened his collar; then he raised him to undo his tunic. The wound was terrible, for the back of his tunic was red with blood. The surgeon undid his coat, and with the swiftness of habit cut his coat up the back; then he called for water.

"Water," repeated Helen in an automatic voice that sounded like an echo.

The river was only fifty paces away, Fritz ran to it and brought back the wooden shoe, with which he was accustomed to bail out the boat, full of water. Helen gave her handkerchief.

The surgeon dipped into the water and began to wash the wounded man's chest, while Benedict supported his body across his knees. It was only then that they saw a clot of blood on his arm, this was a third wound. That on his head was insignificant. That in his chest seemed the most serious at first, but an artery had been cut in his right arm, and the great loss of blood had led to a fainting fit during which the blood had ceased to flow.

Helen, during this sad examination, had not ceased asking.

"Is he dead? is he dead?"

"We are going to see," said the surgeon. And on examination it proved that his blood still flowed. Karl was not dead.

"He lives!" said the surgeon.

Helen cried out and fell on her knees.

"What must we do to bring him to life?" she asked.

"The artery must be tied," said the surgeon, "will you let me take him to the ambulance?"

"Oh, no, no!" cried Helen. "I cannot be parted from him. Do you think he will bear being taken to Frankfort?"

"By water, yes. And I confess to you that considering the interest you take in this young man, I would rather some one else performed this operation. Now, if you have any way of taking him quickly by water—"

"I have my boat," said Fritz, "and if this gentleman" (he pointed to Benedict) "will give me a helping hand we will be in Frankfort in three hours."

"It remains to be seen," said the surgeon, "considering his great loss of blood, whether he will live three hours."

"My God, my God!" cried Helen.

"I don't dare to ask you to look, madam, but the earth is soaked with his blood!"

Helen gave a cry of dismay, and put her hand before her eyes.

While talking, while reassuring, while frightening Helen with the terrible cold-bloodedness of a man used to death, the surgeon was binding up the wound in Karl's chest.

"You say you fear that he has lost too much blood? How much blood can one lose without dying?" asked Helen.

"It depends, madam."

"What have I to fear or hope for?" asked Helen.

"You have to hope that he will live to reach Frankfort, that he has not lost as much blood as I fear he has, and that a clever surgeon will tie up the artery. You have to fear that he will have a second hæmorrhage to-day, or in eight or ten days, when the wound is healed."

"But we can save him, can't we?"

"Nature has so many resources, that we must always hope, madam."

"Well," said Helen, "do not let us lose an instant."

Benedict and the surgeon took the torches, the two soldiers carried the wounded man to the bank. They laid him in the stern of the boat on a mattress and blanket fetched from Aschaffenburg.

"May I try to rouse him?" asked Helen, "or ought I to leave him in his present state?"

"Do not do anything to bring him back to consciousness, madam it is this which stops the hæmorrhage, and if the artery is tied before he wakes, all may be well."

They all took their places in the boat, the two Prussians stood holding the torches; Helen was kneeling, the surgeon supported the wounded man; Benedict and Fritz rowed. Frisk, who did not seem to feel pride in having played such a splendid part, was sitting in the prow. This time, well ballasted, pulled by four arms, vigorous and accustomed to the exercise, the boat sped like a swallow over the surface of the water.

Karl remained unconscious. The doctor had thought that the air, cooler on the water than on the land, would rouse him, but it did not. He remained motionless, and gave no sign of life.

They arrived at Dettingen. Benedict gave a handsome reward to the two Prussian soldiers, and asked the surgeon, whom Helen could only thank by pressing his hands, to tell Frederic all the details of the expedition.

Benedict called Lenhart, who was sleeping on the box of his carriage, and told him to go to Frankfort as fast as possible, and tell some porters to wait with a litter on the banks of the Main at Frankfort. As for him, with Helen and Earl, he continued his journey by water, that being the smoothest road that one can find for a sick man.

Towards Hanau the sky began to get light; a great band of rosy silver stretched itself above the Bavarian mountains.

It seemed to Helen that the wounded man shuddered. She gave a cry that made the two rowers turn, then without another movement, Karl opened his eyes, murmured the name of Helen, and closed them again. All this was so rapid, that if Fritz and Benedict had not seen it with her, she would have doubted it. That opened eye, that gently murmured word did not seem a return to life, but the dream of a dying man.

The sun in rising sometimes has this effect on the dying, and before closing for ever their eyes look for the last time upon the sun. This idea came to Helen.

"Oh, Heaven!" she murmured, with sobs. "Is he breathing his last sigh?"

Benedict left the oar for a moment and went to Karl. He took his hand, felt his pulse; and found it imperceptible. He listened to his heart; it seemed to be still.

At each test Helen murmured: "Oh, Heaven!"

At the last test he shared her doubts. He took out a lancet, which he always carried, and pricked the shoulder of the wounded man, who did not feel or move; but a feeble drop of blood appeared.

"Be of good courage, he is still alive," he said, and again took up his oar.

Helen began to pray.

Since the evening, no one had eaten but Fritz. Benedict broke a piece of bread and gave it to Helen. She refused it with a smile.

They reached Offenbach, and could see Frankfort in the distance silhouetted against the sky. They were due there at about eight o'clock. At eight o'clock, in fact, the boat stopped at the landing-place by the bridge. Soon they saw Lenhart and his carriage, and close to him a litter. They raised the wounded man with the same precautions as before, put him in the litter, and drew the curtains round him.

Benedict wished Helen to go in Lenhart's carriage; the bodice of her dress was stained with blood. She wrapped herself in a large shawl and walked beside the litter. To save time she asked Benedict to go and seek for the same doctor who had attended the Baron von Bülow, Doctor Bodemacker. She herself crossed all the town from the Sachsenhausen Strasse to her mother's house, following the litter which bore Karl. People watched her pass with astonishment, and went to question Fritz who walked behind. And when he said it was a fiancée who was following the body of her lover, and as every one knew that Fräulein Helen von Chandroz was engaged to Count Karl von Freyberg, they recognized the beautiful young lady, and stepped back bowing respectfully.

When they reached the house the door was already open. Her grandmother and sister were waiting on each side of the door, and as she passed Helen took a hand of each.

198

"To my room!" she said.

The wounded man was taken to her room and laid on her bed. At that moment Doctor Bodemacker arrived with Benedict.

The doctor examined Karl, and Benedict looked on with anxiety almost equal to Helen's.

"Who saw this man before me?" asked, the doctor. "Who bound his wounds?"

"A regimental surgeon," answered Helen.

"Why did he not tie the artery?"

"It was at night, by torchlight, in the open air; he did not dare. He told me to get a cleverer man, and I came to you."

The surgeon looked at Karl uneasily. "He has lost a quarter of his blood," he murmured.

"Well?" asked Helen.

The doctor bent his head.

"Doctor," cried Helen, "don't tell me there is no hope: it is always said that people quickly recover lost blood."

"Yes," replied the doctor, "when he can eat. But never mind, a doctor must do all he can. Can you help me?" he asked Benedict.

"Yes," he answered, "I have some idea of surgery."

"You will leave the room, won't you?" the surgeon asked Helen.

"Not for the world!" she cried, "no, no, I will stay to the end."

The operation on the arm was finished with a cleverness which astonished Benedict.

"Now," said the doctor, "ice water must be slowly dropped on that arm!"

Some ice was procured and in five minutes was upon the arm.

"Now," said the doctor, "we shall see."

"What shall we see?" asked Helen anxiously.

"We shall see the effect of the ice water."

All three were standing by the bed, and it would be difficult to say which was the most interested in its success: the doctor, from professional pride; Helen, from her great love of the wounded man; or Benedict, from his friendship with Karl and Helen.

At the first drops of ice water which fell on the arm, Karl shuddered visibly. Then his eyelids trembled, his eyes opened, and he looked round him with surprise until they became fixed on Helen. A faint smile appeared on his lips and the corners of his eyes. He tried to speak and breathed the name of Helen.

"He must not speak," said the doctor, "until to-morrow at least."

"Enough, my beloved," said Helen. "To-morrow you can tell me you love me."

# CHAPTER XXVII. THE PRUSSIANS AT FRANKFORT

In Frankfort all was sorrow and dismay at the news of the defeat. The inhabitants were deeply apprehensive of their treatment by the Prussians since seeing what had occurred in Hanover. On the evening of the battle, as we have said, the news of the disaster had reached Frankfort, and from the next day, the 15th, the conviction that its occupation would be immediate had cast an aspect of mourning over the town. Not a single person was to be seen on the fashionable promenade. The Prussians, so it was said, would make their entry on the 16th after midday.

Night came, and with it a strange solitude in the streets, where, if one met a wayfarer it was evident from his hurry that he was on urgent business, carrying perhaps jewels or valuables for deposit at one of the foreign legations. At an early hour the houses had been shut up. Behind the bolted doors and windows one guessed that the inmates were silently digging holes for the concealment of their treasures.

Morning came and everywhere might be seen affixed placards of the Senate, reading as follows:

"The King of Prussia's royal troops will make their entry into Frankfort and its suburbs; our relations with them will therefore be materially changed from what they were when they were in garrison here. The Senate deplores this change which has been brought about in the relations in question, but the national sacrifices we have already made will render our inevitable pecuniary losses easy in comparison with what we have already lost. We all know that the discipline of the King of Prussia's troops is admirable. In circumstances of great difficulty the Senate exhorts all alike, of whatever rank or position, to give a friendly reception to the Prussian troops."

The Frankfort battalion received orders to hold itself ready, with band in front, to march out and meet the Prussians and do them honour. From ten o'clock in the morning every advantageous spot, all the belfries and housetops from which the suburbs, and particularly the road from Aschaffenburg could be seen, were crowded with curious spectators. Towards noon the Prussians were descried at Hanau. The railway brought them by thousands and they were seen occupying as if by magic all the strategic points along the line, not without certain precautions which indicated their uneasiness as to what might portend.

Nothing occurred, however, until four o'clock. Then successive trains left Hanau bearing the victorious army and rolled up to the town gates until seven o'clock. It was clear that General Falkenstein now waited the submission of the municipality, perhaps believing that the keys of the town would be brought him on a silver salver. He waited in vain.

All was silence. None of the inhabitants moved and the Prussian soldiers, prominent among whom were the cuirassiers who had charged so vigorously in the battle, seemed spectres in their great cloaks and steel helmets. In the evening the Zeil is ever a melancholy place. On this occasion how sad it looked, despair seemed inextricably intermingled with its brooding shadows, in which stood out like a squadron of phantoms the Prussian cuirassiers. Now and again the trumpets sounded sinister fanfares.

The fact that the Prussians were Germans was completely forgotten; their attitude clearly showed that they were enemies.

Suddenly the music of the battalion of Frankfort broke out, coming from the further side of the town. It met the Prussians at the top of the Zeil, drew up in ranks and presented arms to the beating of the drums.

The Prussians did not appear to notice these friendly advances. Two cannons arrived at a gallop. One was trained on the Zeil, the other on the Ross-market. The head of the Prussian column was formed on the Schiller Square and commanded the Zeil: for a quarter-of-an-hour the cavalry remained in line on horseback, then they dismounted and stood awaiting orders. This kind of encampment during which expectation grew tenser lasted until eleven. Then, all at once as the clocks struck, groups of ten, fifteen, or twenty men detached themselves, struck on the doors and invaded the houses.

No order had been given in the town for the provision of rations and wine. So the Prussians, treating Frankfort as a conquered world, chose the most comfortable houses in which to establish themselves.

The battalion remained a quarter-of-an-hour presenting arms; after which the commanding officer ordered muskets to be grounded. The band continued to play. It was ordered to cease.

After two hours, as no word had been exchanged between the battalion and the Prussian army, the former received the order to retire, arms lowered as for a funeral. It was the funeral of Frankfort's liberty.

The whole night passed in the same terrors as if the town had been taken by assault. If doors opened slowly, they were broken; cries of terror were heard in the houses and no one dared to ask what caused them. As the house of Hermann Mumm appeared one of the most important, he had to lodge and board two hundred soldiers and fifteen officers this first night. Another house, that of Madame Luttereth, lodged fifty men, who amused themselves with breaking the windows and furniture, on the alleged pretext that she had given evening parties and balls without inviting the Prussian officers in garrison. Accusations of this kind, accusations which served as the pretext for unheard of violence were preferred against all classes of society. And the Prussian officers said to their men: "You have a right to get all you can from these Frankfort rascals, who have lent Austria twenty-five millions without charging interest."

It was vain to say that the town had never had twenty-five millions in its coffers; that had it had them such a loan could not have been made without a decree of the Senate and the Legislature, and that the most skilful investigator would fail to find a trace of such a decree. The officers persisted, and, as the soldiers had no need to be encouraged in a preliminary pillage while waiting the great day of plunder which had been promised them, they gave themselves up to the most brutal disorders, believing themselves authorized by the hatred of their chiefs towards the unhappy town. From this night commenced what was rightly called the Prussian Terror at Frankfort.

Frederic von Bülow, who knew of the orders to treat Frankfort as a hostile city, had had a guard placed at the Chandroz' house to secure the safety of the family, his pretext being that it had been reserved for General Sturm and his staff.

Daylight dawned and presently, few having slept, all the world was abroad, lamenting their misfortune and enquiring about those suffered by their friends. Then came the billstickers slowly and unwillingly, like men under constraint, fixing up the following notice:

"Authority having been given me over the Duchy of Nassau, the town of Frankfort and its suburbs, as also over that part of Bavaria which is occupied by the Prussian troops and over the Grand-duchy of Hesse, all workmen and functionaries will in future take orders from me. These orders will be duly and formally communicated.

"Dated at Frankfort, July 16th, 1866,

"The Commander-in-Chief of the Army of the Main,

"Falkenstein."

Two hours later the general addressed a note to the Deputies Fellner and Müller, in which he stated that as armies at war could procure what they had need of in the enemy's country, the town of Frankfort would furnish to the army of the Main:

"1. For each soldier a pair of boots to sample.

"2. Three hundred good horses ready saddled to replace those lost by the army.

"3. The pay of the army for a year to be sent instantly to the army treasurer."

By way of recompense the town was to be freed from all imposts, except cigars, the general engaging furthermore to reduce the burden of the military billeting as much as possible.

The total claimed for army pay was 7,747,008 florins.

The two members hastened to General Falkenstein's headquarters, and were admitted to him. His first words were:

"Well, sirs, have you brought my money?"

"We beg leave to submit to your Excellency," said Fellner, "that we have no authority to decree payment of such a sum, as the government of the town having been dissolved, its consent cannot be obtained."

"That does not concern me," said the general, "I have conquered the country and I raise an indemnity. It is perfectly regular."

"Will you allow me to say to your Excellency that a town which does not defend itself cannot be conquered. Frankfort, a free town, relies for its defence on its treaties, and has never thought of opposing your army."

"Frankfort has found twenty-four millions for the Austrians," cried the general, "and can easily find fifteen or eighteen for us. But if it refuses, I myself will find them. Four hours only of pillage and we shall see if your street of the Jews and the coffers of your bankers do not produce twice as much."

"I doubt, general," said Fellner coldly, "whether Germans can be got to treat Germans in such a way."

"Who speaks of Germans? I have a Polish regiment brought expressly."

"We have done no harm to the Poles; we have afforded them a refuge against you whenever they required it. The Poles are not our enemies; the Poles will not pillage Frankfort."

"That is just what we are going to see," said the general, stamping his foot with one of those oaths of which the Prussians enjoy the monopoly. "I don't care a damn if I am called a second Duke of Alva, and I warn you that if at six o'clock to-day the money is not paid, you will be arrested to-morrow and thrown into a dungeon, which you will leave only when the last thaler of the 7,747,008 florins is paid."

"We know your first minister's maxim, 'Might is right.' Dispose of us as you wish," answered Fellner.

"At five o'clock, the men whom I shall order to receive the seven million florins will be at the door of the bank, in readiness to transport the money to my headquarters." Then he added so that the burgomaster could hear the orders: "Arrest and bring before me, the Journalist Fischer, editor in chief of the 'Post Zeitung.' I shall commence with him in dealing with the newspaper men and the newspapers."

Two hours later Fischer was arrested in his house where, after a communication from Fellner he had remained in expectation of the event, and brought to headquarters. General Falkenstein had contrived to keep himself at boiling point, so the moment he saw Fischer:

"Let him enter," he said, in the third person, which in Germany is the sign of the most profound contempt. And, as Fischer did not enter as quickly as the general wished, he cried: "A thousand thunders! if he hangs back, shove him in."

"Here I am," said Fischer; "forewarned of your intention I could have left Frankfort, but it is my custom to face danger."

"Oh! so you knew that you would be in danger, Mr. Pocket-pen, when you reached me."

"An unarmed man is always in danger from a powerful armed enemy."

"You consider me your enemy, then?"

"The indemnity you have exacted from Frankfort and your threats against Herr Fellner are not those of a friend, you will allow."

"Oh! you have no need to await my threats and orders to declare yourself my enemy. We know your paper, and it is because we know it that you are going to sign the following declaration. Sit down there, take a pen, and write."

"I take a pen; but, before using it, what are you about to dictate?"

"You want to know? Well, here it is. I, Dr. Fischer Goullet, Councillor of State, editor in chief.... But you are not writing."

"Finish your sentence, sir, and if I decide to write I will do so."

"Editor-in-chief of the 'Post Zeitung,' acknowledge myself guilty of systematic and calumnious hostility towards the Prussian Government."

Fischer threw down the pen.

"I will never write that, sir," said he; "it is false."

"Tempests and thunders!" cried the general, making a step towards him. "You give me the lie."

Fischer took a newspaper from his pocket.

"This will inform you better than I can, sir," he said; "it is the last issue of my paper published an hour before your entry here. This is what I wrote in it:

"'The history of the days which are to come is written at the point of the bayonet. It is not for the citizens of Frankfort to change anything. For the population of a small and weak state there is nothing else to do but to succour the combatants, whether friends or enemies: they must dress wounds, nurse the sick, exercise charity towards all. Right behaviour is as much the duty of every one as obedience towards the responsible authority.'"

Then, seeing the general shrugging his shoulders, Fischer in his turn took a step forward and holding out his paper:

"Read yourself, if you doubt me," said he.

The general tore it from his hands.

"You wrote that yesterday," he said white with rage, "because yesterday you felt us coming, because, yesterday, you were afraid of us." And tearing up the newspaper he crushed it into a ball and threw it in the Councillor's face, shouting; "You are a coward."

Fischer threw a wild glance around him as if for a weapon with which to avenge this insult; then with his hand to his forehead he staggered, turned round with a strangled cry and fell in a heap, killed by the bursting of a blood vessel in the brain.

The general went to him, pushed him with his foot, and seeing that he was dead:

"Throw this rascal into a corner," said he to his soldiers, "until his family comes to fetch him."

The soldiers dragged the corpse into a corner of the ante-room.

Meanwhile, Fellner, fearing that harm would befall his friend, had run to Hannibal Fischer, the journalist's father, and had told him of the general's orders. Hannibal Fischer was an old man of eighty, he went to the headquarters and asked for his son. The son had been seen going up to the first floor where General Falkenstein held his audiences, but no one had seen him leave. The old man went up and asked for the general. He had gone to lunch and his door was closed.

"Sit down there," said some one, "he may return."

"Cannot you tell him that it is a father who claims his son?"

"What on?" asked one of the soldiers.

"My son, Councillor Fischer, who was arrested this morning."

"Why, it is the father," said the soldier to his comrade.

"If he wants his son, let him take him," said the other.

"How, take him?" said the old man, bewildered.

"Certainly," answered the soldier. "There he is waiting for you." And he pointed to the corpse in the corner.

The father approached the body, knelt on one knee and raised his son's head.

"Then they have killed him?" he asked the soldiers.

"No, indeed, he died of his own accord."

The father kissed the corpse on the forehead.

"These are unhappy days," he said, "in which fathers bury their children."

Then he went down, called a street porter, sent him for three of his mates, mounted again to the ante-chamber and showing them the body:

"Take my son," he said, "and bear him to my house." The men took the body on their shoulders and bore him to a barrow. The father walked before it bare-headed and pale, his eyes bathed in tears; and to all who questioned him about this strange procession, carrying a dead man through the town without a priest, replied: "It is my son, Councillor Fischer, whom the Prussians have killed." And thus the news spread over Frankfort.

# CHAPTER XXVIII. GENERAL MANTEUFFEL'S THREATS

At five o'clock in the afternoon of July 17th, as the general had said, he sent to the bank a squad of eight men under the command of a sergeant-major, accompanied by two men with wheel-barrows for the seven million florins. His notion of the weight of the coin, which in gold would amount to more than fifty tons, must have been a curious one. Seeing his men return without the money, General Falkenstein declared that if it were not forthcoming the next day he would permit pillage and bombardment. Meanwhile the members Bernus and Speltz were arrested and conducted to the guard-room, when, having left them in view behind the bars for two hours to convince every one of his power over the town authorities, he sent them off to Cologne with four soldiers and a letter for the governor.

This act of brutality had its effect. It alarmed a great many influential people who went to find the bank manager and urge him to advance the seven millions demanded. The directors of the bank gave way and the money was paid to the last florin on July 19th.

The same day the city battalion was disbanded in the presence of the Prussian Colonel von der Goltz. The soldiers had not expected this, and some of the oldest of them shed tears.

At the same time, the Prussians took their fill of the townspeople's horses. They requisitioned seven hundred, including two little ponies of Madame de Rothschild. The carriages were then seized, and if a lady happened to take a cab she was obliged when she met an officer in search of one, to get out in the mud and leave him to take her place.

Two orders were circulated. The first enjoined the presentation at the police station every morning, before eight o'clock, of a list of all travellers who had arrived in the hotels and boarding-houses.

Many societies formed for divers purposes such as gymnastics, education, and the like, were called before the commander-in-chief and dissolved. Such of them as had for object military exercises were invited to deposit their arms. Finally the general addressed to the presidents of the societies some kindly words upon the necessity of the measures taken, and upon the actual situation in general. You ask me how kindly words could be uttered by M. de Falkenstein. Reassure yourself, the illustrious general had not altered his habits. Having received his millions at two o'clock he had at once left Frankfort. General Wranzel acted as his deputy for two or three hours and showed a smiling face between two morose ones, for at five o'clock, General Manteuffel arrived. He at once issued the following order:

> "To assure the subsistence of the Prussian troops a storehouse will be at once established in this town of Frankfort-on-the-Main, by order of His Excellency the Lieutenant-General Manteuffel, commander-in-chief of the army of the Main. It will be provisioned as follows:

> 15.000 loaves of bread of 5 lbs. 9 ozs.

> 1,480 hundredweight of sea biscuits.

| | | |
|---|---|---|
| 600 | " | of beef. |
| 800 | " | of smoked bacon. |
| 450 | " | of rice. |
| 450 | " | of coffee. |
| 100 | " | of salt. |
| 5,000 | " | of hay. |

> "A third part of these quantities is to be placed at our disposal in convenient places between now and the morning of the 21st. The second third on the 21st in the evening, and the last third on July 22nd at the latest.

> "Frankfort, July 20th, 1866.

> "The Military Superintendent of the army of the Main.

> "KASUISKIL"

The unhappy townspeople had believed themselves free from these imposts according to General Falkenstein's promise—except, indeed, as regards cigars, of which both the Prussian officers and men required nine provided each day.

The next day, while at breakfast with his family towards ten o'clock, Fellner received a letter from the new commander. It was addressed: "To the Very Illustrious Herren Fellner and Müller, proxies of the town of Frankfort." He turned it and turned it about between his hands without unsealing it. Madame Fellner trembled, Herr Kugler, his brother-in-law, grew pale, and seeing the drops of perspiration on their father's forehead as he sighed deeply, the children began to cry. At last he opened it, but seeing his pallor as he read, all rose to their feet awaiting his first words. But he said nothing, he let his head fall on his breast and dropped the letter on the floor. His brother-in-law picked it up and read:

> "To the Very Illustrious Herren Fellner and Müller, proxies of the government in this town.

> "You are invited by these presents to take the necessary measures for a war indemnity of twenty-five millions of florins to be paid within twenty-four hours to the pay office of the Army of the Main in this town.

> "The Commander-in-Chief of the Army of the Main,

> "MANTEUFFEL"

> "Oh!" murmured Fellner, "my poor Fischer, you are fortunate."

Within two hours bills which Messrs. Fellner and Müller had printed were posted all over the town. They consisted of General Manteuffel's letter to them with this addition:

> "The Burgomasters Fellner and Müller declare that they will die rather than assist in the spoliation of their fellow citizens."

The blow to the city was the more terrible because it was entirely unexpected. The city had just paid more than six millions of florins, had contributed in goods an equivalent sum, and was billeting soldiers at a crushing expense. Some had ten, others twenty, thirty, or even fifty soldiers. General Falkenstein had prescribed the soldiers' rations as for the officers, they were entitled to anything they asked for. A soldier's daily rations comprised, coffee and accessories in the morning; a pound of meat, vegetables, bread, and half a bottle of wine at noon; a collation with a pint of beer in the evening, in addition eight cigars. These cigars had to be specially bought from the dealers coming with the army. Usually the soldiers demanded and got an extra meal at ten in the morning of bread-and-butter and brandy, and after lunch they got coffee. The sergeant-majors had to be treated like officers, being provided with roast meat and a bottle of wine at dinner, with coffee to follow. Havana cigars, eight in number, were insisted on.

The citizens dared not complain, for the soldiers whatever they did were always found to be in the right. But when they heard of this new exaction of General Manteuffel, used as they were to theft and rapine on the part of the Prussians, the Frankfortians, mute with astonishment, looked at each other, not being able to grasp the extent of their misfortune. As soon as the news was actually billed they rushed in crowds to see it with their own eyes. Hours were spent in deploring the enemy's greed, but nothing was done towards obeying the order. Meanwhile, some of the chief citizens, M. de Rothschild among them, had gone to seek General Manteuffel. In reply to their observations he said:

"To-morrow my cannon will be trained upon all the chief points of the town, and if in three days I have not half of the contribution, and the rest in six, I double it."

"General," answered M. de Rothschild, "you know the range of your cannons I do not doubt, but you do not know that of the measures you are taking—if you ruin Frankfort, you ruin the neighbouring provinces."

"Very well, gentlemen," answered Manteuffel, "the contribution, or pillage and bombardment."

In spite of the intervention of the foreign legations, those of France, Russia, England, Spain, and Belgium, on July 23rd, masses of troops were put in movement with loaded cannon. These were ranged on the chief spaces in the town. At the same time batteries were established on the Muhlberger and the Roederberg, as also on the left bank of the Main.

# CHAPTER XXIX. GENERAL STURM

Brigadier-General Roeder, who had replaced General Manteuffel, had brought with him General Sturm and his brigade. Baron von Bülow was the principal staff officer of this brigade, and, as we have related, on the day the Prussians entered Frankfort he had safeguarded the Chandroz family, by placing four men and a serjeant-major in their house. The serjeant-major bore a letter for Madame von Beling, informing her why she was thus garrisoned and urging her to prepare the best rooms on her first floor for General Sturm and his suite. Madame von Beling acted on these instructions, and the men had better rations and cigars supplied to them than if the municipality had catered for them.

After the surgeon's departure Karl lay still unconscious, but his breathing gradually became more perceptible. Towards evening he uttered a sigh, opened his eyes, and by a slight movement of his left hand seemed to beckon Helen. She rushed to him, seized his hand and placed her lips upon it. Benedict wished her to retire, promising to watch over Karl, but Helen refused, saying that no one but herself should nurse him.

Benedict being desirous of ridding himself of the sailor's clothes in which he had descended the river before General Sturm arrived, and having no other suit, left the house to get a new outfit. Lenhart was at the front door with his carriage and, driving to the port, he soon found Fritz and his boat. There was his uniform, with his pistols and carbine. He took them and put them in the carriage. Frisk, who had spent the day incessantly watching for his master, joyfully jumped in. Benedict gave Fritz twenty florins and sent him back to Aschaffenburg. Then Lenhart took him to a tailor where he had no difficulty in obtaining an outfit. Next he took a bath. He had fought during the whole of the 14th and had not closed his eyes during thirty-six hours, so he found it refreshing. Afterwards he allowed Lenhart to take him to his own house, and there he got between the sheets.

When he awoke it was ten o'clock; he had slept for six hours. He rushed to the Chandrozes. He found Helen as he had left her kneeling by Karl's bed. She raised her head and smiled. She also had not slept for thirty hours, but the devotion of women knows no bounds. Nature has intended them for sisters of charity. Love is as strong as life itself.

Karl seemed to sleep; it was evident that, as no blood flowed to it, the brain was in a state of torpor; but every time a spoonful of syrup of digitalis was placed in his mouth he absorbed it better. Benedict's work was to renew the ice which dripped upon the arm, washing the wound made first by the cuirassier's sabre and then by the doctor's lancet.

Towards eight in the morning Emma came into the room for news of the wounded man. She found Helen asking Benedict for more ice. He was an entire stranger to Emma, but by a flash of intuition she guessed him to be the man who had spared her husband's life. She was thanking him when Hans came to announce Fellner. The worthy man was afraid that the Prussians would break into the house, and came to offer his services.

While they were talking, Frederic arrived with the news that his general was only five minutes behind him.

Nothing can describe Emma's joy and happiness in seeing Frederic. The war was nearly over, rumours of peace became stronger, her Frederic was then out of danger. Love is egoistic, scarcely had she thought of what was happening in the city; the entry of the Prussians, their exactions, their imposts, their brutalities, the death of Herr Fischer; all these seemed vague—a letter from Frederic had been the important event. Frederic: it was he whom she embraced. He was safe and sound, unwounded, and no longer in danger. Keenly interested as she was in her sister and Karl and their mutual love, she felt how fortunate Frederic was that he was not Karl.

Frederic went up to Karl, who recognized him and smiled.

While General Sturm ate a splendid dinner, Frederic, to whom Benedict had whispered a few words about the behaviour of the Prussians at Frankfort, went out to judge for himself. He was told that the Senate was sitting and he went in. The Senate declared that the demand made upon it being impossible of fulfilment it submitted itself to the general's clemency.

On leaving the Senate, Frederic saw the cannon trained on the town, the crowds round all the posted bills. He saw besides, entire families driven from their homes by the Prussians, bivouacking on the open spaces. The men were swearing, the women were in tears. A mother was calling for vengeance, as she tended her child of ten, through whose arm a bayonet had been thrust. Without knowing what he did the unfortunate child had followed a Prussian, singing the song that the people of Sachsenhausen had made on the Prussians:

Warte, kuckuck, warte

Bald kommt Bonaparte

Der wird alles wieder holen

Was ihr hobt bei uns gestohlen.[1]

The Prussian had used his bayonet on the lad. But instead of consoling the mother and calling for vengeance with her, the passers-by had signed to her to be quiet, to dry her tears and wipe the blood away; so great was the general terror.

The Prussians, however, had not everywhere had a like experience. One of them lodging with a man of Sachsenhausen, to frighten him had drawn his sabre and placed it on the table. The man without offering any remark had gone out and returned within five minutes with an iron trident, which he in his turn put on the table. "What does this signify?" the Prussian had asked. "Well," was the reply, "you wanted to show me that you had a fine knife, and I have wanted to convince you that I have a fine fork." The Prussian had taken the joke badly, he had tried to make play with his sabre and had been transfixed to the wall with the trident.

Passing by Hermann Mumm's house, the baron noticed him sitting at his door, his head buried in his hands. He touched him on the shoulder. Mumm looked up.

"Is that you?" he said, "and have you pillagers also?"

"Pillagers?" asked Frederic.

"Come and see! Look at my china which my family for three generations has collected—all broken. My cellar is empty, and naturally so, for I have been lodging two hundred soldiers and fifteen officers. Listen to them!" And Frederic heard shouts from within of "wine, more wine! or we blow the place to pieces with cannon balls!"

He went into the house. Poor Mumm's fine house looked like a stable. The floors were covered with wine, straw, and filth. Not a window remained whole, not an article of furniture was unbroken.

"Look at my poor tables," said the unhappy Mumm. "At them have sat for over a century the best people of Frankfort; yes, the king, many princes, and the members of the Diet have dined at them. Not a year ago Frau and Fräulein von Bismarck complimented me on the collation I gave them. And now, days of horror and desolation have come, and Frankfort is lost."

Frederic was powerless and could only leave the place. He well knew that neither General Roeder nor General Sturm would stop the pillaging. Roeder was ruthless, Sturm was mad. He was an old style Prussian general, who when opposed struck down the obstacle.

Presently he met Baron von Schele, the postmaster-general. Since the entry of the Prussians he had received the order to institute a censorship, unsealing letters and drawing up reports upon those who discovered hostile feelings to the Prussian government. He had refused to obey, and, his successor having arrived from Berlin, the censorship was in operation. Von Schele, who looked on Frederic as a Frankfortian rather than a Prussian, told him all this and invited him and his friends to resist.

He reached Fellner's with a broken heart and found all the family in despair. Fellner had just received the official intimation of the refusal of the chief commercial houses to pay the millions demanded by the Prussians and the decree of the Senate in the matter. Although as a member of the Senate he knew its contents, he was re-reading it mechanically, while his wife and children sobbed around him, for all feared what excesses the Prussians might commit on receipt of the refusal. While they sat together, Fellner was informed of the decision just come to by the Legislative Assembly, that a deputation

218

should be sent to the king to obtain the remission of the imposition of twenty-five millions of florins exacted by General Manteuffel.

"Ah," said Frederic, "if only I could see the King of Prussia."

"Why not?" said Fellner, catching at a straw.

"Impossible, my dear Fellner, I am only a soldier. When a general commands I must obey. But, if the millions are going to be found, my family will contribute its share."

Being powerless to assist Fellner, he left him and had walked a few steps when a soldier saluted and asked him to proceed to General Sturm who was waiting for him.

General Sturm was a biggish, strongly made man of about two and fifty. He had a small head, with a high brow. His round face was red and when he was angry, which was often, it became crimson. His large eyes were almost always injected with blood, and he glared with fixed pupils when, as invariably was the case, he wished to be obeyed. All this, with his big mouth, thin lips, yellow teeth, menacing eyebrows, aquiline nose, and thick, short red neck, made him a formidable looking man. His voice was loud and penetrating, his gestures commanding, his movements brusque and rapid. He walked with long strides, he despised danger, but nevertheless seldom encountered any unless it was worth his while.

He had a passion for plumes, red, waving colours, the smell of powder, of gaming; he was as brusque in his words as in his movements; violent and full of pride he brooked contradictions ill and readily flew into a passion. Then his face grew a crimson-violet, his grey eyes became golden and seemed to emit sparks. At such times, he completely forgot all the decencies of life, he swore, he insulted, he struck. Nevertheless he had some common sense, for knowing that he must from time to time have duels to fight, he spent his spare time in sword exercise and pistol shooting with the maître-d'armes of the regiment. And it must be allowed that he was a first-rate performer with both weapons; and, not only so, he had what was called "an unfortunate hand," and where another would have wounded slightly he wounded badly, and frequently he killed his adversary. This had happened ten or twelve times. His real name was Ruhig, which means peaceful, so inappropriate to its owner that he received the surname of Sturm, meaning storm or tempest. By this name he was always known. He had made a reputation for ferocity in the war against the Bavarians in 1848-49.

When Frederic presented himself he was relatively calm. Sitting in a great chair, and it was rare for him to be seated, he almost smiled.

"Ah, it is you," he said. "I was asking for you. General Roeder was here. Where have you been?"

"Excuse me, general," Frederic answered. "I had gone to my mother-in-law for news of one of my friends, who was seriously wounded in the battle."

"Ah! yes," said the general, "I heard about him—an Austrian. It is too good of you to enquire about such imperial vermin. I should like to see twenty-five thousand of them lying on the battlefield, where I would let them rot from the first man to the last."

"But, your Excellency, he was a friend—"

"Oh, very well—the matter is not in question. I am satisfied with you, baron," said General Sturm, in the same voice in which another man would have said, "I loathe you!" "and I wish to do something for you."

Frederic bowed.

"General Roeder was asking for a man with whom I am well pleased, to carry to His Majesty King William I, whom God preserve, the two Austrian and Hessian flags taken by us in the battle of Aschaffenburg. I have thought of you, dear baron. Will you accept the mission?"

"Your Excellency," replied Frederic, "nothing could honour or delight me more. If you recollect, it was the king who placed me near you; to bring me into contact with the king in such circumstances is to do me a favour and to do him, I dare hope, a pleasure."

"Well, you must leave within the hour and not come to me with 'my little wife,' or 'my grandmother.' An hour suffices for embracing all the grandmothers and all the wives in the world, all sisters and children into the bargain. The flags are in the ante-room there. Within the hour jump on the train on your way to Bohemia, and to-morrow you will be with the king at Sadowa. Here is your letter of introduction to His Majesty. Take it."

Frederic took the letter and saluted, his heart full of joy; he had not had to ask for leave; as if the general had read, had known his dearest wish, he had offered it, and with it had done him a favour of which he had not dreamt.

In two bounds he had reached Benedict.

"My dear friend," he said, "I leave for Sadowa in an hour, but hesitate to say with what object."

"Tell me all the same," said Benedict.

"Well, I am taking the flags captured from the Austrians."

"And you can take them without grieving me; for, if all Prussians were like yourself, I should have fought with them and not with the Hanoverians and Austrians," said Benedict. "Now go and say your adieux."

He was still embracing his wife and little child, when the same soldier who had already been sent to him, called to ask him not to take the flags without exchanging a last word with the general.

[1]

> Wait, wait a bit, cuckoo,
>
> Bonaparte is coming, who
>
> Soon will force you to restore
>
> All you stole from us before.

# CHAPTER XXX. THE BREAKING OF THE STORM

The general received Frederic with the same calm and gracious expression as before.

"Excuse me for delaying," he said, "after I was so anxious to speed you; but I have a little service to ask."

Frederic bowed.

"It is about General Manteuffel's subsidy of twenty-five millions of florins. You know about it, don't you?"

"Yes," said Frederic, "and it is a heavy impost for a poor city with some 40,000 inhabitants."

"You mean 72,000," said Sturm.

"No, there are only about 40,000 Frankfortians, the remainder of the 72,000 counted as natives are strangers."

"What does that matter?" said Sturm, becoming impatient. "The statistics say 72,000 and General Manteuffel has made his calculation accordingly."

"But if he has made an error, it seems to me that those who are charged with the execution of his order should point it out."

"That is not our affair. We are told 72,000 inhabitants, and 72,000 there therefore are. We are told 25 million florins, and 25 million florins there are also. That is all! Just fancy! the senators have declared, that we can burn the town, but they will not pay the subsidy."

"I was present," said Frederic quietly, "and the sitting was admirably conducted, with much dignity, calm, and sorrow."

"Ta ta ta ta," said Sturm. "General Manteuffel before leaving gave General Roeder the order to get in these millions. Roeder has ordered the town to pay them. The Senate has chosen to deliberate; that is its own affair.

Roeder came round to me about it, it is true; but I told him that it was nothing to worry about. I said. 'The chief of my staff married in Frankfort; he knows the town like his own land, everyone's fortune even to shillings and half-pence. He will indicate five and twenty millionaires.' There are twenty-five of them here, are there not?"

"More than that," answered Frederic.

"Good; we will commence with them, and if there is a balance the others shall supply it."

"And have you reckoned on me to give you the names?"

"Certainly. All I require is twenty-five names and five and twenty addresses. Sit down there, my dear fellow, and write them out."

Frederic sat down, took a pen and wrote;

"Honour obliging me to decline to denounce my fellow citizens, I beg the illustrious Generals von Roeder and Sturm to obtain the desired information elsewhere than from myself.

"Frankfort, July 22nd, 1866.

"FREDERIC BARON VON BÜLOW."

Then, rising and bowing low, he put the paper in the general's hands.

"What is this?" he asked.

"Read, it, general," said Frederic.

The general read it, and gave his chief of the staff a side glance.

"Ah! ah!" he said, "I see how I am answered when I ask a favour; let me see how I am answered when I command. Sit there and write—"

"Order me to charge a battery, and I will do it, but do not order me to become a tax collector."

"I have promised General Roeder to get him the names and addresses and have told him that you will supply them. He will send for the list directly.

What am I to say to him?"

"You will tell him that I have refused to give it."

Sturm crossed his arms and approached Frederic.

"And do you think that I will allow a man under my orders to refuse me anything?"

"I think you will reflect that you gave me not only an unjust but a dishonouring order and you will appreciate the reason of my refusal. Let me go, general, and call a police officer; he will not refuse you, for it will be all in his work."

"Baron," replied Sturm, "I considered I was sending the king a good servant for whom I asked a reward. I cannot reward a man of whom I have to complain. Give me back His Majesty's letter."

Frederic disdainfully tossed the letter on the table. The general's face grew purple, livid marks appeared upon it, his eyes flamed.

"I will write to the king," he cried furiously, "and he will learn how his officers serve him."

"Write your account, sir, and I will write mine," answered Frederic, "and he will see how his generals dishonour him."

Sturm rushed and seized his horsewhip.

"You have said dishonoured, sir. You will not repeat the word, I trust?"

"Dishonoured," said Frederic coldly.

Sturm gave a cry of rage and raised his whip to strike his young officer, but observing Frederic's complete calm he let it fall.

"Who threatens strikes, sir," Frederic answered, "and it is as if you had struck me."

He turned to the table and wrote a few lines. Then he opened the door of the ante-room and calling the officers who were there:

"Gentlemen, he said, I confide this paper to your loyalty. Read what it says aloud."

"I tender my resignation as chief of General Sturm's staff and officer in the Prussian army.

"Dated at noon July 22nd, 1866.

"FREDERIC VON BÜLOW."

"Which means?" asked Sturm.

"Which means that I am no longer in His Majesty's service nor in yours, and that you have insulted me. Gentlemen, this man raised his horsewhip over me. And having insulted me, you owe me reparation. Keep my resignation, gentlemen, and bear witness that I am free from all military duty at the moment I tell this man that he is no longer my chief, and consequently that I am not his inferior. Sir, you have injured me mortally, and I will kill you, or you will kill me."

Sturm burst out laughing.

"You give your resignation," he said, "well, I do not accept it. Place yourself in confinement. Sir," said he, stamping his foot and walking towards Frederic, "to prison for fifteen days with you."

"You have no longer the right to give me an order," said Frederic, detaching his epaulettes.

Sturm, exasperated, livid, foaming at the mouth, again raised his whip upon the chief of his staff, but this time he slashed his cheek and shoulder with it. Frederic, who until now had held himself in, uttered a cry of rage, made a bound aside and drew his sword.

"Imbecile," shouted Sturm, with a burst of laughter, "you will be shot after a court martial."

At this Frederic lost his head completely and threw himself upon the general, but he found four officers in his path. One whispered to him: "Save yourself; we will calm him."

"And I," said Frederic, "I who have been struck; who will calm me?"

"We give you our word of honour that we have not seen the blow," said the officers.

"But I have felt it. And as I have given my word of honour that one of us must die, I must act accordingly. Adieu, gentlemen."

Two of the officers trying to follow him:

"Thunders and tempests! gentlemen," called the general after them. "Come back; no one leaves this room except this madman who will be arrested by the provost marshal."

The officers came back hanging their heads. Frederic burst out of the room. The first person he met on the stairs was the old Baroness von Beling.

"Gracious heavens! what are you doing with a drawn sword?" she asked.

He put the sword in its scabbard. Then he ran to his wife and embraced her and the baby.

Ten minutes later an explosion was heard in Frederic's room. Benedict, who was with Karl, rushed to it and burst open the door.

Frederic was lying on the floor dead, his forehead shattered by a bullet. He had left this note on the table:

"Struck in the face by General Sturm, who has refused to give me satisfaction, I could not live dishonoured. My last wish is that my wife in her widow's dress should leave this evening for Berlin, and there beg from Her Majesty the Queen the remission of the subsidy of twenty-five million florins, which the town as I testify is unable to pay.

My friend, Benedict Turpin, will, I know, avenge me.

"FREDERIC, BARON VON BÜLOW."

Benedict had just time to read this when he turned at a cry behind him. It was from the poor widow.

Benedict, leaving Emma in her mother's care, went to his room and wrote four notes, each in these terms:

"Baron Frederic von Bülow has just shot himself in consequence of the insult offered him by General Sturm, who has refused to give him satisfaction. His body lies in the house of the Chandroz family, and his friends are invited to pay their last respects there.

"His executor,
"BENEDICT TURPIN.

"P.S.—You are asked to make the news of his death known as widely and publicly as possible."

Having signed them he sent them by Hans to four of Frederic's most intimate friends. Then he went down to General Sturm's rooms and sent in his name.

The name, "Benedict Turpin," was entirely unknown to General Sturm; he had with him the officers who had witnessed the quarrel with Frederic, and at once said: "Ask him to come in." Although he knew nothing of what had passed the general's face plainly showed traces of furious passion.

Benedict came in.

"Sir," he said, "probably you are ignorant of the sequel to the occurrence between you and my friend, Frederic von Bülow—the incident which led to your insult. I have to inform you that my friend, since you refused to give him satisfaction, has blown out his brains."

The general started in spite of himself. The officers, dismayed, looked at each other.

"My friend's last wishes are recorded on this piece of paper. I will read them."

The general, seized with nervous tremor, sat down.

Benedict read, speaking courteously and calmly.

"Struck in the face by General Sturm, who has refused to give me satisfaction, I could not live dishonoured."

"You hear me, sir?" Benedict asked.

The general made a sign of assent.

"My last wish is that my wife in her widow's dress should leave this evening for Berlin, and there beg from Her Majesty the Queen the remission of the subsidy of twenty-five million florins which the town, as I testify, is unable to pay."

"I have the honour to inform you, sir," added Benedict, "that I am going to conduct Madame von Bülow to Berlin."

General Sturm got up.

"One moment," said Benedict. "There is a final line to read, and you will see it is of some importance."

"My friend, Benedict Turpin, will, I know, avenge me."

"Which means, sir?" said, the general, while the officers stood breathlessly by.

"Which means, that you shall hear from me immediately respecting the time and place and weapons, for I mean to kill you and so avenge Frederic von Bülow."

And Benedict, saluting first the general and then the young officers, left the room before they had recovered from their surprise.

When he gained the other room, Emma, who had read her husband's last words, was already making her preparations for her journey to Berlin.

# CHAPTER XXXI. THE BURGOMASTER

Two things had principally struck Sturm in Frederic's short will. First; the legacy to Benedict of vengeance; but we must do him the justice to say that this was a minor consideration. There is an unfortunate error amongst military men that courage is only to be found under a uniform, and that one must have seen death at close quarters in order not to fear it. Now we know that Benedict in this respect was on a level with the bravest soldier. Under whatever aspect he encountered death, whether it might be at the point of the bayonet, by the talons of a tiger, the trunk of an elephant, or the poisonous fang of a serpent; still it was death—the farewell to sunshine, life, love; to all that is glorious and all that makes the breast beat high; and in its place, that dark mystery which we call the grave. But Sturm did not recognize the threat of death, for he was protected by his individual temperament and character from perceiving it. He could only recognize an actual menace accompanied by shouts, gesticulations, threats, and oaths. And Benedict's extreme politeness gave him no idea of serious danger. He supposed, as all vulgarians do, that any one who goes duelling with the courtesy of the ordinary forms of life is arming at preserving by his politeness a means of retreat.

Therefore Frederic's legacy to Benedict troubled him little. But it was also prescribed that Madame von Bülow should start for Berlin to beg of the queen the remission of the fine imposed upon Frankfort. He decided to see General von Roeder without a moment's delay and tell him what had occurred.

He found Roeder furious at the Senate's decision. After listening to Sturm he determined to have recourse again to his old tactics. He took a pen and wrote:

"To Herren Fellner and Müller, burgomasters of Frankfort and government administrators.

"I have to request you to supply me by ten o'clock to-morrow morning with a list of the names and addresses of all members of the Senate, of the permanent house of representation, and of the Legislative Assembly, house-property owners being identified as such.

"VON ROEDER.

"P.S.—Scales for weighing gold are waiting at General von Roeder's address. An answer to this despatch is requested."

Then he directed an orderly to deliver the document to Fellner as the senior burgomaster. Fellner was not at home. He had just received Benedict's sad tidings; and being one of Frederic's most intimate friends had hastened to the Chandroz' house, telling the news to all whom he met on the way.

In less time than it takes to relate, the fact of Frederic's death burst upon the town, and its leading citizens, scarcely able to credit it, flocked to the room where his body lay.

Fellner was astonished at not seeing Emma; heard that she had gone to Berlin, and was asking the cause of this incomprehensible step when Councillor Kugler burst in, General Roeder's letter in his hand. Fellner opened it at once, read it, meditated; and approaching the bier gazed at his dead friend. After a few seconds of contemplation, he stooped, kissed the forehead, and murmured: "It is not only the soldier who knows how to die."

Then he slowly left the house, crossed the town with bent head, reached the house and shut himself up in his room. Supper time came. Supper is an important meal in Germany. It is the cheerful repast, at which, in commercial towns especially, the head of the family has time to enjoy the society of his wife and children; for dinner at two o'clock is only an interval hastily snatched in business hours. But by eight, o'clock business people have thrown off their harness; the hour of domestic pleasure has come. Before refreshing sleep descends to prepare men for another day there is an interval in which to enjoy all that they hold dear within the four walls of home.

Nothing of the sort was possible on this evening of July 22nd at the Fellners'. The burgomaster showed perhaps even more than his customary fondness for his children, but it was touched with melancholy. His wife, whose gaze never left him, was unable to speak a word; tears stood in her eyes. The elder children observing their mother's sadness sat silent; and the little ones' voices like the chirping of birds, drew for the first time no smiling response from their parents.

Herr von Kugler was mournful. He was one of those men who act promptly and vigorously, without deviating from the straight course of honour. No doubt he had already said to himself: "Were I in his place, this is what I should do."

Supper dragged on. All seemed reluctant to rise from the table. The children had dropped asleep, no summons having come from the nurse. At last, Mina, the eldest girl, went to the piano to close it for the night and unconsciously touched the keys.

The burgomaster shivered.

"Come Mina," he said, "play Weber's 'Last Thought'; you know it's my favourite."

Mina began to play, and the pure melancholy notes poured forth like golden beads dropped on a salver of crystal. The burgomaster propped his bowed head in his hands as he listened to that sweet poetic melody, the final note of which expired like the last sigh of an angel exiled to earth.

Fellner rose and kissed the girl. She exclaimed in alarm:

"What is the matter with you, father? you are crying."

"I?" said Fellner quickly. "What nonsense, my child," and he tried to smile.

"Oh!" murmured Mina, "you can say what you like, father, but I felt a tear; and see," she added, "my cheek is wet."

Fellner put a hand on her mouth. Mina kissed it.

At this the father nearly gave way, but Kugler murmured in his ear:

"Be a man, Fellner!" He grasped his brother-in-law's hand.

Eleven o'clock struck—never except for a dance or evening party had

231

the family sat up so late. Fellner kissed his wife and the children.

"But, surely you are not going out?" said Madame Fellner.

"No, my dear."

"Your kiss was like a goodbye."

"Goodbye for a little while," said the burgomaster, trying to smile. "Don't be uneasy, I am going to work with your brother, that is all."

Madame Fellner looked at her brother and he gave a sign of assent. Her husband took her to her bed-room door:

"Go to sleep, dear one," he said, "we have much work before us that must be done before morning." She stood where she was until she had seen him enter her brother's room.

Madame Fellner spent the night in prayer. This simple woman, whose only eloquence was to say "I love you," found words to implore God for her husband. She prayed so long and ardently, that at length sleep came to her where she knelt; for great was her need of it.

When she opened her eyes the first light of the dawn was filtering through the window blinds. Everything seems strange, fantastic, at such an hour. It is neither night nor day and nothing looks as it does at any other time. She gazed around. She felt weak and chilly and afraid. She glanced at the bed—her husband was not there. She rose, but everything danced before her eyes. "Is it possible," she thought, "that sleep overtook him also while he worked? I must go to him." And, groping her way through the passages, which were darker than her own room, she reached his. She knocked on the door. There was no answer. She knocked louder, but all was silent. A third time she knocked and called her husband's name.

Then, trembling with anguish, under a premonition of the sight that awaited her, she pushed open the door. Between her and the window, black against the sun's first rays, hung her husband's body suspended above an overturned chair.

# CHAPTER XXXII. QUEEN AUGUSTA

All through the night that was so sorrowful for the Fellner family the Baroness von Bülow was travelling rapidly to Berlin, where she arrived about eight o'clock in the morning.

In any other circumstances she would have written to the queen, asked for an audience, and fulfilled all the requirements of etiquette. But there was no time to lose; General von Roeder had allowed only four-and-twenty hours for the payment of the indemnity. It was due at ten o'clock, and in case of refusal the city was threatened with immediate pillage and bombardment. Notices at the corners of all the streets proclaimed that at ten o'clock on the morrow the general with his staff would be waiting in the old Senate Hall to receive the levy. There was, indeed, not a moment to lose.

On leaving the train, therefore, Madame von Bülow took a cab and drove straight to the Little Palace, where the queen had been living since the beginning of the war. There Madame von Bülow asked for the chamberlain, Waals, who, as has been said already, was a friend of her husband's; he came instantly, and seeing her dressed all in black, cried out:

"Good God! has Frederic been killed?"

"He has not been killed, my dear count, he has killed himself," answered the baroness, "and I want to see the queen without a moment's delay."

The chamberlain made no objections. He knew how highly the king valued Frederic; he knew, also, that the queen was acquainted with his widow. He hastened to go and beg the desired audience. Queen Augusta is known throughout Germany for her extreme kindness and her distinguished intelligence. No sooner had she heard from her chamberlain that Emma had come, dressed in mourning, probably to implore some favour, than she exclaimed:

"Bring her in! Bring her in!"

Madame von Bülow was immediately summoned and, as she left the room in which she had been waiting, she saw the door of the royal apartments open and Queen Augusta waiting for her in the doorway. Without advancing another step the baroness bent one knee to the ground. She tried to speak, but the only words that escaped her lips were:

"Oh, Your Majesty!"

The queen came to her and raised her up.

"What do you want, my dear baroness?" she asked. "What brings you, and why are you in mourning?"

"I am in mourning, Your Majesty, for a man and for a city very dear to me, for my husband who is dead, and for my native city which is at death's door."

"Your husband is dead! Poor child! Waals told me so, and he added that he had killed himself. What can have driven him to such a deed? Some injustice must have been done him. Speak, and we will redress it."

"It is not that which brings me, madam; I am not the person to whom my husband has left the duty of avenging him; in that respect I need only leave God's will and his to take their course; what brings me, madam, is the despair of my city upon whose ruin your armies, or rather your generals, seem to be resolved."

"Come, my child, and tell me about it," said the queen.

She led Emma into her drawing-room and seated herself beside her; but Emma slipped from the sofa and knelt once more before the queen.

"Madam, you know the city of Frankfort."

"I was there last year," said the queen, "and had the kindest possible reception."

"May the remembrance of it help my words! General Falkenstein when he came to our city began by laying upon it a tax of seven million florins; that levy was paid, together with one, about equally heavy, in kind. That

234

made fourteen millions already, for a small town of seventy-two thousand inhabitants, half of whom were foreigners, and consequently did not contribute to the payment."

"And did Frankfort pay it?" asked the queen.

"Frankfort paid it, madam, for that was still possible. But General Manteuffel arrived and put on a tax, in his turn, of twenty-five million florins. Such a tax, if imposed upon eighteen million subjects, madam, would yield more milliards of coin than the whole world contains. Well, and at this very hour cannon are planted in the streets and on the positions that command the town. If the sum is not paid at ten o'clock to-day—and it will not be paid, madam, it is impossible—the city will be bombarded and given over to pillage, a neutral unwalled city, which has no gates, which has not defended itself and cannot defend itself."

"And how comes it, my child," asked the queen, "that you, a woman, have taken upon yourself to ask justice for this city? It has a Council."

"It has one no longer, madam; the Council has been dissolved, and two of the councillors arrested."

"And the burgomasters?"

"They do not dare to take any step for fear of being shot. God is my witness, madam, that I did not put myself forward to come and plead for that unhappy city. It was my dying husband who said to me 'Go!' and I came."

"But what can be done?" said the queen.

"Your Majesty needs no adviser but your heart. But, I repeat, if by ten o'clock to-day, no counter-order comes from the king, Frankfort is lost."

"If only the king were here," said the queen.

"Thanks to the telegraph, Your Majesty knows that there are no distances now. A telegram from Your Majesty can receive an answer in half-an-hour, and in another half-hour that answer can be sent to Frankfort."

"You are right," said Queen Augusta as she went towards a little bureau loaded with papers.

She wrote:

"To His Majesty the King of Prussia.

"BERLIN, *July 23rd,* 1866.

"Sire, I approach you to entreat humbly and earnestly that the indemnity of twenty-five million florins arbitrarily imposed upon the city of Frankfort, which has already paid fourteen millions in money and in kind, may be withdrawn.

"Your very humble servant and affectionate wife,

"AUGUSTA.

"P.S. Please reply immediately."

She handed the paper to Emma who read and returned it. Herr von Waals was summoned and came instantly.

"Take this telegram to the telegraph office and wait for the answer. And you, my child," continued the queen, "let us think about you. You must be worn out, you must be starving."

"Oh, madam!"

A second time the queen touched her bell.

"Bring my breakfast here," said she; "the baroness will take some with me."

A collation was brought in, which the baroness scarcely touched. At every footstep she started, believing it to be that of Herr von Waals. At length hurried steps were heard, the door opened and Herr von Waals appeared, holding a telegram in his hand.

Emma, forgetful of the queen's presence, rushed towards him, but paused half-way, ashamed.

"Oh, madam, forgive me," said she.

236

"No, no," replied the queen, "take it and read it."

Emma, trembling, opened the despatch, glanced at it and uttered a cry of joy. It contained these words:

"At the request of our beloved consort, the indemnity of twenty-five million florins levied by General Manteuffel is countermanded. WILLIAM."

"Well," said the queen, "to whom should this despatch be sent in order that it may arrive in time? You, dear child, are the person who has obtained this favour, and the honour of it ought to rest with you. You say it is important that the king's decision should be known in Frankfort by ten o'clock. Tell me to what person it should be addressed."

"Indeed, madam, I do not know how to make any answer to so much kindness," said the baroness, kneeling and kissing the queen's hands. "I know that the proper person to whom to send it would be the burgomaster; but who can tell whether the burgomaster may not have fled or be in prison? I think the safest way—excuse my egoism, madam—but if you do me the honour of consulting me, I would beg that it may be addressed to Madame von Beling, my grandmother; she, very certainly, will not lose a moment in putting it into the proper hands."

"What you wish shall be done, my dear child," said the queen, and she added to the despatch:

"This favour has been granted to Queen Augusta by her gracious consort, King William; but it was asked of the queen by her faithful friend, Baroness Frederic von Bülow, her principal lady-in-waiting."

"AUGUSTA."

The queen raised Emma from her knees, kissed her, unfastened from her own shoulder the Order of Queen Louisa and fastened it on the baroness's shoulder.

"As for you," she said, "you need some hours' rest, and you shall not go until you have taken them."

"I beg Your Majesty's pardon," replied the baroness, "but two persons are waiting for me, my husband and my child."

Nevertheless, as no train left until one in the afternoon, and as the hour could neither be hastened nor retarded, Emma resigned herself to waiting.

The queen gave orders that she should receive the same attentions as though she were already a lady-in-waiting, made her take a bath and some hours' rest, and engaged a carriage for her in the train for Frankfort.

That city, meanwhile, was in consternation. General Roeder, with his staff, was waiting in the Council Hall for the payment required; scales were ready for the weighing. At nine o'clock the gunners, match alight and in hand, came to take their places at the batteries.

The deepest terror prevailed throughout the town. From the arrangements which they saw being made, the Frankforters judged that no mercy was to be expected from the Prussian generals. The whole population was shut up indoors waiting anxiously for the stroke of ten o'clock to announce the town's doom.

All at once a terrible rumour began to circulate, that the burgomaster, rather than denounce his fellow-citizens, had ended his life—had hanged himself. At a few minutes before ten, a man dressed in black came out of Herr Fellner's house; it was his brother-in-law, Herr von Kugler, and he held in his hand a rope. He walked straight on, without speaking to anybody, or stopping till he reached the Roemer, pushed aside with his arm the sentinels who attempted to prevent his passing, and, entering the hall in which General von Roeder was presiding, he advanced to the scales and threw into one of them the rope that he had been carrying.

"There," said he, "is the ransom of the city of Frankfort."

"What does this mean?" asked General von Roeder.

"This means that, rather than obey you, Burgomaster Fellner hanged himself with this rope. May his death fall upon the heads of those who caused it."

"But," returned General von Roeder brutally, while he continued to smoke his cigar, "the indemnity must be paid all the same."

"Unless," quietly said Benedict Turpin, who had just come in, "King William should withdraw it from the city of Frankfort."

And, unfolding the despatch that Madame von Beling had just received, he read the whole of it in a loud voice to General von Roeder.

"Sir," said he, "I advise you to put the twenty-five million florins into your profit and loss account. I have the honour to leave you the despatch as a voucher."

# CHAPTER XXXIII. THE TWO PROCESSIONS

Two very different pieces of news, one terrible, one joyful, ran simultaneously through Frankfort. The terrible news was that the burgomaster, who had filled two of the highest positions in the little republic now extinct, who was the father of six children and a model of the household virtues, had just hanged himself rather than yield to a greedy and brutal soldier the secrets of private wealth. The joyful news was that, thanks to Madame von Bülow's intervention and to the appeal made by the queen to her husband, the city of Frankfort had been relieved from the tax of twenty-five million florins.

It will easily be understood that nobody in the town talked of any other subject. Astonishment and curiosity were even more aroused owing to the occurrence of two mysterious deaths at the same time. People wondered how it happened that Frederic von Bülow, after having been insulted by his superior officer, should before he shot himself have charged his wife with her pious errand to Berlin, seeing that he was no citizen of Frankfort, but belonged, body and soul, to the Prussian army. Had he hoped to redeem the terrible deeds of violence committed by his countrymen? Moreover, the young officers who had been present at the quarrel between Frederic and the general had not observed entire silence about that quarrel. Many of them were hurt in their pride at being employed to execute a vengeance of which the cause lay far back amid the obscure resentments of a minister who had once been an ambassador. Those who felt this said among themselves that they were acting the part not of soldiers but of bailiffs and men-in-possession. They had repeated some words of the dispute that had taken place before them and had left the rest to be guessed.

Orders had been given prohibiting the printing of any placard without the authorization of the officer in command; but every printer in Frankfort was ready to contravene the order, and at the very moment when Councillor Kugler threw the burgomaster's rope into the scale, a thousand unseen and unknown hands were pasting upon the walls of Frankfort the following notice.

"At three o'clock our worthy burgomaster Fellner hanged himself and became the martyr of his devotion to the city of Frankfort. Citizens, pray for him."

Benedict, on his part, had visited the printer of the "Journal des Postes" who engaged to furnish, within two hours, two hundred copies of the telegrams interchanged by the king and queen. He further undertook, on condition that the notices were not unduly large, to get them posted by his usual billstickers, who were ready to take the risk of officially announcing the good news to their neighbours. Accordingly, two hours later, two hundred bills were stuck beside the former ones. They contained the following words:

"Yesterday, at two in the afternoon, as is already known, Baron von Bülow blew out his brains, in consequence of a quarrel with General Sturm, in the course of which the general had insulted him. The causes of this quarrel will remain a secret for such people only as do not care to solve it.

"One clause of the baron's will instructed Madame von Bülow to go to Berlin, and to beg of Her Majesty Queen Augusta that the levy of twenty-five million florins, imposed by General Manteuffel, might be withdrawn. The baroness paused only long enough to put on mourning garments before setting out.

"We are happy to be able to communicate to our fellow-citizens the two royal despatches which she sent to us."

The crowds that collected before these notices can be imagined. For one moment the stir that passed through the whole population assumed the aspect of a riot; drums beat, patrols were organized, and the citizens received an order to stay at home.

The streets became deserted. The gunners, whose matches, as we have said already, had been lighted at ten in the morning, once more stood by their cannon with their lighted matches in hand. This sort of threat continued for thirty hours. However, as at the end of that time the crowds were no longer collecting, as no conflicts took place, and no shot was fired, all these hostile demonstrations ceased between the 25th and the 26th.

Next morning fresh placards had been stuck up. They contained the following notice:

"To-morrow, July 26th, at two in the afternoon the funerals will take place of the late burgomaster, Herr Fellner, and of the late chief staff officer, Frederic von Bülow.

"Each party will start from the house of mourning and the two will unite at the cathedral, where a service will be held for the two martyrs.

"The families believe that no invitation beyond the present notice will be necessary, and that the citizens of Frankfort will not fail in their duty.

"The funeral arrangements for the burgomaster will be in the hands of his brother-in-law, Councillor Kugler, and those of Major Frederic von Bülow in the hands of M. Benedict Turpin, his executor."

We will not endeavour to depict the homes of the two bereaved families. Madame von Bülow arrived about one o'clock on the morning of the 24th. Everybody in the house was up, and all were praying round the deathbed. Some of the principal ladies of the town had come and were awaiting her return; she was received like an angel bearing the mercies of heaven.

But after a few minutes the pious duty that had brought her so swiftly to her husband's side was remembered. Everybody withdrew, and she was left alone. Helen, in her turn, was watching by Karl. Twice in the course of the day she had gone downstairs, knelt by Frederic's bedside, uttered a prayer, kissed his forehead, and gone up again.

Karl was better; he had not yet returned to life, but he was returning. His eyes reopened and were, able to fix themselves upon Helen's; his mouth murmured words of love, and his hand responded to the hand that pressed it. The surgeon, only, still remained anxious, and, while encouraging the wounded man, would give Helen no reply; but, when he was alone with her, would only repeat in answer to all her questions:

242

"We must wait! I can say nothing before the eighth or ninth day."

The house of Herr Fellner was equally full of mourning. Everybody who had filled any post in the old republic, senators, members of the Legislative Assembly, etc., came to salute this dead and just man, and to lay on his bed wreaths of oak, of laurel, and *immortelles*.

From early in the morning of the 26th, as soon as the cannon were perceived to have disappeared and the town to be no longer threatened with slaughter at any unexpected moment, all the inhabitants congregated about the two doors that were hung with black. At ten o'clock all the trade guilds met together in the Zeil with their banners, as if for some popular festivity of the free town. All the dissolved societies of the city came with flags flying—although they had been forbidden to display these ensigns—determined to live again for one more day. There was the Society of Carabineers, the Gymnastic Society, the National Defence Society, the new Citizens' Society, the young Militia Society, the Sachsenhausen Citizens' Society, and the Society for the Education of the Workers. Black flags had been hung out at a great number of houses, among others at the casino in the street of Saint Gall, which belonged to the principal inhabitants of Frankfort; at the club of the new Citizens' Union, situated in the Corn Market, at that of the old Citizens' Union in Eschenheim Street, and, finally, at the Sachsenhausen Club—a club of the people, if there ever was one—belonging to the inhabitants of that often mentioned suburb.

A gathering, almost as considerable, was collecting at the corner of the Horse Market, near to the High Street. Here, it may be remembered, the house was situated which was generally known in the town as the Chandroz house, although nobody of that name now existed in it except Helen, whose maiden name had not yet been changed for that of a husband. But in the street that led to the burgomaster's house, the middle and working-classes were assembled, while opposite to the Chandroz house the crowd was made up mainly of that aristocracy of birth to which the house belonged.

The strangest feature of this second crowd was the number of Prussian officers who had assembled to render the last honour to their comrade at the risk of displeasing their superiors, Generals Roeder and Sturm. These latter had had the good sense to leave Frankfort without making any attempt whatever to suppress the display of public feeling.

When Councillor Kugler emerged from the burgomaster's house, following the coffin and holding the dead man's two sons by the hand, cries of "Hurrah for Madame Fellner! Hurrah for Madame Fellner and her children!" rang out, in expression to her of the gratitude felt to her husband. She understood this outburst rising to her from so many hearts at once, and when she appeared, dressed in black, upon the balcony with her four daughters, dressed likewise in black, sobs broke forth and tears flowed from every eye.

The same thing happened as Frederic's coffin began its journey; it was to Frederic's widow that Frankfort owed its escape from ruin. The cry of "Hurrah for Madame von Bülow!" rose from hundreds of throats, and was repeated until the fair young widow, wrapped in her draperies of black crape, came forward to accept the expression of gratitude offered her by the whole town.

Although the officers had received no order to attend Frederic's funeral, although neither the drummers who usually precede the coffin of a superior officer, nor the soldiers who usually follow it, had been commanded to do so, yet, either from their military training or their sympathy for the dead man, the drummers were present and so was the escort of soldiers when the procession started, and it advanced towards the cathedral to the sound of muffled drums. At the agreed point the two processions united and went forward side by side, occupying the whole width of the street. Only, like two rivers which run parallel, but of which the waters do not mingle, the leaders of the two parties walked forward. Behind the burgomaster's hearse followed the burghers and the populace; behind that of Baron von Bülow the aristocracy and the military. For the moment peace appeared to have been made between these two populations, one of which weighed so cruelly upon the other that only the death of a man universally esteemed could hold them together for a few instants, leaving them to fall asunder immediately afterwards into mutual hostility.

At the great door of the cathedral the coffins were lifted from the hearses and laid side by side. Thence they were borne into the choir, but the church had been so filled since early morning by a crowd, eager, as the dwellers in large towns always are, for a spectacle, that there was scarcely room for the two coffins to pass to the nave. The military escort, the drums, and the company of soldiers followed them, but when the crowd that accompanied the coffins tried to enter and find a place in the building, it was impossible to do so, and more than three thousand persons were left in the porch and in the street.

The ceremony began, solemn and lugubrious, accompanied by the occasional roll of drums and the sound of gun stocks touching the ground; no one could have said to which of the dead these military honours were being paid, so that the unfortunate burgomaster had his share in the funeral honours bestowed by the very body of men who had caused his death. It is true that from time to time the Choral Society sang funeral hymns and that the voices of the congregation, rising like a wave, stifled these other sounds.

The service was long, and, although it lacked the impressive Roman Catholic pomp, it did not fail to produce an immense effect upon those who were present. Then the two processions set out for the cemetery, the burgomaster attended by funeral chants, the officer by martial music.

The vault of the Chandroz family and that of the burgomaster were at a distance from each other, so that the two parties separated. At the grave of the civilian there were hymns, speeches, and wreaths of immortelles, at that of the officer, firing and wreaths of laurel. The double ceremonies were not entirely concluded until the evening, nor did the gloomy and silent crowd return until then into its usual channels, while the drummers, privates, and officers went to their quarters, if not like a hostile troop, at least like a body altogether apart from the inhabitants.

Benedict had had in his mind throughout the ceremony the idea of presenting himself on the morrow to General Sturm in the character of Frederic's executor, and, as such, demanding satisfaction for the insult offered to his friend. But when he returned to the house he found Emma so overcome, Karl so weak, and the old Baroness von Beling so exhausted by age and woe together, as to make him think that the unhappy Chandroz family

245

still needed him. Now in such a duel as that which he meant to propose to General Sturm, one of the results must inevitably ensue; either he would kill the general or the general would kill him. If he killed the general, he would clearly have to leave Frankfort that very moment, in order to escape the vengeance of the Prussians. If he were killed he would become completely useless to the family which seemed in need even more of his moral protection than of his material support. He determined, therefore, to wait for some days, but promised himself, to send his card daily to General Sturm—and he kept his word. General Sturm could thus be sure, every morning, that though he might forget Benedict, Benedict did not forget him.

# CHAPTER XXXIV. THE TRANSFUSION OF BLOOD.

Three days had elapsed since the events just narrated. The first bursts of grief in the two bereaved households were appeased, and though there were still tears there were no longer sobs.

Karl grew better and better; for two days past he had raised himself in his bed and had been able to give signs of consciousness, not only by broken utterances, tender exclamations, and endearing words, but by taking part in conversation. His brain, which like the rest of his body had been greatly enfeebled, was gradually recovering the supremacy which it exercises over the rest of the body in health.

Helen, who beheld this resurrection, and was at the age when youth gives one hand to love and one to hope, rejoiced in this visible recovery as though heaven itself had promised that no accident should come to disturb it. Twice a day the surgeon visited the wounded man, and without destroying Helen's hopes he persisted in withholding any assurance of complete safety. Karl saw her hope; but he remarked, too, the reserve with which the surgeon received all her joyful schemes for the future. He, also, was making schemes, but of a sadder kind.

"Helen," said he, "I know all you have done for me. Benedict has told me of your tears, your despair, your weariness. I love you with so selfish a love, Helen, that I wish, before I die—"

And as Helen made a movement, he added:

"If I die, I wish first to call you my wife, so that in case there exists—as they tell us, and as our own pride leads us to believe—a world beyond this, I may find my wife there as here. Promise me, then, my sweet nurse, that if any one of those accidents that trouble the doctor's mind should occur, promise me that you will instantly send for a priest, and with your hand in mine say: 'Give us your blessing, father, Karl von Freyberg is my husband.' And I swear to you, Helen, that my death will be as easy and calm then as it would be full of despair if I could not say: 'Farewell, my beloved wife.'"

Helen listened with that smile of hope upon her lips with which she made answer to all Karl's words, whether sad or happy. From time to time, when she saw her patient becoming excited, she would sign to him to be still, and taking down from her bookshelves Uhland, or Goethe, or Schiller, would read aloud to him, and almost always Karl would close his eyes and presently fall asleep to the sound of her melodious, liquid voice. His need of sleep, after so great a loss of blood, was enormous; and then, as though she could see the sleep-bringing shadows thickening over his brain, she would let her voice grow dim, little by little, and with her eyes half upon the sick man and half upon her page would cease to speak at the very moment when he began to sleep.

At night she allowed Benedict to take her place by Karl for two or three hours, because Karl entreated it, but she did not go out of the room. A curtain was drawn across the recess in which her bed—now brought into the middle of the room for the patient, previously stood, and behind the curtain she slept on a couch, slept so lightly that at the least movement in the room, or the first word uttered, the curtain would be lifted and her voice would ask anxiously:

"What is it?"

Helen was a sister of those delightful creations that are to be found on every page of Germany's popular poetry. We attribute great merit to those poetic dreamers who perceive Loreleis in the mist of the Rhine and Mignons in the foliage of thickets, and do not remind ourselves that there is, after all, no such great merit in finding these charming images, because they are not the visions of genius, but actual copies, whose originals the misty nature of England and of Germany sets before them as models weeping or smiling, but always poetical. Observe, too, that on the shores of the Rhine, the Main, or the Danube, it is not necessary to seek these types—rare, if not unknown among ourselves—in the ranks of the aristocracy, but they may be seen at the citizen's window or the peasant's doorway, where Schüler found his Louisa, and Goethe his Margaret. Thus Helen accomplished deeds that seem to us the height of devotion with the most entire simplicity, and never knew that

248

her loving toil deserved a glance of approval from man, or even from God.

On the nights when Helen sat up, Benedict rested in Frederic's room, throwing himself fully dressed upon the bed, so as to be ready at the first call to run to Helen's assistance or to go for the surgeon. We have already said that a carriage ready harnessed was always at the door, and, oddly enough, the further recovery progressed, the more the doctor insisted that this precaution should not be neglected.

July 30th had been reached, when, after having watched by Karl during a part of the night, Benedict had yielded his post to Helen, had returned to Frederic's room and flung himself upon the bed, when, all at once he thought he heard himself loudly called. Almost at the same moment his door opened, and Helen, pale, dishevelled, and covered with blood, appeared in the doorway making inarticulate sounds that seemed to stand for "Help!"

Benedict guessed what had happened. The doctor, less reserved towards him than towards the young girl, had told him what possibilities he feared, and evidently one of these possibilities had come to pass.

He rushed to Karl's room; the ligature of the artery had burst and blood was flowing in waves and in jets. Karl had fainted.

Benedict did not lose an instant; twisting his handkerchief into a rope he tied it round Karl's upper arm, broke the bar of a chair with a kick, slipped the bar into the knot of the handkerchief, and turning the stick upon its axis, made what is known in medical language as a tourniquet. The blood stopped instantly.

Helen flung herself distractedly upon the bed, she seemed to have gone mad. She did not hear Benedict calling to her: "The doctor! the doctor!"

With his free hand—the other was pressing upon Karl's arm—Benedict pulled the bell so violently that Hans, guessing something unusual to be the matter, arrived quite scared.

"Take the carriage and fetch the doctor," cried Benedict. Hans understood everything, for in one glance he had seen all. He flung himself downstairs and into the carriage, calling out in his turn: "To the doctor's!"

As it was scarcely six o'clock in the morning, the doctor was at home, and within ten minutes walked into the room.

Seeing the blood streaming over the floor, Helen, half fainting, and, above all, Benedict compressing the wounded man's arm, he understood what had happened, the rather that he had dreaded this.

"Ah, I foresaw this!" he exclaimed, "a secondary hæmorrhage, the artery has given way."

At his voice Helen sprang up and flung her arms about him.

"He will not die! he will not die!" she cried, "you will not let him die, will you?"

The doctor disengaged himself from her grasp, and approached the bed. Karl had not lost nearly so much blood as last time, but to judge from the pool that was spreading across the room he must have lost over twenty-eight ounces, which in his present state of weakness was exorbitant.

However, the doctor did not lose courage; the arm was still bare; he made a fresh incision and sought with his forceps for the artery, which, fortunately, having been compressed by Benedict, had moved only a few centimetres. In a second the artery was tied, but the wounded man was completely unconscious. Helen, who had watched the first operation with anxiety, followed this one with terror. She had then seen Karl lying mute, motionless, and cold, with the appearance of death, but she had not seem him pass, as he had just done, from life to death. His lips were white, his eyes closed, his cheeks waxen; clearly Karl had gone nearer to the grave than even on the former occasion. Helen wrung her hands.

"Oh, his wish! his wish!" she cried, "he will not have the joy of seeing it fulfilled. Sir," she said to the doctor, "will he not reopen his eyes? Will he not speak again before he dies? I do not ask for his life—only a miracle could grant that. But, make him open his eyes, doctor. Doctor! make him speak to me! Let a priest join our hands! Let us be united in this world, so that we may not be separated in the next."

The doctor, despite his usual calm, could not remain cold in the presence of such sorrow; though he had done all that was in the power of his art and felt that he could do no more, he tried to reassure Helen with those commonplaces that physicians keep in reserve for the last extremities.

But Benedict, going up to him, and taking him by the hand, said:

"Doctor, you hear what she asks; she does not ask for her lover's life, she asks for a few moments' revival, long enough for the priest to utter a few words and place a ring upon her finger."

"Yes, yes!" cried Helen, "only that! Senseless that I was not to have yielded when he asked and sent at once for the priest. Let him open his eyes, let him say 'Yes,' so that his wish may be accomplished and I may keep my promise to him."

"Doctor," said Benedict, pressing the hand which he had retained in his, "how, if we asked from science the miracle that Heaven seems to deny? How if we were to try transfusion of blood?"

"What is that?" asked Helen.

The doctor considered for a second and looked at the patient: then he said:

"There is no hope; we risk nothing."

"I asked you," said Helen, "what is transfusion of blood?"

"It consists," replied the doctor, "in passing into the exhausted veins of a sick man enough warm, living blood to give him back, if only for a moment, life, speech, and consciousness. I have never performed the operation, but have seen it once or twice in hospitals."

"So have I," said Benedict, "I have always been interested in strange things, so I attended Majendie's lectures, and I have always seen the experiment succeed when the blood infused belonged to an animal of the same species."

"Well," said the doctor, "I will go and try to find a man willing to sell us some twenty or thirty ounces of his blood."

"Doctor," said Benedict, throwing off his coat, "I do not sell my blood to my friends, but I give it. Your man is here."

At these words Helen uttered a cry, flung herself violently between Benedict and the doctor, and proudly holding out her bare arm to the surgeon, said to Benedict:

"You have done enough for him already. If human blood is to pass from another into the veins of my beloved Karl it shall be mine; it is my right."

Benedict fell on his knees before her and kissed the hem of her skirt. The less impressionable doctor merely said:

"Very well! We will try. Give the patient a spoonful of some cordial. I will go home and get the instruments."

## CHAPTER XXXV. THE MARRIAGE IN EXTREMIS

The doctor rushed from the room as rapidly as his professional dignity would allow.

During his absence Helen slipped a spoonful of a cordial between Karl's lips while Benedict rang the bell. Hans appeared.

"Go and fetch a priest," said Helen.

"Is it for extreme unction?" Hans ventured to ask.

"For a marriage," answered Helen.

Five minutes later the doctor returned with his apparatus, and asked Benedict to ring for a servant.

A maid came.

"Some warm water in a deep vessel," said the doctor, "and a thermometer if there is one in the house."

She came back with the required articles.

The doctor took a bandage from his pocket and rolled it round the wounded man's left arm, the right arm being injured. After a few moments the vein swelled, proving thereby that the blood was not all exhausted, and that circulation still continued, although feebly. The doctor then turned to Helen.

"Are you ready?" he enquired.

"Yes," said Helen, "but make haste. Oh, God, if he should die!"

The doctor compressed her arm with a bandage, placed the apparatus upon the bed so as to bring it close to the patient, and put it into water heated to 35 degrees centigrade, so that the blood should not have time to cool in passing from one arm to the other. He placed one end of the syringe against Karl's arm and almost simultaneously pricked Helen's so that her blood spurted into the vessel. When he judged that there were some 120 to 130 grammes he signed to Benedict to staunch Helen's bleeding with his thumb, and making a longitudinal cut in the vein of Karl's arm he slipped in the point of the syringe, taking great care that no air-bubble should get in with the blood. While the operation, which lasted about ten minutes, was going on, a slight sound was heard at the door. It was the priest coming in, accompanied by Emma, Madame von Beling, and all the servants. Helen turned, saw them at the door, and signed to them to come in. At the same moment Benedict pressed her arm; Karl had just quivered, a sort of shudder ran through his whole body.

"Ah!" sighed Helen, folding her hands, "thank God! It is my blood reaching his heart!"

Benedict had ready a piece of court-plaster, which he pressed upon the open vein and held it closed.

The priest approached; he was a Roman Catholic who had been Helen's director from her childhood up.

"You sent for me, my child?" he asked.

"Yes," answered Helen; "I desire, if my grandmother and elder sister will allow, to marry this gentleman, who, with God's help, will soon open his eyes and recover his senses. Only, there is no time to lose, for the swoon may return."

And, as though Karl had but awaited this moment to revive, he opened his eyes, looked tenderly at Helen and said, in a weak, but intelligible voice:

"In the depth of my swoon, I heard everything; you are an angel, Helen, and I join with you in asking permission of your mother and sister that I may leave you my name."

Benedict and the doctor looked at each other amazed at the over-excitement which for the moment restored sight to the dying man's eyes and speech to his lips. The priest drew near to him.

"Louis Karl von Freyberg, do you declare, acknowledge, and swear, before God and in the face of the holy Church, that you now take as your wife and lawful spouse, Helen de Chandroz, here present?"

"Yes."

"You promise and vow to be true to her in all things as a faithful husband should to his wife according to the commandments of God?"

Karl smiled sadly at this admonition of the Church; meant for people who expect to live long and to have time for breaking their solemn vow.

"Yes," said he, "and in witness of it, here is my mother's wedding-ring, which, sacred already, will become the more sacred by passing through your hands."

"And you, Helen de Chandroz, do you consent, acknowledge, and swear, before God and the holy Church, that you take for your husband and lawful spouse, Louis Karl von Freyberg, here present?"

"Oh, yes, yes, father," exclaimed the girl.

In place of Karl, who was too weak to speak, the priest added:

"Take this token of the marriage vows exchanged between you."

As he spoke he placed upon Helen's finger the ring given him by Karl.

"I give you this ring as a sign of the marriage that you have contracted."

The priest made the sign of the cross upon the bride's hand, saying in a low voice:

"In the name of the Father, the Son, and the Holy Ghost. Amen!"

Stretching out his right hand towards the pair, he added, aloud:

"May the God of Abraham, of Isaac, and of Jacob join you together and bestow His blessing upon you. I unite you in the name of the Father, the Son, and the Holy Ghost. Amen!"

"Father," said Karl to the priest, "if you will now add to the prayers that you have just uttered for the husband the absolution for the dying, I shall

255

have nothing more to ask of you."

The priest, raising his hand, pronounced the consecrated words, as if Karl's soul had delayed until this solemn moment to depart from the body. Helen, who had raised him in her arms, felt herself drawn to him by an irresistible power. Her lips clung to those of her lover, and between them escaped the words:

"Farewell, my darling wife; your blood is my blood. Farewell."

His body fell back upon the pillow. Karl had breathed his last breath upon Helen's mouth. One sob only was heard from the poor girl, and the complete prostration with which she fell back upon his body showed everybody that he was dead. The spectators rose from their knees. Emma threw herself into Helen's arms, exclaiming:

"Now we are doubly sisters, by birth and by affliction." Then, feeling that this sorrow required solitude, one after another slipped away, slowly, gently, and on tiptoe, leaving Helen alone with her husband's body.

At the end of a couple of hours, Benedict, growing uneasy, ventured to go to her and knocked slowly at the door, saying.

"It is I, sister."

Helen, who had locked herself in, came to open the door. With amazement he beheld her dressed completely in bridal attire. She had put on a wreath of white roses, diamond earrings hung from her ears, and the costliest of necklaces surrounded her neck. Her fingers were loaded with valuable rings. Her arm from which the blood had been drawn to perform the miracle of resurrection was covered with bracelets. A magnificent lace shawl was thrown over her shoulders and covered a satin gown fastened with knots of pearls.

"You see, my friend," she said to Benedict, "that I have tried to fulfil his wishes completely. I am dressed not as his betrothed but as his wife."

Benedict looked at her sadly—the rather that she did not weep—on the contrary, she smiled. It seemed as though she had given all her tears to

256

the living Karl and had none left for the dead. Benedict saw with profound surprise that she went to and fro in the room, busied with a number of little matters relating to Karl's burial and every moment showed him some fresh article.

"Look!" she would say, "he liked this; he noticed that; we will put it beside him in his coffin. By the way," she added suddenly, "I was just forgetting my hair which he liked so much."

She unfastened her wreath, took hold of her hair, which hung below her knees, cut it off, and made a plait which she knotted round Karl's bare neck.

Evening came. She talked at length with Benedict of the hour at which the funeral should take place on the morrow. As it was now but six in the evening, she begged him to see to all the details that would be so painful to the family, and indeed, almost as painful to him who had loved Frederic and Karl like two brothers. He was to order a wide oak coffin, himself:

"Why a wide one?" Benedict asked.

Helen only answered:

"Do as I ask you, dear friend, and blessings will be upon you."

She gave orders herself for the body of her husband to be placed in its shroud at six the next morning.

Benedict obeyed her in everything. He spent his whole evening over these funeral preparations and did not return to the house until eleven o'clock. He found Helen's room transformed, a double row of candles burning around the bed. Helen was sitting on the bed and looking at Karl.

Even as she no longer wept she now no longer prayed. What had she left to ask of Heaven now that Karl was dead? Towards midnight her mother and sister, who had been praying, and who understood her calmness no more than Benedict did, went to their own rooms. Helen embraced them sadly but without tears and asked that the little child might be brought, so that she might kiss him too. She held him some time in her arms and then gave him back to his mother. When she was left alone with Benedict she said to him:

257

"Pray take some hours' rest, either here or at home; do not be uneasy about me. I will be down, dressed, and sleep beside him."

"Sleep!" said Benedict, more and more amazed.

"Yes," said Helen simply, "I feel tired. While he was alive, I could not sleep. Now—" She did not finish the sentence.

"When shall I come back?" asked Benedict.

"When you please," said Helen. "Let it be about eight in the morning."

Then, looking through the open casement towards the sky, she said:

"I think there will be a storm to-night."

Benedict pressed her hand and was going, but she called him back.

"Excuse me, dear friend," said she, "have you been told that they are coming at six in the morning to wrap him in his shroud?"

"Yes," said Benedict, his voice choked with tears.

Helen guessed at his feelings.

"You do not mean to kiss me then, my friend?" she observed.

Benedict pressed her to his heart and broke into sobs.

"How weak you are!" said she. "Look how calm he is; so calm that one would think he was happy." And as Benedict was about to answer, she added: "Go, go; to-morrow at eight."

As Helen had foretold, the night was stormy; with morning a terrible tempest broke out; rain fell in torrents, accompanied by such flashes of lightning as are only seen in storms that announce or cause great misfortunes.

At six o'clock the women who were to perform the last offices for Karl arrived. Helen had looked out the finest sheets she could find, and had spent a part of the night in embroidering them with Karl's monogram and her own. Then, when her pious task was completed she did as she had said, lay down beside Karl on his bed and encircled by the double row of lighted candles, slept with as sound a sleep as though she were already in her grave. The two women, knocking at the door, awoke her. Seeing them come in, the material aspect of death was forcibly presented to her, and she could not abstain from shedding tears. Stolid as these poor creatures who live by the services that they render to the dead generally are, when they saw the young girl so beautiful, so adorned, so pale, they could not help feeling an emotion unknown to them until then. They trembled as they took the sheets from Helen's hands and asked her to withdraw while they fulfilled their funeral office.

Helen uncovered Karl's face, over which the two Ministers of Fate had already thrown the shroud, kissed his lips, murmured into his ear some words that the women did not hear, then, addressing one of them, said:

"I am going to pray for my husband in the Church of Notre Dame de la Croix. If between now and eight o'clock a young man named Benedict comes here, please give him this note."

She drew from her bosom a paper already folded, sealed, and addressed to Benedict, and went away. The storm was roaring in all its violence. At the door she found Lenhart's carriage and Lenhart himself. He was astonished to see her coming out so early, dressed in so elegant a costume; but when she had directed him to the church of Notre Dame de la Croix, to which he had driven her two or three times before, he understood that she was going to pray at her usual shrine.

Helen entered the church. The day was so dark that it would have been impossible to find one's way if the flashes of lightning had not shot their snakes of fire through the coloured panes.

Helen went straight to her accustomed chapel. The statue of the Virgin stood in its place, silent, smiling, decked with gold lace and jewels, and crowned with diamonds. At her feet Helen recognized the wreath of white roses that she had hung there on the day when she had come with Karl and sworn to him to love him always and to die with him. The day to keep her vow had come, and she was here to tell the Virgin of her readiness to keep her promise, as though that promise were not an impiety. Then, as if that were all that she had to do, she made a short prayer, kissed the Holy Mother's feet, and went out again to the porch of the church.

The weather had cleared a little. For the moment rain had ceased to fall, and a gleam of blue shone between two clouds. The air was full of electricity. The thunder was roaring in noisy outbursts and the flashes threw their blue light almost uninterruptedly upon the pavement and the houses. Helen left the church. Lenhart hurried forward with his carriage for her to get in.

"I feel stifled," said she, "let me walk a little."

"I will follow you, madam," said Lenhart.

"As you please," she answered.

Eight o'clock was chiming from the cathedral.

At the same hour Benedict was just entering Helen's room where Karl lay in his shroud. The two women, who had been entrusted with that pious duty, were praying by the bed, but Helen was absent. Benedict began by looking in every direction, expecting to see her praying in some corner, but not perceiving her in any, he enquired where she could be.

One of the women replied:

"She went out an hour ago, saying that she would go to the Church of Notre Dame de la Croix."

"How was she dressed?" asked Benedict. "And," he added, with an uneasy presentiment, "did she not say anything or leave any message for me?"

"Are you the gentleman called M. Benedict?" returned the woman who had answered his previous questions.

"Yes," said he.

"Then here is a letter for you."

She handed him the note that Helen had left. He opened it hastily. It contained only these few lines:

"MY BELOVED BROTHER,

"I promised Karl, before Notre Dame de la Croix, not to outlive him; Karl is dead, and I am about to die.

"If my body is recovered, see, my dear Benedict, that it is placed in my husband's coffin; this was the reason why I asked you to have it made wide. I hope that God will permit me to sleep in it by Karl's side throughout eternity.

"I bequeath a thousand florins to the person who finds my body, if it should be some boatman or fisherman, or poor man with a family. If it should be some person who cannot or will not accept the money, I leave him my last blessing.

"The morrow of Karl's death is the day of mine.

"My farewells to all who love me."

"HELEN."

Benedict was finishing the reading of this letter when Lenhart appeared in the doorway, pale and dripping with water, and calling out:

"Oh, how shall I tell you, M. Benedict! Madame Helen has just thrown herself into the river. Come, come at once!"

Benedict looked round, seized a handkerchief that was lying on the bier, still perfumed and damp with the poor girl's tears, and rushed from the room. The carriage was at the door; he sprang into it.

"To your house," he called sharply to Lenhart. The latter, accustomed to obey Benedict without asking why, put his horses to the gallop; moreover, his house was on the way to the river. The house being reached, he leaped from the carriage, took the staircase in three strides, and opening the door, called:

"Here! Frisk!"

The dog rushed out after his master and was in the carriage as soon as he.

"To the river!" cried Benedict.

Lenhart began to understand; he whipped up his horses and they

261

galloped on as quickly as before. As they drove, Benedict divested himself of his coat, waistcoat, and shirt, retaining only his trousers. When they arrived at the river bank, he saw some sailors with boathooks who were raking the water for Helen's body.

"Did you see her throw herself into the water?" he enquired of Lenhart.

"Yes, your honour," he answered.

"Where was it?"

Lenhart showed him the spot.

"Twenty florins for a boat!" shouted Benedict.

A boatman brought one. Benedict, followed by Frisk, sprang into it. Then, having steered it into the line along which Helen's body had disappeared, he followed the current, holding Frisk by the collar, and making him smell the handkerchief that he had taken up from Karl's bed.

They came to a place in the river where the dog gave a melancholy howl. Benedict let him loose, he sprang out and disappeared at once. An instant later he came to the surface and swam about above the same place howling dismally.

"Yes," said Benedict, "yes, she is there."

Then he, in his turn, dived, and soon reappeared bearing Helen's body on his shoulder.

As Helen had wished, her body was, by Benedict's care, laid in the same coffin as Karl's. Her bridal garments were allowed to dry upon her and she had no other shroud.

# CHAPTER XXXVI. "WAIT AND SEE"

When Karl and Helen had been laid in their place of eternal rest, Benedict considered that the time had now arrived when, having no more services to perform for the family to which he had devoted himself, he might remind Sturm that he was Frederic von Bülow's executor.

Always obedient to convention he dressed himself with the greatest care, hung the Cross of the Legion of Honour and the Guelphic Order to his buttonhole by a line gold chain and sent in his name to General Sturm. The general was in his study. He ordered Benedict to be shown in at once, and as he entered rose from his seat, showed him a chair, and sat down again. Benedict indicated that he preferred to stand.

"Sir," said he, "the succession of misfortunes which has befallen the Chandroz family leaves me free, earlier than I expected, to come and remind you that Frederic, when he was dying, bequeathed to me a sacred duty—that of vengeance."

The general bowed and Benedict returned his bow.

"Nothing now keeps me in Frankfort but my wish to fulfil my friend's last injunction. You know what that injunction was, for I have told you; from this moment I shall have the honour of holding myself at your disposal."

"That is to say, sir," said General Sturm, striking his fist upon the writing-table before him, "that you come here to challenge me?"

"Yes, sir," answered Benedict. "A dying man's wishes are sacred, and Frederic von Bülow's wish was that one of us—either you or I—should disappear from this world. I deliver it to you the more readily because I know you, sir, to be brave, skilful in all bodily exercises, and a first-rate swordsman and shot. I am not an officer in the Prussian army; you are in no sense my chief. I am a Frenchman, you are a Prussian; we have Jena behind us and you have Leipzig; we are therefore enemies. All this makes me hope that you will place no difficulty in my way, and will consent to send me two seconds to-morrow, who will find mine at my house between seven and eight in the morning, and will do me the pleasure of announcing to them the hour, place, and weapons that you have chosen. Everything will be acceptable to me; make what conditions you like in the best way you can. I hope that you are satisfied."

General Sturm had shown frequent signs of impatience during Benedict's speech; but had controlled himself like a well-bred man.

"Sir," said he, "I promise you that you shall hear from me by the hour you name, and perhaps earlier."

This was all that Benedict wanted. He bowed and withdrew, delighted that everything had passed off so properly. He was already at the door when he remembered that he had omitted to give the general his new address, at Lenhart's. He went to a table and wrote the street and number below his name on his card.

"Excuse me," said he, "I must not fail to let your Excellency know where I am to be found."

"Are you not my neighbour?" asked the general.

"No," said Benedict. "I have left this house since the day before yesterday."

On the same evening, since he expected to leave Frankfort immediately after next day's duel—unless, indeed, some wound should detain him—Benedict left cards of farewell at all the houses where he had visited, withdrew his money from the bank, and, his banker having detained him, remained at his house until eleven o'clock, and then took leave to return to Lenhart's. But, as he was crossing the corner of the Ross Market an officer accosted him and, saying that he had a communication to make on behalf of the officer in command of the town, begged Benedict to accompany him. The latter made no difficulty about entering the market place where military were quartered, and there, at a sign from the officer, soldiers surrounded him.

"Sir," said the officer, "will you kindly read this paper, which concerns you."

Benedict took the paper and read it:

"By order of the colonel in command of the town and as a measure of public safety, M. Benedict Turpin is instructed to leave Frankfort instantly upon receipt of the present order. Should he refuse to obey willingly, force is to be employed. Six privates and an officer will accompany him to the station, enter the same carriage in the Cologne train and only leave him at the frontier of the Prussian territory.

"This order to be carried out before midnight.

"Signed ***."

Benedict looked round; he had no possible means of resistance.

"Sir," said he, "if I had any way of escaping from the order that I have just read, I declare to you that I would do anything in the world to get out of your hands. The great man who is your minister, and whom I admire although I do not like him, has said 'Might is right.' I am ready to yield to force. But I should be greatly obliged if one of you would go to 17, Beckenheim Street, to a man who lets out carriages, named Lenhart, and kindly ask him to bring me my dog, of which I am very fond. I will take occasion to give him some orders in your presence that are of no particular consequence, but rather important to a man who has been living in a town for three months and is leaving when he had no expectation of doing so."

The officer ordered a soldier to fulfil Benedict's wish.

"Sir," said he, "I know that you were intimate with a man to whom we were all attached, Herr Frederic von Bülow; although I have not the honour of your personal acquaintance, I should be sorry that you should carry away a bad impression of me. I was ordered to arrest you in the manner that I have done. I hope you will pardon an action entirely outside my own wishes, and which I have tried to perform with as much courtesy as possible."

Benedict held out his hand.

"I have been a soldier, sir; and therefore I am obliged to you for an explanation that you might easily have refrained from making."

A minute or so later Lenhart arrived with Frisk.

"My dear Lenhart," said Benedict, "I am leaving Frankfort unexpectedly; be so kind as to collect any things belonging to me that you may have and send them to me, in two or three days, unless you prefer to bring them yourself to Paris, which you do not know and where I would try to make you spend a pleasant fortnight. I do not offer any terms; you know that you may safely leave such matters in my hands."

"Oh, I will go, sir, I will go," said. Lenhart. "You may be sure of that."

"And now," said Benedict, "I think it must be time for the train; no doubt you have a carriage waiting; let us go if you have nothing more to wait for, and if you have not a travelling companion to give me."

The soldiers lined up and Benedict passed between them to the carriage that was waiting. Frisk, always delighted to go from one place to another, leapt in first, as if to invite his master to follow. Benedict stepped in, the officer followed him; four privates followed the officer, a fifth seated himself beside the driver, a sixth jumped up behind, and the conveyance set out for the station.

The engine was just ready to start as the prisoner arrived; he had not even the trouble of waiting a few minutes. At the carriage door Frisk was, as usual, the first to jump in, and although it is not customary, especially in Prussia, for dogs to travel first-class, Benedict obtained for him the favour of remaining with them. Next morning they were at Cologne.

"Sir," said Benedict to the officer, "I am accustomed, every time that I pass through this town, to provide myself with Farina's eau-de-Cologne for my dressing-table. If you are not pressed for time I would propose two things to you: in the first place my word of honour to play fair and not give you the slip before reaching the frontier; in the second place, a good breakfast for these gentlemen and you, all breakfasting together at the same table without any distinction of rank, like brothers. Then we will take the midday train, unless you prefer to trust my word that I will go straight to Paris."

The officer smiled.

"Sir," said he, "we will do what you please. I should like you to carry away the impression that we are only uncivil and tormentors when we are ordered to be. You want to stay; then let us stay! You offer me your word; I accept it. You wish to have us all breakfast with you; although it does not conform either to Prussian habits or Prussian discipline, I accept. The only precaution we will take—and that rather to do you honour than because we doubt your word—will be to see you off at the station. Where do you wish us to meet you again?"

"At the Rhine Hotel, if you please, gentlemen, in an hour's time."

"I need not say," added the officer, speaking in French that the soldiers should not understand him, "that after the way I have behaved to you I ought to be cashiered."

Benedict bowed with an air that seemed to say "You need be under no uneasiness, sir."

Benedict went away to the cathedral square, where Jean Marie Parina's shop is situated, and the officer took off his men in another direction.

Benedict supplied himself with eau-de-Cologne, which he could the more easily do because, having no other luggage, he could carry his purchase with him, and then proceeded to the Rhine Hotel, where he was accustomed to stay. He ordered the best breakfast that the proprietor could promise him, and awaited his guests, who appeared at the agreed time.

The breakfast was a thoroughly cheerful one; the prosperity of France and the prosperity of Prussia were toasted, the Prussians courteously setting the example; and after breakfast Benedict was escorted to the station, and, by military order, had a carriage to himself, instead of sharing one with six private soldiers and an officer.

At the moment of the train's starting the officer put into Benedict's hand a letter, which the traveller opened as soon as the train had passed out of the station. He gave a glance at the signature. It came, as he expected, from

General Sturm and contained these words:

"MY DEAR SIR,

"You will understand that it does not become a superior officer to set a bad example by accepting a challenge of which the object is to avenge an officer who was punished for disobedience to his chief. If I were to fight you for a reason so contrary to all military discipline I should be setting a fatal example to the army. I refuse, therefore, for the present, to meet you, and in order to avoid a scandal, I employ one of the most courteous measures at my disposal. You, yourself, were so good as to acknowledge that I had a reputation for courage, and you added that you knew me to be a first-rate shot and swordsman. You cannot, therefore, attribute my refusal to any fear of facing you. A proverb, common to all countries, says: 'Mountains do not meet, but men do.' If we meet anywhere else than in Prussia, and if you are still desirous of killing me, we will see about settling this little matter; but I warn you that the result is by no means a foregone conclusion, and that you will have more trouble than you expect in keeping your promise to your friend Frederic."

Benedict refolded the letter with the utmost care, placed it in his pocket-book and slipped his pocket-book into his pocket, arranged himself as comfortably as he could in a corner, and closing his eyes for sleep, murmured: "Well, well, we will wait and see!"

268

# CONCLUSION

The presence of the Prussians in Frankfort and the terror that they caused there did not end with the events which have just been related, and to which the present narrative ought to confine itself. A few lines only must be added that our work may close as it opened, by a page of politics.

Towards the end of September 1866 it was announced that the city of Frankfort, losing its nationality, its title of a free town, its privilege of having the Diet held there, and finally its rights as a member of the Confederation, was to be united on October 8th to the kingdom of Prussia.

The morrow was gloomy and rainy; no house had hung out the black-and-white flag; no citizen, sad or cheerful, was in the streets, every window was shuttered, every door closed. It seemed a city of the dead. The flag flew only over the barracks, the Exchange, and the post office.

But in the Roemer Square there was an assemblage of some three or four hundred men, all belonging to the suburb of Sachsenhausen. It was a curious thing that each of these men had a dog of some description with him: a bulldog, mastiff, spaniel, hound, griffon, greyhound, or poodle. Amidst these bipeds and quadrupeds, Lenhart went up and down relating what fine things he had seen in Paris, and holding everybody's attention. He it was who had devised this meeting of his fellow inhabitants of Sachsenhausen, and who, by whispered instructions, had invited them to bring their dogs. Men and dogs alike gazed towards the window from which the proclamation was to be made. They had been waiting there since nine in the morning.

At eleven the members of the Senate, the Christian and Jewish clergy, the professors, the chief officials, and Major-General Boyer, with the officers of the garrison, were gathered together in the Hall of the Emperors in the Roemer, to witness the taking possession of the formerly free town of Frankfort by His Gracious Majesty, the King of Prussia.

The civil governor, Baron Patow, and the civil Commissioner, Herr von

Madaï, came from the Senate Hall (once the hall in which the Emperors of Germany were elected) into the great hall. After some little preamble on Baron Patow's part he read to the persons present the patent by which the former free town of Frankfort was taken into possession, and then the royal proclamation which announced that the town had been added to the Prussian dominions.

The same documents were now to be read to the people of Frankfort. The window was opened to an accompaniment of joyful murmurs and mocking acclamation from the men of Sachsenhausen and the yawns of their dogs. The square was occupied, we forgot to mention, not only by the men from Sachsenhausen but by a company of the 34th regiment of the line and its band.

Herr von Madaï read aloud the following proclamation:

"The very high and very powerful proclamation of His Majesty the King of Prussia to the inhabitants of the former free town of Frankfort."

Either because the voice of Herr von Madaï was particularly disagreeable to his hearers or because the words "former free town of Frankfort" aroused their sensibility, several dogs howled dismally. Herr von Madaï paused until silence was restored, and continued, still in the king's name:

"By the patent that I cause to be published to-day I unite you, inhabitants of the city of Frankfort-on-the-Main and its suburbs, to my subjects, your German neighbours and brothers."

Five or six howls protested against this union. Herr von Madaï seemed to give no heed to them and proceeded.

"By the decision of the war and the reorganization of our common German Fatherland, you are deprived of the independence which you have hitherto enjoyed, and now enter the union of a great country, whose population is sympathetic to you by language, customs, and identity of interests."

This news did not appear agreeable to the prejudices of some hearers;

270

there were complaints, growls, and a certain number of lamentations. Herr von Madaï seemed to understand these sad protestations.

"If," said he, "it is not without pain that you resign former connections that were dear to you, I respect such feelings and esteem them as a guarantee that you and your children will be faithfully attached to me and my house."

An enormous bulldog replied by a single bark, which appeared, however, to speak the opinion of the two or three hundred companions around him. The interruption did not disturb Herr von Madaï, and he went on:

"You will recognize the force of accomplished facts; if the fruits of an obstinate war and of bloody victories are not to be lost to Germany, the duty of self-preservation and care for national interests imperatively demand that the town of Frankfort shall be joined to Prussia, solidly and for ever."

At this moment a dog broke its chain and despite shouts of "Arrest the rebel! Arrest the rebel!" and the pursuit of some five or six Sachsenhausen urchins, disappeared into the Jewry.

"And, as my father of blessed memory declared," resumed Herr von Madaï, "it is solely for the profit of Germany that Prussia has enlarged its boundaries. I offer this for your serious reflection, and I confide in your upright German good sense to swear allegiance to me with the same sincerity as my own people. May God grant it!"

"WILLIAM"

"Given at my castle of Babelsberg, October 3rd, 1866."

And raising his voice, Herr von Madaï added, by way of peroration:

"Hurrah for King William! Hurrah for the King of Prussia!"

At the same instant the black-and-white flag was hoisted on the topmost gable of the Roemer. No shout replied to Herr von Madaï's, only the voice of Lenhart was heard like that of a drill sergeant:

"And now, my little doggies, as you have the honour to be Prussian dogs, shout 'Hurrah for the King of Prussia!'"

271

Then every man pressed his toe upon the tail, the ear, or the paw of his dog, and there arose such frightful uproar, including the deepest and the shrillest notes, as could only be covered by the band of the 34th Prussian Regiment playing "Heil dir im Siegeskranze," which means "Hail to thee in the crown of victory."

Thus was the former free town of Frankfort united to the kingdom of Prussia. But many people say that it is not stitched, but only tacked on.

# EPILOGUE

On June 5th, in the year 1867, a young man of some twenty-five to twenty-seven years of age, elegantly dressed, and wearing at his buttonhole a ribbon half red and half blue-and-white, had just finished his cup of chocolate at the Café Prévôt, which was at the corner of the Boulevard and the Rue Poissonière. He asked for the "Étandard" newspaper.

He had to repeat the name twice to the waiter, who, not having the paper on the premises, went out to the Boulevard for a copy and brought it to his customer. The latter cast his eyes rapidly over it, looking evidently for some article that he knew to be there. His glance settled at last upon the following lines:

"To-day, Wednesday, June 6th, the King of Prussia will enter Paris. We give a complete list of the persons who will accompany His Majesty:

"M. de Bismarck.

"General de Moltke.

"Count Puckler, Lord Marshal.

"General de Treskow.

"Count de Goltz, Brigadier-General.

"Count Lehendorff, Aide-de-Camp to the king.

"General Achilles Sturm—"

Doubtless the young man had seen all that he wanted to see, for he carried no further his investigations into the persons accompanying His Majesty.

But he tried, to discover at what hour King William was to arrive, and found that he was expected at a quarter-past four at the Gare du Nord.

He immediately took a carriage and placed himself upon the road which the king would have to follow in going to the Tuileries.

The king and his escort were some minutes behind their time. Our young man was waiting at the corner of the Boulevard de Magenta; he placed himself at the end of the procession, and accompanied it to the Tuileries, keeping his eyes particularly, as he did so, upon the carriage which contained General von Treskow, Count von Goltz, and General Achilles Sturm. That carriage entered the courtyard of the palace with the King of Prussia's, but came out again, almost immediately, with the three generals who occupied it, in order to go to the Hôtel du Louvre.

There the three generals alighted; they were clearly intending to lodge in the neighbourhood of the Tuileries where their sovereign was staying. Our young man, who also had alighted, saw a waiter lead them to their several rooms. He waited a moment, but none of them came out again. He got into his carriage again and disappeared round the corner of the Rue des Pyramides. He knew all that he wanted to know.

Next morning, about eleven o'clock, the same young man was walking in front of the café belonging to the hotel, and smoking a cigarette. At the end of ten minutes his expectation was satisfied. General Sturm came from the Hôtel du Louvre into the restaurant, sat down at one of the marble tables arranged just inside the windows and asked for a cup of coffee and a glass of brandy. This was just opposite the Zouave Barracks.

Benedict entered the barracks and came out a minute later, with two officers. He led them in front of the window and showed them General Sturm.

"Gentlemen," said he, "that is a Prussian general with whom I have so serious a quarrel that one of us must be left upon the field. I have applied to you to do me the favour of acting as my seconds, because you are officers, because you do not know me, and do not know my adversary, and consequently, will not have any of those little delicate considerations for us that fashionable people have towards those for whom they act as seconds. We will go in and sit down at the same table with him. I will reproach him with what I have to reproach him with, and you will see whether the matter is serious enough for a duel to the death. If you judge it to be so, you will do me the honour of being my seconds. I am a soldier like yourselves; I went through the Chinese war with the rank of lieutenant, I fought at the battle of Langensalza as orderly to Prince Ernest of Hanover, and, finally, I fired one of the last shots at the battle of Aschaffenburg. My name is Benedict Turpin, and I am a knight of the Legion of Honour and of the Guelphic Order."

The two officers stepped back a pace, exchanged a few words in a low voice, and returned to Benedict's side, to tell him that they were at his command.

All three then entered the café and went to seat themselves at the general's table. The latter looked up and found himself face to face with Benedict, whom he recognized at the first glance.

"Ah, it is you, sir," said he, growing rather pale.

"Yes, sir," answered Benedict. "And here are these gentlemen who are still unacquainted with the explanation that I am about to have with you and are here to hear what I say, and will be kind enough to assist me in our combat. Will you allow me to explain to these gentlemen, in your presence, the cause of our meeting, and afterwards will you give them details of our antecedents as we go together to the place decided upon? You remember, sir, that, nearly a year ago you did me the honour of writing to me that mountains did not meet, but that men did, and that whenever I had the honour of meeting you outside the kingdom of His Majesty, King William, you would put no difficulty in the way of giving me satisfaction."

The general rose.

"It is useless," said he, "to prolong an explanation in a café where everybody can hear what we say; you can give any explanations to these gentlemen of the grounds of complaint which you consider yourself to have against me, and which I am not in any degree bound to disclaim to you. I wrote to you that I was ready to give you satisfaction; I am. Give me time to go into the hotel and fetch two friends. That is all I ask of you."

"Do so, sir," said Benedict, bowing.

Sturm left the café. Benedict and the two officers followed him. He went into the Hôtel du Louvre. The three gentlemen waited at the door.

In the ten minutes during which they waited Benedict told them the whole story, and was just concluding it as the general reappeared with his seconds—two officers of the king's retinue. All three came towards Benedict and bowed to him. Benedict introduced his own seconds to those of the general by a wave of the hand. All four drew apart a little. Presently Benedict's seconds came back to him.

"You have left the choice of weapons to the general?" said he.

"Yes, sir, and he has chosen the sword; we are to go to a sword cutler and choose a couple of blades that neither of you will have seen before; then we are to go to the nearest convenient spot for the meeting. We suggested the fortifications, and these gentlemen have agreed; they are to take an open carriage, we are to take another; and, as they do not know the way and we do, we shall guide them along the boulevard, and at the first sword-cutler's we will buy the swords."

Everything was arranged accordingly. Two waiters were sent for two carriages. The seconds suggested that the surgeon-major of the Zouaves should accompany the party, and the suggestion being accepted, one of the officers went to fetch him. He joined Benedict and the two Frenchmen, while General Sturm and his seconds followed at some distance.

At the sword-cutler's—which was Claudin's, Benedict said in an aside to the shopman, whom he knew:

"The swords are to be charged to me; let the gentlemen who are in the second carriage choose them."

Three different swords were shown to General Sturm, who selected the one that best suited his hand, and asked its price; he was told that they were paid for. The two carriages went as far as the Étoile turnpike by way of the Maillot gate. Thence they followed the line of the fortifications for a short distance, then, when they had reached a tolerably deserted spot, the two Zouave officers alighted from their chaise, looked up and down the fosse, and finding it empty beckoned their adversaries to join them. In another minute

276

the whole party was standing at the base of the walls. The ground was level and offered every facility for a combat of the kind that was now to take place.

The general's seconds presented the two swords to Benedict who had not previously seen them; he cast a quick glance at them and saw that they were montées en quarte, a circumstance which suited his designs admirably. Apparently it suited General Sturm's, also, since he had chosen the swords.

"When is the fight to stop?" asked the seconds.

"When one of us is killed," answered the two antagonists together.

"Coats off, gentlemen!" said the seconds.

Benedict threw aside his jacket and waistcoat, displaying his shirt.

"Are you ready, gentlemen?" asked the seconds.

"Yes," replied both at the same time.

One of the Zouave officers took one sword and put it into Benedict's hands; one of the Prussian officers took the other and put it into General Sturm's hands.

The seconds crossed the two swords at a distance of three inches from the points, and, moving aside to leave the combatants face to face, said:

"Now, gentlemen!"

The words were scarcely uttered when the general swiftly made himself master of his opponent's sword by a double engagement, making as he did so a stride forward with all the usual impetuosity of a man who knows himself an adept in fencing.

Benedict leapt back; then, looking at the general's guard:

"Ah, ah!" he murmured, "a quick fellow on his feet. Attention!"

He exchanged a quick glance with his seconds, to tell them not to be uneasy.

But at the same moment, and without any interval, the general, while entangling the sword by a skilful pressure advanced in a crouching attitude, and lunged with so rapid a dégagement that it needed all Benedict's close handling to parry by a counter quarte, which, quick though it was, could not save his shoulder from a graze. The shirt tore upon the sword's point and became slightly tinged with blood.

The return thrust came so swiftly that the Prussian by luck or by instinct had not time to resort to a circular parry and mechanically employed the parade de quarte and was now on the defensive. The thrust was parried, but it had been given with such energy that General Sturm staggered on his legs and could not deliver his counter thrust.

"He is a pretty fencer, after all," thought Benedict. "He gives one something to do."

Sturm stepped back and lowered his point.

"You are wounded," said he.

"Come, come," returned the young man, "no nonsense! Here's a fuss about a scratch. You know very well, general, that I have got to kill you. One must keep one's word, even to a dead man." He put himself in position again.

"You? Kill me! Upstart!" exclaimed the general.

"Yes, I, greenhorn as you think me," replied Benedict. "Your blood for his, although all yours is not equal to one drop of his."

"Cursed rascal!" swore Sturm, growing crimson. And, rushing upon Benedict, he made as he came, two successive coups de seconde, so hasty and so furious that Benedict had barely time to parry them, by twice retiring, and then a parade de seconde delivered with such precision and energy that the loose shirt was torn above the waistband, and Benedict felt the cold steel. Another stain of blood appeared.

"What! Are you trying to tear off my shirt?" said Benedict, sending his enemy a high thrust de quarte, which would have run him through, but that, feeling himself in danger, he flung himself forward in such a manner that the hilts touched, and the two adversaries stood with their swords up face to face.

278

"Here!" cried Benedict, "this will teach you to steal my thrust."

And before the seconds could interpose their swords to separate them, Benedict, freeing his arm like a spring, drove the two hilts like the blow of a fist in his adversary's face, who staggered back, his face lacerated and bruised by the blow.

Then followed a scene which made those who beheld it shudder.

Sturm drew back for an instant, his mouth half-open and foaming, his teeth clenched and bleeding, his lips turned back, his eyes gleaming, bloodshot and almost starting from their sockets, his whole countenance reddish purple.

"Blackguard! Dog!" he yelled, waving his stiff-held sword and crouching back for his guard like a jaguar ready to spring.

Benedict stood calm, cold, contemptuous. He extended his sword towards him.

"You belong to me, now," he said in a solemn voice. "You are about to die."

He fell back to his guard, exaggerating the pose as a sort of challenge. He had not to wait long.

Sturm was too good a fencer to throw himself unprotected upon his enemy. He advanced sharply one pace, making un double engagement, of which Benedict turned aside the second by a dégagement fait comme on les passe au mur.

Anger had disturbed Sturm's guard, he was lunging with his head down—an attitude which, for this once at least, saved him. The dégagement merely grazed his shoulder by the neck. Blood appeared.

"A sleeve for a sleeve," retorted Benedict, falling back quickly to his guard, and leaving a great distance between the general and himself. "Now for it!"

The general found himself too far off, took a step forward, gathered all his powers, made a frenzied beating with his sword and struck straight, lunging at the full stretch of his body. All his soul, that is to say, all his hope, was in that blow.

This time Benedict, planted firmly on his feet, did not yield an inch; he caught the sword par un demi cercle, executed in due form, with his nails held upwards as though he were in a fencing school, and standing over the point of his sword inclined towards his feet:

"Now then," he said, delivering his thrust.

The sword entered the upper part of the chest and disappeared completely in the general's body where Benedict left it, as he sprang back—as a bull fighter leaves his dagger in the breast of the bull. Then, folding his arms, he waited.

The general remained standing for a second, staggered, tried to speak; his mouth became full of blood, he made a movement with his sword and the sword fell from his hand; then he, himself, like an uprooted tree, fell full length upon the turf.

The surgeon rushed to the body of Sturm; but he was already dead.

The point of the sword had gone in below the right shoulder blade, and come out on the left hip, after passing through the heart.

"Sapristi!" muttered the surgeon, "that's a man well killed."

Such was Sturm's funeral oration.

THE END

# About Author

His father, General Thomas-Alexandre Dumas Davy de la Pailleterie, was born in the French colony of Saint-Domingue (present-day Haiti) to Alexandre Antoine Davy de la Pailleterie, a French nobleman, and Marie-Cessette Dumas, a black slave. At age 14 Thomas-Alexandre was taken by his father to France, where he was educated in a military academy and entered the military for what became an illustrious career.

Dumas' father's aristocratic rank helped young Alexandre acquire work with Louis-Philippe, Duke of Orléans, then as a writer, finding early success. Decades later, after the election of Louis-Napoléon Bonaparte in 1851, Dumas fell from favour and left France for Belgium, where he stayed for several years, then moved to Russia for a few years before going to Italy. In 1861, he founded and published the newspaper L'Indipendente, which supported Italian unification, before returning to Paris in 1864.

Though married, in the tradition of Frenchmen of higher social class, Dumas had numerous affairs (allegedly as many as forty). In his lifetime, he was known to have at least four illegitimate children; although twentieth-century scholars found that Dumas fathered three other children out of wedlock. He acknowledged and assisted his son, Alexandre Dumas, to become a successful novelist and playwright. They are known as Alexandre Dumas père ('father') and Alexandre Dumas fils ('son'). Among his affairs, in 1866, Dumas had one with Adah Isaacs Menken, an American actress then less than half his age and at the height of her career.

The English playwright Watts Phillips, who knew Dumas in his later life, described him as "the most generous, large-hearted being in the world. He also was the most delightfully amusing and egotistical creature on the face of the earth. His tongue was like a windmill – once set in motion, you never knew when he would stop, especially if the theme was himself."

**Early life**

Dumas Davy de la Pailleterie (later known as Alexandre Dumas) was born in 1802 in Villers-Cotterêts in the department of Aisne, in Picardy,

France. He had two older sisters, Marie-Alexandrine (born 1794) and Louise-Alexandrine (born 1796, died 1797). Their parents were Marie-Louise Élisabeth Labouret, the daughter of an innkeeper, and Thomas-Alexandre Dumas.

Thomas-Alexandre had been born in the French colony of Saint-Domingue (now Haiti), the mixed-race, natural son of the marquis Alexandre Antoine Davy de la Pailleterie, a French nobleman and général commissaire in the artillery of the colony, and Marie-Cessette Dumas, a slave of Afro-Caribbean ancestry. At the time of Thomas-Alexandre's birth, his father was impoverished. It is not known whether his mother was born in Saint-Domingue or in Africa, nor is it known from which African people her ancestors came.

Brought as a boy to France by his father and legally freed there, Thomas-Alexandre Dumas Davy was educated in a military school and joined the army as a young man. As an adult, Thomas-Alexandre used his mother's name, Dumas, as his surname after a break with his father. Dumas was promoted to general by the age of 31, the first soldier of Afro-Antilles origin to reach that rank in the French army. He served with distinction in the French Revolutionary Wars. He became general-in-chief of the Army of the Pyrenees, the first man of colour to reach that rank. Although a general under Bonaparte in the Italian and Egyptian campaigns, Dumas had fallen out of favour by 1800 and requested leave to return to France. On his return, his ship had to put in at Taranto in the Kingdom of Naples, where he and others were held as prisoners of war.

In 1806, when Alexandre was four years of age, his father, Thomas-Alexandre, died of cancer. His widowed mother, Marie-Louise, could not provide her son with much of an education, but Dumas read everything he could and taught himself Spanish. Although poor, the family had their father's distinguished reputation and aristocratic rank to aid the children's advancement. In 1822, after the restoration of the monarchy, the 20-year-old Alexandre Dumas moved to Paris. He acquired a position at the Palais Royal in the office of Louis-Philippe, Duke of Orléans.

**Career**

While working for Louis-Philippe, Dumas began writing articles for magazines and plays for the theatre. As an adult, he used his slave grandmother's surname of Dumas, as his father had done as an adult. His first play, Henry III and His Courts, produced in 1829 when he was 27 years old, met with acclaim. The next year, his second play, Christine, was equally popular. These successes gave him sufficient income to write full-time.

In 1830, Dumas participated in the Revolution that ousted Charles X and replaced him with Dumas' former employer, the Duke of Orléans, who ruled as Louis-Philippe, the Citizen King. Until the mid-1830s, life in France remained unsettled, with sporadic riots by disgruntled Republicans and impoverished urban workers seeking change. As life slowly returned to normal, the nation began to industrialise. An improving economy combined with the end of press censorship made the times rewarding for Alexandre Dumas' literary skills.

After writing additional successful plays, Dumas switched to writing novels. Although attracted to an extravagant lifestyle and always spending more than he earned, Dumas proved to be an astute marketer. As newspapers were publishing many serial novels, in 1838, Dumas rewrote one of his plays as his first serial novel, Le Capitaine Paul. He founded a production studio, staffed with writers who turned out hundreds of stories, all subject to his personal direction, editing, and additions.

From 1839 to 1841, Dumas, with the assistance of several friends, compiled Celebrated Crimes, an eight-volume collection of essays on famous criminals and crimes from European history. He featured Beatrice Cenci, Martin Guerre, Cesare and Lucrezia Borgia, as well as more recent events and criminals, including the cases of the alleged murderers Karl Ludwig Sand and Antoine François Desrues, who were executed.

Dumas collaborated with Augustin Grisier, his fencing master, in his 1840 novel, The Fencing Master. The story is written as Grisier's account of how he came to witness the events of the Decembrist revolt in Russia. The novel was eventually banned in Russia by Czar Nicholas I, and Dumas was prohibited from visiting the country until after the Czar's death. Dumas refers to Grisier with great respect in The Count of Monte Cristo, The Corsican

Brothers, and in his memoirs.

Dumas depended on numerous assistants and collaborators, of whom Auguste Maquet was the best known. It was not until the late twentieth century that his role was fully understood. Dumas wrote the short novel Georges (1843), which uses ideas and plots later repeated in The Count of Monte Cristo. Maquet took Dumas to court to try to get authorial recognition and a higher rate of payment for his work. He was successful in getting more money, but not a by-line.

Dumas' novels were so popular that they were soon translated into English and other languages. His writing earned him a great deal of money, but he was frequently insolvent, as he spent lavishly on women and sumptuous living. (Scholars have found that he had a total of 40 mistresses.) In 1846, he had built a country house outside Paris at Le Port-Marly, the large Château de Monte-Cristo, with an additional building for his writing studio. It was often filled with strangers and acquaintances who stayed for lengthy visits and took advantage of his generosity. Two years later, faced with financial difficulties, he sold the entire property.

Dumas wrote in a wide variety of genres and published a total of 100,000 pages in his lifetime. He also made use of his experience, writing travel books after taking journeys, including those motivated by reasons other than pleasure. Dumas traveled to Spain, Italy, Germany, England and French Algeria. After King Louis-Philippe was ousted in a revolt, Louis-Napoléon Bonaparte was elected president. As Bonaparte disapproved of the author, Dumas fled in 1851 to Brussels, Belgium, which was also an effort to escape his creditors. About 1859, he moved to Russia, where French was the second language of the elite and his writings were enormously popular. Dumas spent two years in Russia and visited St. Petersburg, Moscow, Kazan, Astrakhan and Tbilisi, before leaving to seek different adventures. He published travel books about Russia.

In March 1861, the kingdom of Italy was proclaimed, with Victor Emmanuel II as its king. Dumas travelled there and for the next three years participated in the movement for Italian unification. He founded and led a newspaper, Indipendente. While there, he befriended Giuseppe Garibaldi, whom he had long admired and with whom he shared a commitment to liberal republican principles as well as membership within Freemasonry. Returning to Paris in 1864, he published travel books about Italy.

Despite Dumas' aristocratic background and personal success, he had to deal with discrimination related to his mixed-race ancestry. In 1843, he wrote a short novel, Georges, that addressed some of the issues of race and the effects of colonialism. His response to a man who insulted him about his African ancestry has become famous. Dumas said:

My father was a mulatto, my grandfather was a Negro, and my great-grandfather a monkey. You see, Sir, my family starts where yours ends.

**Personal life**

On 1 February 1840, Dumas married actress Ida Ferrier (born Marguerite-Joséphine Ferrand) (1811–1859). He had numerous liaisons with other women and was known to have fathered at least four children by them:

Alexandre Dumas, fils (1824–1895), son of Marie-Laure-Catherine Labay (1794–1868), a dressmaker. He became a successful novelist and playwright.

Marie-Alexandrine Dumas (5 March 1831 – 1878), the daughter of Belle Krelsamer (1803–1875).

Micaëlla-Clélie-Josepha-Élisabeth Cordier (born 1860), the daughter of Emélie Cordier.

Henry Bauer, the son of a woman whose surname was Bauer.

About 1866, Dumas had an affair with Adah Isaacs Menken, a well-known American actress. She had performed her sensational role in Mazeppa in London. In Paris, she had a sold-out run of Les Pirates de la Savanne and was at the peak of her success.

These women were among Dumas' nearly 40 mistresses found by scholar Claude Schopp, in addition to three natural children.

**Death and legacy**

At his death in December 1870, Dumas was buried at his birthplace of Villers-Cotterêts in the department of Aisne. His death was overshadowed by the Franco-Prussian War. Changing literary fashions decreased his popularity. In the late twentieth century, scholars such as Reginald Hamel and Claude Schopp have caused a critical reappraisal and new appreciation of his art, as well as finding lost works.

In 1970, the Alexandre Dumas Paris Métro station was named in his honour. His country home outside Paris, the Château de Monte-Cristo, has been restored and is open to the public as a museum.

Researchers have continued to find Dumas works in archives, including the five-act play, The Gold Thieves, found in 2002 by the scholar Réginald Hamel [fr] in the Bibliothèque Nationale de France. It was published in France in 2004 by Honoré-Champion.

Frank Wild Reed (1874–1953), the older brother of Dunedin publisher A. H. Reed, was a busy Whangarei pharmacist who never visited France, yet he amassed the greatest collection of books and manuscripts relating to Dumas outside France. It contains about 3350 volumes, including some 2000 sheets in Dumas' handwriting and dozens of French, Belgian and English first editions. This collection was donated to Auckland Libraries after his death. Reed wrote the most comprehensive bibliography of Dumas.

In 2002, for the bicentennial of Dumas' birth, French President Jacques Chirac had a ceremony honouring the author by having his ashes re-interred at the mausoleum of the Panthéon of Paris, where many French luminaries were buried. The proceedings were televised: the new coffin was draped in a blue velvet cloth and carried on a caisson flanked by four mounted Republican Guards costumed as the four Musketeers. It was transported through Paris to the Panthéon. In his speech, President Chirac said:

With you, we were D'Artagnan, Monte Cristo, or Balsamo, riding along the roads of France, touring battlefields, visiting palaces and castles—with you, we dream.

Chirac acknowledged the racism that had existed in France and said that the re-interment in the Pantheon had been a way of correcting that wrong, as Alexandre Dumas was enshrined alongside fellow great authors Victor Hugo and Émile Zola. Chirac noted that although France has produced many great writers, none has been so widely read as Dumas. His novels have been translated into nearly 100 languages. In addition, they have inspired more than 200 motion pictures.

In June 2005, Dumas' last novel, The Knight of Sainte-Hermine, was published in France featuring the Battle of Trafalgar. Dumas described a fictional character killing Lord Nelson (Nelson was shot and killed by an unknown sniper). Writing and publishing the novel serially in 1869, Dumas had nearly finished it before his death. It was the third part of the Sainte-Hermine trilogy.

Claude Schopp, a Dumas scholar, noticed a letter in an archive in 1990 that led him to discover the unfinished work. It took him years to research it, edit the completed portions, and decide how to treat the unfinished part. Schopp finally wrote the final two-and-a-half chapters, based on the author's notes, to complete the story. Published by Éditions Phébus, it sold 60,000 copies, making it a best seller. Translated into English, it was released in 2006 as The Last Cavalier, and has been translated into other languages.

Schopp has since found additional material related to the Saints-Hermine saga. Schopp combined them to publish the sequel Le Salut de l'Empire in 2008.

Dumas is briefly mentioned in the 1994 film The Shawshank Redemption. The inmate Heywood mispronounces Dumas' last name as "dumbass" as he files books in the prison library.

Dumas is briefly mentioned in the 2012 film Django Unchained. The Southern slaveholder Calvin Candie expressed admiration for Dumas, owning his books in his library and even naming one of his slaves D'Artagnan. He is surprised to learn from another white man that Dumas was black. (Source: Wikipedia)

CPSIA information can be obtained
at www.ICGtesting.com
Printed in the USA
BVHW030607270819
556835BV00002B/350/P

9 789353 852023